very good

"The butterfly," Antonia hissed between clenched teeth when she saw the sparkling gem pinned to my breast. "You have the butterfly. It is mine!" She snapped to my grandfather. "You know it should be mine!"

My grandfather's face darkened. "I know no such thing," he glowered.

"I have more right to it than this—this—imposter!" Antonia spat, pointing at me.

People were turning to look at us now. I felt my face flame.

"Imposter!" My grandfather stood up and loomed over the tiny Antonia. "Imposter, indeed! My granddaughter is the true descendant of the Montoyas," he roared, "the legitimate one!"

Antonia's face flushed and she spun to face me. "You will be sorry," she said furiously, leaning close to my face. "You will be very sorry . . ."

SUCCUMB TO THE TERROR AND PASSION OF THESE ZEBRA GOTHICS!

THE MISTRESS OF HARROWGATE   (772, $2.25)
by Jessica Laurie
Margaret could not avoid the intense stare of Elizabeth Ashcroft's portrait—for the elegant bejeweled woman could have been her identical twin! When Margaret heard and saw impossible things, she feared that Elizabeth was trying to send her a dangerous and terrifying message from beyond the grave . . .

THE LORDS OF CASTLE WEIRWYCK   (668, $1.95)
by Elaine F. Wells
It didn't take long for hired companion Victoria Alcott to discover there were dreadful secrets in the old lady's past. As Victoria slowly became enmeshed in a web of evil, she realized she could not escape a terrible plot to avenge a murder that had been committed many years ago . . .

THE LADY OF STANTONWYCK   (752, $2.50)
by Maye Barrett
Despite her better judgment, Olivia took the job at Stantonwyck and fell in love with broodingly handsome Mark Stanton. Only when it was too late did she learn that once she lost her heart, she was destined to lose her life!

THE VANDERLEIGH LEGACY   (813, $2.75)
by Betty Caldwell
When Maggie discovered a Buddhist shrine hidden deep in the woods of Jonathan Vanderleigh's New Jersey estate, her curiosity was aroused. And the more she found out about it—that it was related to her father's death—the more her own life was endangered!

Available wherever paperbacks are sold, or order direct from the Publisher. Send cover price plus 50¢ per copy for mailing and handling to Zebra Books, 475 Park Avenue South, New York, N.Y. 10016. DO NOT SEND CASH.

The Cursed Heiress

BY JUNE HARRIS

ZEBRA BOOKS
KENSINGTON PUBLISHING CORP.

To Ron, who told me so . . .

ZEBRA BOOKS

are published by

KENSINGTON PUBLISHING CORP.
475 Park Avenue South
New York, N.Y. 10016

Printed in the United States of America

Chapter One

Sometimes our lives are changed by trivial things—a tossed coin, a left turn instead of a right, a decision made on the spur of the moment. I believe I decided, ultimately, to go to my grandfather's ranch in California because there were no lilacs there.

My father died in April. I was in the garden behind our little house cutting lilacs for the table when Mrs. Graham, our part-time cleaning lady, came to tell me that Mr. Leigh was waiting in the parlor to see me. Tom Leigh was my father's business associate, and I was surprised that he would come here during the day without him. We were not on such terms that he was accustomed to dropping in unexpectedly.

I followed Mrs. Graham into the house, pausing in the kitchen to put the lilacs in water and to remove my apron. Tom Leigh stood in the parlor, turning his hat in his hands.

The late-afternoon sun slanted through the lace curtains and gleamed on the polished wood floor. Tom Leigh was staring at the window, and he started when I spoke his name.

"Mr. Leigh?" He turned toward me; his face was tight and his jaws were clenched. "Do be seated," I said, indicating a chair beside the red plush sofa where I seated myself.

"Miss Cole—Melinda—I—I—" He was pale and seemed very agitated. He sat down, then stood up again and paced the rug in front of me.

"Mr. Leigh, what's wrong? What is it?"

He paced back and forth in front of me, paused, cleared his throat, and finally turned and said, "Melinda, there's been a —sort of—accident with your father."

"Accident?" I stood up. "Is he hurt? Can you take me to him? Is it—" Then I stopped. The look on his face told me that there was nothing I could do. I sat down slowly and looked up at him. "He's dead, isn't he?"

A curious sort of numbness seemed to seep into me. I felt as if I were moving outside my body, watching myself sitting on the sofa, seeing myself from a long distance, but only as a detached observer. I heard my voice, far away, ask, "How did it happen?"

"It was a gunshot, Melinda." He shifted his weight from one foot to the other and mopped his damp brow. I stared at the pattern of sunlight on the floor as if expecting to see something of significance there. Then that same, distant voice asked, "But who, Mr. Leigh? Who would have shot my father?"

Tom Leigh hesitated for a long moment. "The wound was—ah—self-inflicted, Melinda."

Self-inflicted! I was back inside my body, and the pain was sudden and sharp. My father had killed

6

himself. I stared at Mr. Leigh stupidly, and he must have thought I was going to faint, because he rummaged in his pockets for a vial of smelling salts that he tried to hold beneath my nose.

I waved them away. "No, I'm all right, Mr. Leigh. I'm not going to faint. It's just that—"

"You've had a great shock." His round face expressed concern and he looked close to tears. "Shouldn't I call your housekeeper? Could I send for the doctor?" The poor man was almost more overwrought than I was, and I had a sudden image of myself comforting *him*.

"Why, Mr. Leigh? Why would my father do such a thing? I thought things were just beginning to go well for us. We had managed to buy this house. Papa said we had some money in savings. Why now?"

He looked at the floor, and then back at me, the strain of his unwelcome task evident on his face. He shifted his bulky shape in the chair, uncomfortable in this chore, and said, "Melinda, couldn't we talk more about this later? You've got enough to deal with right now. Maybe next week we could go over this when you're feeling more up to it."

I considered what he was saying, and shook my head. I felt that I could only handle this if I could do it all at once. A quick amputation, so to speak.

"Mr. Leigh, my father was the only family I had in the world. Now he's killed himself—" I found myself gasping, trying to get the words out. Tom Leigh started to talk, but I raised my hand to stop him, "—and I want to know what would cause him to do such a thing. Why would he do this to himself?" I stopped, then whispered, "Why would he do this to me?"

Leigh leaned toward me, struggling for words.

"Melinda, your father had been having some business problems for quite some time now. Perhaps you knew about that."

I knew. It was difficult to escape the talk of "financial crisis" and "panic" in business these days. Still, we had always seemed to have money. I had thought we were doing fine.

"At any rate," he went on, "your father had access to some company funds which were, shall we say, discretionary. He could have used the money for any number of things, with the understanding that it had to be accounted for and that limited amounts were to be drawn and to be replaced. Do you understand what I'm saying?"

I nodded, although I was not sure that I did.

"At any rate, I'm sure your father intended to put the money back." He wiped his forehead. "I believe he thought that he would be able to. It's just that, well, he—he got behind, somehow. He wasn't able to account for all that he had borrowed."

" 'Borrowed'? Mr. Leigh, are you telling me that my father had been stealing from the business?"

Leigh was perspiring, and he avoided my eyes. "I'm sure he didn't intend to, Melinda. I know he would have replaced the money. It's just that times are hard, right now, and he kept thinking things would get better, that then he could put the money back."

"But—" I had not yet comprehended all that I had heard. I groped for words to put some meaning

8

to all of this. "I just—Was it so much, Mr. Leigh? Didn't he have any hope of making it good?"

"It was quite a lot, Melinda. The auditors had discovered the loss and your father was given ninety days to make it good. If he was unable to do so, he was—he was to face criminal charges."

"Criminal charges?"

"Embezzlement." The word fell between us like a stone. I looked up at him and he dropped his eyes, embarrassed. "You see, in a way he was thinking of you, Melinda. He wanted to spare you the humiliation of his . . . disgrace."

"I see," I said, but I was not sure that I did. In fact, I was sure that I did not. An hour ago, I had been cutting lilacs in my own backyard, my life had been pleasant and smooth, for perhaps the first time in my nineteen years. And now it was gone. All of that was gone. My pleasant life, my security, the first I'd ever known, gone. And I realized something else.

"The money my father took, Mr. Leigh—it will have to be replaced, will it not?"

"As much as can be recovered, Melinda."

"That means, then, that this house, the savings, everything that was my father's, will have to go to account for it. Is that correct?"

Leigh looked at the floor, nodded and sighed. "I would imagine so, Melinda. I'm sure that the amount they will recognize from the sale of this house won't satisfy the debt, but—"

"But the company will be entitled to all of my father's assets to make good as much of it as they can. Am I right?"

"I—I believe you are right."

I was silent a moment as the implications of the situation sank in. I would have no place to live. I had no money. I had no profession. I had no relatives. I had awakened this morning with a bright future, but would go to bed this night with only memories. I thanked Tom Leigh for his help and saw him to the door, my mind alternately blank and crowded with images.

I refused his offer to send a doctor. I told him I would be fine with Mrs. Graham, but I sent her home as soon as he was gone. I wanted to be alone for a while to try to sort out the thoughts that were racing around in my mind.

My father was dead. My handsome, generous, weak, kind, loving father was dead. Ned Cole had been the center of my life, and now he was dead, I was alone, and my life had little purpose.

I had lost my mother when I was three. She died in childbirth with my little brother, and the baby died soon after. I didn't remember her, but I had a miniature of her that I wore on a chain around my neck. My father had adored her, and after her death there had never been anyone who could replace her for him.

He had met her when she was fourteen. He was eighteen then, and had been sailing for two years. He had sailed into San Francisco, and, curious about the city, had wandered into the exclusive residential area where my mother was visiting her aunt.

"She had skin like a gardenia petal," he used to say, "and black, black eyes. You have her eyes, Melinda."

"And your hair," I would add, referring to the mop of carrot-colored hair we both had. He would smile then, remembering.

Margarita McCarthy, she had been. And my father had sworn that it was love at first sight. Still, she was only fourteen, little more than a child, so my father had told her he would be back when she was of age and he had some money.

He kept his promise. Three years later, he showed up with a ring and money in his pockets, but when he knocked at the door of the house where they had met, he was told that Margarita wasn't there, and in fact, had never lived there. She had only been visiting, he was told. She lived on a ranch a day's ride away. Furthermore, he wouldn't be welcome at the ranch. Margarita was engaged to be married—and who was he, anyway?

Father hadn't come that far to be stopped by a mere engagement. "I had kept her face in my mind for three years," he would say. "I wasn't leaving until she told me to go."

Finding the ranch proved to be no problem. The McCarthy ranch was better known as the old Montoya place, and it was easy enough to locate. Getting to see Margarita was something else, but he finally managed it. Margarita seldom went out by herself, but sometimes she did ride down to the old mission alone, and having learned that, he waited for her there.

Would she remember him? Of course. "I have

prayed every day that you would come back to me,'' she whispered on that first meeting. But there were problems. She was engaged to marry a young man whose ranch joined her family's, and it was unlikely that her father would consider letting her break the engagement. Still, she was her father's only child, a much-loved, indulged daughter. She had every reason to think that perhaps she could induce him to grant her wishes in this.

But her father was furious at the suggestion. Who was this Ned Cole, anyway? An upstart, a nobody, a nothing—a sailor! Marry Margarita Teresa Montoya McCarthy? There was no way her father would hear of it. She cried, she pleaded, she begged to have the wedding postponed. Her father was adamant. The wedding would go on as planned.

And so she simply ran away with my father. On the night before she was to be married to another man, she asked to go down to the mission to pray. Her father allowed her to go, but made sure she was accompanied by her old nurse. My mother prayed for a very long time, knowing that eventually the nurse would drop off to sleep. And when that finally happened, she slipped out of the church to join my father, who was waiting for her.

They were married in San Francisco, then sailed back to Boston where I was born a year later.

My father had stopped sailing before he married my mother and had gone into business. After she died, though, he stopped working for a long time, and we moved from place to place, each one a little worse than the last. I changed schools too often to have any friends, and as a result, I grew up feeling distant from people my own age. My father was my only company, and I was his. He had been orphaned at sixteen. After my mother's death, he had a series of nurses and housekeepers for me until we became too poor to pay them. By that time I was old enough to do most of the housekeeping myself.

My father worked at an occasional odd job to keep us going until the year I was sixteen. One day he suddenly looked up at me as if from a bad dream, and said, "Melinda, what are you doing in that shabby dress?"

I must have looked at him as if stunned.

"Papa, I've been wearing this dress for months now. I wear it every day. You've seen it." I didn't know what else to say. The dress was indeed shabby. It was cheap to begin with, and the brown color was quite drab. The sleeves were too short, and I had let the hem down as far as it would go, but it was getting too short again. My father was tall, and I was going to inherit that from him.

"Don't you have any other dresses?"

"Not for every day, Papa. You know that."

"Well, yes, I guess I do. I just hadn't thought of it. I guess I'll have to do something about that. You're getting too big to have to live like this any more."

That afternoon he went out, dressed in a suit left over from the old days, and when he came back, he told me to pack, we were moving out. I thought we were moving to another of the dingy little places we had lived in for the last few years, but I was wrong. The place we moved to was a nicer apartment than we had lived in for some time. Papa had gone to old friends he hadn't seen since he and Mother were to-gether, and they helped him get a job in his old business. Our lives began to improve steadily.

In a year, Papa managed to buy our little house. "It isn't much, Melinda, but it's ours. In a few years, I'll get a really nice place for you."

Suddenly, everything was for me. It was as if, having almost forgotten me for all those years, he was now trying to make up to me for what I had missed. I must have piano lessons, I must have new clothes, I must have all the things I hadn't had.

Then, six months ago, there was the panic. Papa hadn't seemed to worry, and life went on as it had for two years. The last two months he had been more withdrawn, and had mentioned business problems, but he always assured me that everything would be fine.

Guilt overwhelmed me as I remembered those days. The signs had been there—why had I not seen them? Why had I not gone to him and made him tell me about his problems? I had believed what I had wanted to believe. I had been preoccupied with my new life, my new possessions. I had not wanted to know that there was anything wrong. I had taken his word and gone about doing what I wanted.

Now he was dead. He had stolen to give me what he thought I should have, and now I had lost the thing I had wanted above all others: my father.

Mr. Leigh handled the funeral arrangements. The parlor was dim and filled with baskets of flowers, mostly lilacs, and the scent was overpowering. After the funeral, Mr. Leigh sat down with me to discuss my plans for the future.

"I'm going to look for a job, Mr. Leigh. I know there isn't much I can do, but I can perhaps get a job as a governess or a teacher in one of the private schools. They sometimes take on people my age and without experience."

"We—the company—have made some inquiries, Melinda, and we think we can help you find a position. It isn't easy, these days, you know. There are many young women looking for work, the economy being what it is."

"I can imagine. But if I can have a little while to look for a job, I feel sure I can find something." I attempted a small smile. "I'm not hard to please, you know. It isn't as if I'm unaccustomed to work."

His face was grim, and he didn't return the smile. "Melinda, the company can give you only until next week before they take over the house."

I felt my jaw drop. "Next week! But I had thought—at least a month—"

He was nervous, and I felt sorry that he was the one who had to deal with the mess my life had become.

"I'm sorry, Melinda. I tried to get longer for you, but they—the company officials—said that they wanted to get started right away to recoup their losses. The company has problems, you know, times being the way they are. They said if you were out of the house next week, they would see that no word of the scandal got out." He looked down at his hands, his face guilty and embarrassed. "Of course, legally, you could stay until court action was completed,

15

but . . ." He let the sentence trail off, but I understood the unspoken message.

"In other words, if I leave quietly, my father's name will be protected, but if I do not, the whole thing will be exposed and everyone will know my father for a thief. I think the word for that sort of an agreement is 'blackmail.' Am I correct?"

My words sounded harsh, and Mr. Leigh flinched. He raised miserable eyes to my face. "Melinda, the company has no wish to be cruel to you. They have even made arrangements for a position for you if you wish to take it. But they do have their own losses to consider."

I sighed. "I know. And I've no wish to sound bitter, Mr. Leigh. It's just that this has been so sudden for me that I have hardly had time to think. And I didn't intend to be unkind to you. I'm sure that I would be grateful for the position. What sort of job is it?"

"It's a teaching position. At a private school, such as you mentioned. One of the company officials is on the board of trustees for the school, and they need a young woman to work with the girls there. The pay is minimal, but you would have room and board."

"Right now, Mr. Leigh, it sounds like a godsend. Where is the school?"

"It's here in Boston," he said, and he gave the address. "It is called Westhaven School for Young Ladies. Not one of the better-known schools, but very well thought of."

"I'm not familiar with it, but then, I didn't go to private schools myself."

16

"The school term will be out soon, but the school has agreed to take you on during the summer as a tutor for some of the girls who come for special help during vacation."

Even through my misery, I could see that I was fortunate. I knew that the private schools were having a difficult time these days. As business got worse, more and more families were forced to remove their children from private schools, and more schools were releasing teachers than were hiring. I wondered at my good luck. I thanked Mr. Leigh sincerely, and he left, evidently relieved—I realized later, because I had been so easily handled. I suppose that I could have caused problems for the company, or at least have hurt their public image severely. One wretched, penniless girl against a large corporation—it would not have looked good for them. But I simply didn't have the strength to fight.

By the middle of the following week, I was packed and ready to leave for the school. Most of our furniture had already been taken from the house; it was empty except for the few things in my room which were to go last.

On the last night, I climbed into my bed, pulled the covers up to my chin, and stared at the ceiling. I looked around the room for the last time. The house was empty, and the sounds it made seemed ominous. Always before, the creaking of the house had been comforting; it had been my place, with its own familiar sounds. But now it was not mine, and I was alien to it: I was an outsider. I didn't belong. It was hard to fall asleep. I had never felt so alone in my life.

Chapter Two

My first impression of Westhaven School was deceptive, but as I have since learned, I am often deceived by first appearances. I tend to see things at first as better, more attractive, than they actually turn out to be. It's only later that I see the flaws that would have been evident to a careful observer from the very first.

Westhaven was housed in a large old brick building, and surrounded by green lawns and lovely, spreading trees. The grounds were somewhat narrow, but they stretched out behind the building for some distance. When I arrived, I could see groups of girls sitting under the trees and walking on the lawns, and it looked so like the sort of school I had wanted to attend, that I felt fortunate to be there.

The building itself had wide steps leading up to large, carved-oak doors. I entered a foyer which had a polished parquet floor and a lovely staircase curving up to the next floor. Urns filled with flowers were placed beside the doors and at the bottom of the stairs. It was an impressive entryway, and, I was to learn, was kept in splendid condition to impress visitors. This and the visitors' sitting room were generally all that parents saw of the school, and they believed, from these glimpses, that all of the school was as beautifully kept, as elegant, as this polished entry.

I was not a parent to be kept in blissful ignorance, however, and my disillusion was not only inevitable but desirable.

Mrs. Melrose met me in her office just off the foyer.

Agatha Melrose was the owner and headmistress of Westhaven. She was a tall, thin woman, about fifty years old, I guessed, with pale skin and greenish eyes. She had thin, fine hair which was braided and twisted into a knot on the back of her neck. It was a color I have heard called "iron gray," and certainly the "iron" part applied to Mrs. Melrose; she could have been cast of it. She stood as straight as a statue. She wore a severe black dress, unrelieved by even a touch of color, and her face was set in lines which, I was to learn, altered only when she was trying to charm a parent. I never saw her smile except on those occasions, and then the expression was so foreign to her face that it seemed ludicrous there.

On this first morning, she motioned me into her office and had me be seated in a straight-backed chair in front of her desk.

"Miss Cole. You seem very young." No welcome, no greeting, just those words, in a tone calculated to make me feel suddenly as if I were a child called to the principal's office.

"I'm almost nineteen, Mrs. Melrose."

19

"You've had no experience in a school of this sort, I understand."

"No—no, not really. Not in teaching."

"Oh? You attended a private school, then?"

"No—no, I didn't."

"Private tutoring, I suppose."

"No. I went to public school."

Her eyebrows went up just enough to indicate the poor recommendation *that* admission was. "Well, I suppose it can't be helped now."

I had never before felt, or had been made to feel, that I was so inadequate. Even in our worst times, I had felt as if I were a person of at least some worth. Now I felt my lack of age, of experience, of education, like dead weights. I was to learn that Mrs. Melrose was an expert in fostering just that sense of near-idiocy.

"You will be working with the ten- and eleven-year-old girls. You will teach history, English, arithmetic, and penmanship. You will also supervise their needlework and their exercise period. Do you speak French?"

Another mark against me. "No, Mrs. Melrose."

"Pity. But of course, languages are not taught in public schools." In her mouth, "public schools" sounded faintly obscene.

In an effort to acquit myself with some degree of competence, I said, "I know I must seem rather inexperienced, Mrs. Melrose, but I am well-read, and I have some ideas about things that I could do with the girls—"

"We are not interested in your ideas, Miss Cole." She paused to let that sink in, and I blushed, angry

20

at her rudeness. "And you are wrong when you say you *seem* inexperienced. You *are* inexperienced. Totally. That, however, is not without its merits. You have no bad habits to unlearn. The courses you will teach are thoroughly outlined. You are to follow those outlines exactly. Do you understand?"

"Yes." I must have sounded abrupt, because she again raised her eyebrows, ever so slightly.

"Our classes are designed to give a thorough background in all the educational essentials. Parents send their girls here to learn the fundamentals, not to get radical ideas. You will adhere to the course outlines strictly. Here are your materials." She handed me a stack of books and notebooks. "Other things that are necessary for you to learn, you will be told as you go along. You will have, as do the other teachers, responsibility for some of the housework. I assume you have had some experience with that."

The sarcasm was not lost on me. "Yes, I am familiar with housework," I answered, as coolly as I could manage.

"I have asked Miss Sherwood to show you to the room you and she will be sharing. She will also show you the grounds and instruct you as to the routine. She is in the sitting-room."

She rose and escorted me into a small room off her office. It, like the foyer, was lovely and well-kept. There were small sofas and comfortable-looking chairs grouped in front of a marble fireplace, lace curtains and vases of flowers. It was the room where visiting parents sat with their daughters I was to learn, and so received the same loving care as the entry.

Seated in one of the chairs was a woman of my own age. She rose when we entered the room.

"Miss Sherwood, this is Miss Cole. She will be taking Miss Winthrop's place." Miss Sherwood nodded. "Please show her to her quarters and acquaint her with her duties. You will be responsible for her until she becomes familiar with our routine." She managed to make the last statement sound like a threat, and when she turned and left, Miss Sherwood, who had nodded and smiled while receiving her orders, now stuck out her tongue at the back of the departing figure. I was so startled by this that I clapped my hand over my mouth to strangle a giggle.

Miss Sherwood turned merry blue eyes on me. "Welcome to Worsthaven. I'm Mavis Sherwood."

" 'Worsthaven'?"

"That's what the girls call it. Leave it to them to think of that. What's your first name?"

"Melinda."

"That's pretty. Come with me, Melinda, and I'll show you around. How did you happen to have the bad luck to come here?"

"It seemed like good luck at the time," I said. "My father died and I had no family and no money."

"That sounds about right. That's the sort she usually hires. Ones who have to come here. Those who can do better, soon do."

"That sounds ominous."

"Ha! that's not the half of it. No, no," she put out a hand to stop me as I started up the curving stairway. "We don't use those stairs. Those are for appearance only. This way." She led me down a dark, narrow hallway, her blond curls bouncing ahead of me.

We approached a steep, narrow flight of stairs and she said, "These are our stairs. She wants to keep the others looking perfect for company."

We went up the stairs, and up two more flights just like them. We finally arrived at the small attic room we were to share.

"Well, this is it. Your new home. I'll bet it's not like your old one."

I looked around the room. The roof sloped on both sides so that one could only stand upright in the middle of the room. The floors were warped, and there was only one small window in the end of the room to let in the bit of light we got. I put my things on the bed that Mavis had indicated, and turned to smile at her.

"Well, it isn't like the one I just left, but I've lived in worse."

"You have?" Her eyes were round. "I'd have taken you for one of those rich girls on hard times."

"Well, we had good times and we had bad." I sighed. "Mostly bad. But if this place is as bad as you say, how did you end up here? You seem much too pretty to be—I mean—I'd have thought you'd have been married or something."

She smiled. "I don't know about the 'or something,' but I do plan to be married. I came here because we had eight in the family, and Papa had trouble providing for all of us. I had enough schooling to get this job, and so I took it. The little money helps."

"You're going to be married, you said?" I was curious.

"Can you keep a secret? If Old Lady Melrose knew, she'd get rid of me right away. She doesn't want any of her teachers having anything to do with men. A bad example for the girls, she says.

I assured her I could keep a secret.

"Of course you can. You're not a chatterbox like I am. Sam—he's my fiancé—wants me to leave at the end of this term, but I think we need a little more money saved. If I can stay until the end of next year, we'll have enough to buy some furniture, and we won't have to live with Sam's folks. Or mine."

She looked at me appraisingly. "We'll have to see who Sam knows that we could introduce you to."

I smiled. "I'm afraid I'm not the sort that appeals to men very much, Mavis. I was always one of those girls at school that no one wanted to dance with."

"Oh, nonsense." She waved away my objections. "With all that red hair? Men are simply dotty about redheads. Even Sam. I told him—" We were interrupted by the sound of a ringing bell.

"Uh-oh, we've got to run. That's the start of afternoon exercise. Come with me. You might as well get started right away."

The next few days destroyed any remaining illusions I might have had about Westhaven. Behind the polished and pretty facade was a cold, grimy, badly-kept, uncomfortable place. Mrs. Melrose's genius, according to Mavis and the evidence of my own eyes, lay in running a cheap school while

24

preserving, for the parents' sake, an image of gentility.

"You think it's bad now," Mavis said. "Just wait until next winter. She's so stingy with the coal that it's all you can do to keep from freezing to death. Start saving now for some warm clothes and an extra blanket. Two, if you can manage. You'll need them."

The food was another area where Mrs. Melrose's corner-cutting was evident. Breakfast was cold, lumpy oatmeal and lukewarm tea so weak we could see the bottoms of our cups through it. At midday, we usually had food left over from the previous night's dinner. For dinner, potatoes (always), turnips, sometimes a stew with what might have been a shred of beef in it, or a watery soup.

The food was cold, even when it was scorched, which was often. It was badly prepared and unseasoned. The girls always complained about it, and I asked Mavis why they didn't tell their parents how bad it was.

"Oh, they do. Often. The problem, you see, is that the parents don't really take them seriously. They think all children complain about school food."

"Doesn't anyone ever come to see how it is?" I couldn't believe that all parents were so uncaring.

"Sometimes a parent will come by to see for herself. A mother, of course. Fathers never. You know how Mrs. Melrose made you feel when you came here? Well, she does the same thing with the parents. They end up apologizing for coming. Or, if they insist on seeing for themselves, she has a special meal cooked up so they can eat with the girls. Nothing fine, mind you, just good enough so the parent thinks the child was exaggerating.''

"And they never check any further?''

"Melinda, you are such an idealist. Parents don't want to know there's a problem. They want things to go along smoothly, so they can be sure their judgment in sending the girls here was right. Tell me, didn't you think this was a perfectly lovely place when you walked in?''

"Well, yes, I really did. That lovely curving staircase, that polished floor—it all seemed so beautiful.''

"And what do you think parents think when they walk in? She puts them in that nice little sitting room, with flowers in the vases, or a fire in the fireplace.''

"I'm sure they're impressed. I know I was.''

"Of course they are. Most of the parents didn't go to private schools themselves. This represents a step up for them. They don't know what to expect, and they're easily intimidated. Besides, she charges lower prices then the 'name' schools. Parents think they've found a little jewel at a bargain price. They don't want to know differently.''

The girls, on the whole, didn't seem to suffer much from the routine, possibly because most of them had spending money to supplement their meals with whatever they chose to buy from the nearby pastry shops and markets. When their day's activities were finished in the late afternoons, they had time, before dinner, to go shopping as long as one of us chaperoned them. Most of the teachers were willing to go on occasion, and Mavis could always be counted on to accompany them. It gave her a chance to see her beloved Sam for a few minutes.

It was during one of these recesses that I became friends with Emmaline.

I had noticed her earlier, and had asked Mavis about her. She attended classes with the other girls, but she looked like a sparrow in a cage of parrots. She was small for her age, very thin, and plainly dressed almost to the point of raggedness. Her dresses were always patched, worn, and too small. Still, she was the brightest student in my classes, eager to learn even the dry stuff we were forced to serve up as "fit material for young minds." (When Mrs. Melrose had said that she was eliminating "radical" ideas, she had included as radical anything that might be interesting, thought-provoking, original, or in any way entertaining. What was left was absolutely soporific.)

I was drawn to Emmaline. She reminded me of myself in many ways. I had been that sort of child—thin, plain, ragged—and had also used my studies to escape from an uncomfortable world.

"Her parents must be sacrificing to send her here," I had said to Mavis.

"Oh, her parents are dead. Emmaline is charity."

"Charity? I wouldn't have guessed that Mrs. Melrose had it in her to give charity."

"Don't be misled. Mrs. Melrose doesn't *give* anything. This is one of those gestures that impresses parents."

"Oh?"

"Every year Mrs. Melrose makes a big show of choosing a promising child from the public schools to attend under 'sponsorship.' She gets some well-to-do business organization to pay half of the tuition, and the child works for the other half. It's a way of getting another servant. Not for free, either. She gets paid for the work they do."

"What do they do?"

"Emmaline works in the kitchen. I don't know how that little scrap of a thing does it. She works almost all the time she isn't in class, but she's still miles ahead of anyone in her group."

During the afternoon recesses, I chose to work in the kitchen as my share of the housework so I could talk to Emmaline. We would peel potatoes and talk, and as the weeks passed, grew close. She told me that her father had been killed when she was small, and her mother had died about two years ago of tuberculosis.

"They were going to put me in the orphanage," she said, "but then I got to come here under sponsorship. I'm glad. I wouldn't want to go to the orphanage."

I failed to see how her life could have been much worse at an orphanage than at Westhaven. Surely she wouldn't have had to work like this for every bite she ate.

"Emmaline, I just don't understand how you can do all this and keep up your studies, too."

She looked up at me and smiled, her thin little face brightened by the sudden change. "It isn't hard, Miss Cole. Most of the other girls need to study to pass the tests because they don't listen in

28

class. I found out that if I listen real hard, I don't have to do much outside.''

When the school year ended, Emmaline and I were thrown together even more closely. Mavis went home to her family in the summer, and I stayed on to tutor the day-pupils who came during the summer months.

The time passed with a monotonous regularity. Emmaline had more time free, and she would join me in my attic room where we would read, or when the room became too stifling to bear, we would move to the lawn and sit under the trees.

By the time September came, I had become resigned to my situation, and could look down the long corridor of my future without the sense of devastation I had had when I first came. I could see myself years from now, getting old, still working with the girls, doing what I did year after year. It was not a pleasant future, not the one I would have chosen, but at least I could face it now without flinching, knowing that my options were limited and that I was capable of making the best of what was offered. At least, that was what I thought then. I had not reckoned on that something within me which was not willing to be so resigned.

Mavis returned in September, and I was delighted to see her again. I hadn't realized how much I had missed her. She brought me a warm muffler and gloves she had knitted herself, and bedsocks her mother had made for both of us. "You'll need them, believe me."

She also brought a large box of cookies and other

goodies that we ate as we sat on our beds and giggled over the latest gossip.

"Sam says we're definitely getting married at the end of the school year," she said. "He says he doesn't want to put it off any longer." She giggled. "In fact, it was all I could do to talk him into waiting that long, but we do so need the money. And the family needs the little bit I can send them until my next sister goes to work this summer."

I told her about my summer with Emmaline. "I don't know how that child is going to make it through the winter," I said. "She needs everything—warm shoes, stockings, a coat. I don't know how she can stay as thin as she is and still outgrow everything, but she does."

"Well, she should get a few things from the girls, now that term is starting," Mavis said. "They usually bring back their hand-me-downs for her in the fall. At least, a few of them do. And if that's not enough, I'll write to Mama and see what we've got at home. We're poor, heaven knows, but my mama can always manage to find something."

The fall was beautiful. The trees around Westhaven changed color, and the vases in the sitting room were filled with chrysanthemums. But the nights had begun to get chilly, and in our little attic room, cold seemed to pour through every crack.

"I'm surprised there isn't ice in this pitcher," I said to Mavis as we dressed for breakfast one morning. "When does Awful Agatha loosen up and part with a few pieces of coal?"

"My dear, there will be ice you have to break

before Aggie decides it's cold enough to warrant coal. This is just nippy."

"Nippy! I think I'm getting frostbite in my fingers. And poor Emmaline! That room of hers is worse than ours."

"I know. I was thinking about her. I know she doesn't have enough covers, either."

"What did she do last winter?"

"Well—she spent part of the worst of the winter . . . um . . . with someone else."

"With someone . . . ? Mavis, you took her in with you."

"Well, I couldn't just let the poor little thing freeze."

I threw my arms around her and hugged her. "Oh, Mavis, you are so dear. If we push our beds together, we can bring her in with us when it gets really cold. That'll help."

"We have to be careful not to let you-know-who find out, though. I'm surprised she hasn't called you in to give you her lecture about 'undue familiarity' with the students."

"You mean she would be upset if we helped Emmaline?"

"Of course. It makes her look bad. After all, she's doing this marvelous thing by taking in the little charity case. She doesn't want any implications that the child is neglected or mistreated."

"But she is neglected. And mistreated."

"Don't let Aggie hear you say that."

The weather got colder and Mavis was right. There was ice in the pitcher before we received any coal. When it was issued, we got so little that I thought it was meant for one or two days; it was to last for a week.

"I can't believe this is a week's supply of coal, Mavis. Surely there's some mistake."

"Oh, there's no mistake, Mel. This has to do. We'll just ration it out. Besides, Sam will sneak us in a bit more. He manages to get some extra where he works, and he wraps it up like a parcel and gives it to me when he sees me." She smiled. "The girls think he's so romantic, giving me presents. If they only knew."

The weather continued to get colder, and we started having Emmaline sleep with us. By combining all our blankets and our coal, we managed to keep somewhat warm. My attentions to Emmaline had not gone unnoticed, however, and I was summoned to Mrs. Melrose's office for an "interview" shortly after Christmas.

"Miss Cole, it has been brought to my attention that you have been showing marked partiality to the little charity case."

The little charity case! as if she didn't even have a name!

"Do you mean Emmaline Bower, Mrs. Melrose?"

"Of course."

"I'm not sure I know what you mean by 'marked partiality,' Mrs. Melrose."

She raised her eyebrows. "I'm quite sure you *do* know, Miss Cole. However, if you choose to feign ignorance, I will enlighten you. I understand that when there is dessert, you often give yours to her. I am also told that you spend some time with her, to the exclusion of the other girls. Are these things true?"

I often have an unfortunate inability to govern my temper, even when it is in my best interest to do so, and the sight of this smug, cruel, well-fed woman, secure in her warm, clean apartment, snapped the rein I thought I had placed on my tongue.

"If you are referring to the fact that I gave Emmaline my serving of that abominable bread pudding, you are correct. I'm not sure I was doing her any favors, but the amount of food the girls are served is insufficient for any growing child, and she needed it more than I did."

"I'm not certain how you came by your expertise on growing children, Miss Cole. Do they teach that in public schools?"

I felt my face grow red, but I said nothing.

"At any rate, the other girls seem to be doing quite well. Emmaline no doubt has a poor constitution."

"The other girls can afford to buy food for themselves outside school. Emmaline cannot. She doesn't have a poor constitution. She's merely undernourished."

"And, according to your judgment, under-clothed, apparently."

"I bought her a pair of stockings and some gloves. The child was cold."

"Then perhaps she needs more work to keep her blood circulating more thoroughly."

More work! What had I done to poor Emmaline?

"I hardly think so, Mrs. Melrose. Adequate clothing should suffice."

"She has adequate clothing. The girls bring her perfectly good used clothing from their homes, of a quality she could not possibly hope to obtain otherwise. She is a charity case, after all. She isn't meant to be a fashion-plate.''

"I didn't make a fashion-plate of her. I only wanted to have her warm.''

"If you have money to throw away on such items, Miss Cole, perhaps you are overpaid. Perhaps a salary reduction is in order.''

Salary reduction! Because of those cheap little stockings and gloves that I had scrimped so to buy! I couldn't believe the callousness of the woman.

"I hardly think that is the point, Mrs. Melrose.''

Her eyebrows went up again. "Oh? And what do you consider to be the point, Miss Cole?''

"The point is that the child is hungry and cold.''

"The point is, Miss Cole, that were it not for me, she would be hungrier and colder. It is only through my good graces that she is not begging on the streets at this moment.'' She paused to let this statement sink in, then added, "The poor will always play on our sympathies if we let them, Miss Cole. You need to develop a more objective attitude toward these things.''

When I said nothing, she sat back slightly in her chair and looked at her desk. "Of course,'' she continued in a milder tone, "if you are unable to come to terms with what you obviously perceive as my great cruelty,'' she looked up at me as a malicious smile flickered across her face, "you are always at liberty to find employment elsewhere. And a place for Emmaline if she chooses to go.''

I think it was then that I first understood the meaning of hatred. I felt trapped, both by my own

34

inadequacy and by my concern for Emmaline. The woman knew that I had nowhere else to go, and now she knew that I wouldn't leave Emmaline.

"I don't think that will be necessary," I mumbled, and I rose to leave.

"I should hope not, Miss Cole," she said, self-satisfied and triumphant.

The weather continued to grow colder, and late in January, Mrs. Melrose found out that Emmaline had been sharing the attic room with Mavis and me.

She ordered Emmaline back to her own little room and threatened Mavis and me with the loss of our jobs if we disobeyed her orders. Mavis and I gave Emmaline all of the blankets we could spare, and shared the rest. Mavis gave her the extra coal we got from Sam, and we did our best to keep her as comfortable as we could.

But early in February, she developed a hacking cough. Mavis gave her a cough remedy her mother had mixed, and we warmed blankets over the fire and wrapped her up each night, but the cough grew worse.

One night we were awakened by a tapping at the door, and Mavis opened it to find Emmaline standing there barefoot, in her skimpy little nightgown, face flushed with fever, eyes glazed.

"Emmaline!" Mavis snatched a blanket off our bed, and wrapped her up. I threw another piece of coal on the grate.

"What are you doing? Get back to your bed, you'll catch your death." Mavis felt her forehead, then muttered, "If you haven't already."

"I'm . . . not feeling . . . very . . . well," Emmaline whispered, and sank into a small heap on the floor. I helped Mavis put her in our beds.

"I think she's delirious," Mavis said. "Did you feel her forehead?"

"She's burning up with fever." I looked at Mavis. "She's got to have a doctor."

"Not much chance of that. Aggie would never pay for a doctor for a charity case."

"If she doesn't, Emmaline might die."

Mavis looked at me. "Do you think she's that bad?"

"I'm sure of it. Feel her forehead. Listen to her."

Emmaline was gasping for breath, a hoarse rasping in her chest.

"Pneumonia." Mavis and I looked at the small figure on the bed. "What can we do?" she whispered.

I began to pull on my clothes. "I'm going for a doctor," I answered. "We'll get one, one way or another."

"But, Mel, you don't have money for a doctor, and Mrs. Melrose will never pay for one."

"I'll bet she will when I'm through with her." My teeth were clenched, and I was warmed by my anger. "I'm going to make her get one."

I slammed the door and raced down the stairs. Mrs. Melrose lived in an apartment behind the office, and I hammered on the office door. Soon I saw a light beneath the door, and then Mrs. Melrose opened it.

"Mrs. Melrose, we have to send for the doctor. One of the girls is sick."

"Oh, yes, I see," she said, turning toward her desk. She set the lamp on her desk and reached for her writing materials. "I'll send a note to Dr. Blackwood over in the next street. Which of the girls is it?"

"Emmaline Bower."

"Emmaline Bower!" She stood up from the desk and ripped up the note she had been writing. "You got me up at this time of night for your little pet? I have no intention of paying for a doctor to treat sniffles in a child like that."

I leaned toward her, struggling to control my fury. "Mrs. Melrose, Emmaline Bower has pneumonia. She might die of it if we don't get a doctor. Write the note. I'll take it myself."

"Nonsense. Go out in the kitchen and heat up the kettle. Some steam should take care of—"

I grabbed her shoulders and swung her around to face me. She drew back startled, and spat, "Miss Cole! What do you think you're doing?"

"Let me ask you something, Mrs. Melrose," I glared. "How do you think the parents of the other girls here are going to like your lovely little school when they find out that one of your students died through neglect and overwork?"

"Don't be absurd. She's a charity case, and she isn't dead yet."

"She will be if she doesn't get a doctor."

"Even so, how could they know unless—"

"Unless I tell them, Mrs. Melrose?" I was too angry now to care what I said, but I was going to get a doctor for Emmaline if I had to shake this vicious woman into submission. "I promise you that if you don't send for a doctor, I will write letters to the parents of every girl in this school and tell them about conditions here. I will write letters to newspapers, to City Hall, to the trustees, to anyone who can read. If you don't think that will damage your reputation, then try it, Mrs. Melrose. See what happens.''

She stared at me for a moment, her eyes filled with malice, naked hate on her face. Then she turned to her desk and wrote the note. ''Here's the note. Now get out of here. And I want you out for good by the end of the week.''

My victory had given me a small sense of power, and I turned back to her at the door. ''I'll leave at the end of the term, Mrs. Melrose. Not before.'' I slammed the door and raced for the doctor.

By the time the doctor arrived, Emmaline had lost consciousness. He did what he could, but he said, ''If you had only called me sooner . . .'' and shook his head. Emmaline was dead by the next afternoon.

Chapter Three

Emmaline's death left me shaken and drained. It was as if I had used all of my fight for her, and now that she was gone, I existed in a sort of trance. Mavis and I comforted each other, but Mavis had Sam, and I had no one. There were gaps in my days now, without Emmaline, and time dragged on through the winter, into a rainy, late spring.

I knew I had to start looking for another position, and I didn't want to face it. I'd never be able to get a recommendation from Mrs. Melrose, and without it, my chances of getting a good job were limited. I had another two months at Westhaven, and after that I didn't know what to do.

By April, Mavis had given notice to Mrs. Melrose that she would be leaving at the end of the term. She was now at liberty to see Sam openly, so she spent all of her free time with him, planning their wedding.

Mrs. Melrose had avoided me since Emmaline's death, and so I was a bit surprised when she summoned me to her office one day during the afternoon recess.

Her manner toward me was not what I had

expected. It could hardly have been called cordial, but it was certainly less frigid than I would have anticipated.

I soon learned the reason for her change of attitude.

"Miss Cole," she said, "there is a gentleman here to see you."

"A gentleman?" I was at a bit of a loss. "To see me? But I don't know any gentlemen."

"I know. He will explain his purpose to you. Let me just say that if there is anything I can do to help you, you must feel free to ask."

"Help me?" I must have sounded quite stupid.

"I am not at liberty to explain. Please go into the sitting room. The gentleman is Mr. Stephen Matson."

The day was warm. Sunlight fell on a table containing a vase filled with lilacs. Warmed by the sun, the flowers gave off a fragrance I found almost overpowering. The scent struck me as I entered the room, and brought flooding back memories of my father's death. This, combined with my confusion at Mrs. Melrose's amazing change of attitude and my already depressed state, rendered me almost somnambulistic as I entered the room. I was certainly not feeling myself as I approached the elderly gentleman who was sitting in one of the wingback chairs.

"Mr. Matson?"

He rose quickly and extended his hand. "Are you Melinda Cole?" he asked, peering at me over his glasses.

"Yes, I am."

"The daughter of Edward Taylor Cole and Margarita McCarthy Cole?"

"Margarita Teresa Montoya McCarthy Cole, to be quite precise." I managed a tight little smile. "Why do you want to know?" I was a bit blunt, but I was not concerned about my manners. I was past caring about formalities. I was almost past caring for anything.

Mr. Matson smiled fondly at me and patted my hand before he released it. "Oh, child, only Maggie's daughter would know that mouthful of names. We've certainly had the devil's own time finding you."

"Finding me? I'm sorry if I appear confused, Mr. Matson, but I haven't the faintest idea who you are or why you would want to find me or how you know my mother was called Maggie."

"Of course you don't, my dear. Do let's sit down. I have a great deal to tell you."

We sat down on one of the chintz sofas, and Mr. Matson paused a moment, gathering his thoughts. He had white hair and bright blue eyes, and was so elegantly and expensively dressed that I understood why Mrs. Melrose was impressed.

"First, I must explain to you who I am," he said. "I am with the law firm of Matson, Engles, and Lawhon in San Francisco. I represent your grandfather, James Brian McCarthy."

"My grandfather? I didn't, I mean, I hadn't thought—"

"You didn't know you had one, is that it?" He smiled at me.

"Frankly, Mr. Matson, I hadn't thought about it

41

in one way or another for years. My father's parents are dead, you know, and my mother's family was simply never mentioned.''

"Then you knew nothing of your relatives in California?"

"I suppose I knew I had some, but after my mother died, my father and I didn't discuss her family. I don't believe they approved of him, and he didn't mention them at all.''

"Probably, my dear, your father didn't know much about them. He never met most of them, you see, and I don't know how much your mother would have told him. At any rate, your grandfather has been searching for you for some years now. He wants very much for you to come to California and live with him. Or at least visit for a while.''

"California? You will forgive me, Mr. Matson, if I seem a bit confused, but right now California sounds like the end of the earth. And this is rather sudden, you know.''

"Oh, yes, my dear, I'm sure. I'm not doing this very well, am I?'' He shook his head and chuckled. "I'm not very good at these things, I'm afraid. I'm getting ahead of myself. I'd better go back to the beginning.''

He paused, then said, "When your father and mother eloped, your grandfather was, as you probably know, extremely—er—upset. He had his heart set on your mother's marriage to another young man, a neighbor, of sorts. When she ran away with your father on the very eve of that wedding, well—'' He spread his hands in a loss of words. "You understand how he felt.''

I felt a wry smile tug at the corners of my mouth. "I think you're rather understating the case, Mr. Matson. I would imagine my grandfather would be absolutely furious."

"Well, yes. Yes, I suppose that is more precise." He smiled at me. "You do understand. However, Maggie was his only child. He did love her dearly, in spite of his anger, and as time passed, he missed her more and more. He attempted to reach her, but he had few clues to follow. He knew that your father was a sailor and that he sailed out of Boston, but that wasn't much information.

"Finally, we traced your father to his business, the business he was in when he was younger, but he had left that and had dropped out of sight. For years your grandfather looked for you, but there was no trace."

All those years we'd been moving from place to place, leaving little or no evidence of our passing.

"At any rate, in the last few years your father had, apparently, gone back to his old business. Since we made it a practice to check with them periodically, we finally had some success last year. We received a letter from a Mr. Thomas Leigh telling us that you were here. I came as soon as I could."

I considered what he had told me for a few moments. "I see," I said. "And now you—or rather my grandfather—want me to come to California."

"Oh, yes. Very much so. He is most eager to meet you."

"Oh," I said vaguely, my mind spinning from this sudden turn of events. I had a grandfather. I had *family*. I should have been delighted at this news, but somehow those lilacs and their fragrance and my father's death and Emmaline kept getting mixed up in my mind with what I had just heard, and I had a difficult time sorting out my thoughts.

The room was silent, and Mr. Matson, in an effort to make conversation, said, "It's certainly nice to smell lilacs again. I do miss lilacs in the spring in California."

I looked at him, grateful to be able to pull my scattered thoughts together on at least one subject, and said, "They don't have lilacs in California?"

"No," he sighed. "I've tried to raise them but it just won't do, you know. The gardeners say it's something to do with lilacs needing a cold winter. The winters in California, at least where your grandfather and I live, simply don't get cold enough."

Suddenly the thought of never having to smell that fragrance again was extremely appealing to me. Leaving Westhaven, leaving the site of so much of the unhappiness and discomfort in my life, going somewhere new and different, struck me as a marvelous idea.

"When did you intend to leave for California, Mr. Matson?"

"Oh, as soon as possible, my dear. Haste is of the essence, so to speak. Your grandfather's health is not at all good; that's why he didn't come himself. But he is so eager to see you, now that he has found you, that we would want to leave right away."

"How would we be traveling?"

"We'd go by rail. It is, I suppose, less comfortable than traveling by ship, but it is much faster now that the new tracks cross the country. And as I say, speed is important. Am I to take it that you are willing to return with me?"

My heart pounded, and I gazed at him for a long moment. He was leaning a bit toward me, waiting expectantly for my answer. I took a deep breath and responded, "Yes. Yes, I think it would be best."

And so was set the first link of the chain of events which was to bind my entire future.

The night before we were to leave, I had difficulty falling asleep. When I finally did drop off, I had troublesome dreams. In one of them, a figure in a dark hood approached me with her arms outstretched, seeming to implore me to do something— but what, I couldn't understand. I tried to run to her, but my legs moved slowly, as if I were running in water, and my body felt weighted and weak.

Finally, when I reached her, the hood fell away, and it was my mother, her arms outstretched, fading from me even as I tried to touch her, her face filled with fear. She was shouting some kind of warning to me, but I couldn't hear her, and something was holding me, keeping me from reaching her as she faded away.

Then I awakened, and there was Mavis, shaking me and saying, "Mel, Mel, stop it! Wake up, it's just a bad dream!"

The nightmare had been so real that it took me a minute to realize where we were. The moonlight streamed through the little window and fell across my bed. In its glow, everything seemed ghostly, and I was holding Mavis and trembling.

"Are you all right?" Mavis' voice sounded far away.

"I—I think so. Yes, yes, of course," I said. "Of course. It was just a bad dream." But I was still shaking.

"It must have been a real terror. You were crying and calling someone. Scared me to death. Are you sure you're all right?"

"Yes, of course I am." I was steadier now. "It's just that it seemed so real. You know how dreams are." I forced my voice to sound reassuring.

"That one must have been a real nightmare. Look, Mel, you don't have to go to California if you don't want to. Even now it isn't too late."

"I know, Mavis, but what can I do? You know I can't stay here. I don't even want to, now that you're going and Emmaline—"

"Sam and I talked it over. You could live with us and we'd help you find something. It would work out. You don't have to go."

I patted her hand and tried to sound self-assured. "It's going to be fine, really it is. I have family there. You don't know how much I've longed for family, especially after listening to you talk about yours. And besides," I added with all the bravado I could muster, "if it doesn't suit me, I can always come back. It isn't as if I were going to Africa, you know."

"I know," she said doubtfully, "but it's awfully far away, even so. Promise you'll write."

"I've already promised, and I promise again. And

you must answer.''

"Of course I will. Now I'm going back to bed. *I* still have classes tomorrow, you know."

When she went back to bed, I stared at the moonlit patch on my bed and watched it until it faded in the light of dawn. I kept turning the dream over and over in my mind, but it made no more sense. Although I hadn't dreamed of her in years, it had been my mother. The face was the face on the miniature, and she had seemed to want to warn me of something. Warn me of what? Why was I so frightened? I finally gave up trying to sleep and dressed. That day I was to begin a new life.

Chapter Four

Traveling across the continent was, as Mr. Matson had said, uncomfortable to some extent, but once we were underway, I found that I hardly noticed. The trip was exciting, and I stared out the windows at the passing scenery from dawn until it became too dark to see.

I had never been farther from Boston than an occasional trip into the country would take us, and all of this was very new to me. The Midwest, the Great Plains, the Sierra Nevada—places I had only studied in my geography books—were real, and I was getting to see them. I was glad we had not taken the ocean route; I would have missed so much.

As we traveled, Mr. Matson told me about my grandfather's ranch and about the family.

"The ranch itself was owned for almost a hundred years by the Montoya family. At least, the old part of the ranch and the old ranch house was. It's much bigger now than it was then. Your grandfather has added to it considerably. Most of the *haciendas* are getting smaller, but your grandfather has kept building up the original Montoya holdings."

"Haciendas?"

"Spanish word for ranch, loosely translated. Originally, 'hacienda' was to 'ranch' as 'plantation' was to 'farm' in the South. Now they're called ranches for the most part, although the Spanish ways and terms still cling, as you will find when you get there."

" 'Montoya' was one of my mother's names. She was half Spanish, wasn't she?"

"Yes. Your grandmother was Susana Montoya, the only daughter of Don Diego Montoya, last of the Montoya line. Your grandfather owned a small ranch attached to the Montoya hacienda, and Don Diego loved him like a son. Your grandfather was the son of Irish immigrants, and he came west to get land. He fell in love with Susana Montoya, and Don Diego was delighted."

"I'm surprised at that. I'd have thought Don Diego would have preferred to have his daughter marry one of the other Spanish landholders."

"Don Diego was an unusual man for his time. He admired your grandfather because he was a self-made man. He thought your grandfather had strength of character, and said that the sons of all the other landowners had grown soft and would eventually be unable to hold their property. Time has proved that he was right."

"They did lose the land?"

"Most of them. Only your grandfather's ranch has increased, as I say, and most of the old landowners have had to sell, or have lost their land through poor management."

"Whatever happened to the young man my

mother was supposed to marry?"

"He was killed two years later in a gambling house brawl in San Francisco." Mr. Matson stared out the window for a moment at the passing scenery. "I'm sure that's one of the things that made your grandfather regret his unyielding attitude toward Maggie's marriage. He realized he had used poor judgment in the situation. The young man came of a good family, but," he sighed, "perhaps too much emphasis is placed on such things as family. He had no character."

I wondered what Mr. Matson would say if he knew the circumstances of my father's death. I was certain that he would judge my father as lacking in character, also. I decided to change the subject.

"My grandmother has been dead for some years, has she not?"

"Yes. She died when your mother was about ten. I thought it might kill your grandfather, too. That was probably one reason he was so set on tying Maggie to a marriage that would keep her close to him. She was all he had left."

"Poor Grandfather. He must have been very lonely all these years."

"Yes, I'm sure he was for some time. Of course, about five years ago, he remarried, and I would imagine things have been less lonely for him since."

This bit of information came as something of a surprise to me, since Mr. Matson had never made any reference, even obliquely, to my grandfather's second wife.

"I didn't realize he was married. What is his wife like?"

50

"I'm sorry I hadn't mentioned it," he said, but he seemed a bit hesitant about discussing her. "I would have to describe Sybil as—elegant. A very attractive woman." I had the feeling that he was choosing his words very carefully.

"Sybil? Is that her name?"

"Yes. Sybil Harrington, she was. She has a son, a few years older than you are, I'd guess. Lane Harrington."

"But I find that exciting, Mr. Matson," I said. "I suppose you think it's silly of me to be sentimental about such things, but if you knew how much I have always wanted a family, and how much I have envied other people theirs—" I stopped. My eyes had filled with tears, and I turned to the window.

"There, there." He patted my hand awkwardly. "I understand perfectly. But I must warn you that Sybil and Lane may be different than you expect."

"How do you mean, different?"

"Well, Sybil comes from a very wealthy family in San Francisco, and she and Lane tend to be more, shall we say, sophisticated than the rest of us about some things."

"You mean they might think me a perfect ninny for getting all weepy over my long-lost family?" I said, trying to make a joke of my tears.

"Oh, I wouldn't say that, exactly," he said in a tone which indicated that he would say just that, exactly.

"Don't worry, Mr. Matson. I won't make a fool of myself in front of my elegant new grandmother or my elegant new—what would Lane be? my uncle?"

"Yes, I suppose technically he would be your

uncle. Although that does sound strange. He's not much older than you are."

He warned me that they might seem distant at first, but said that I was not to take it to heart. That was just their way, he said, and I must not be put off by it.

I thought about this as we traveled along. I felt that he was giving me a subtle warning that there were those at the ranch who would not necessarily welcome me, who might, in fact, resent my presence there. I was not sure I understood that, but I did feel a stirring of something unpleasant in the back of my mind.

It would be different than I had expected. Somehow I had managed to build a picture of just my grandfather and myself, both of us alone in the world, and both of us finding comfort together. Pure sentimental nonsense, Melinda, I scolded myself. Of course as lonely as he'd been, he would look for someone else. He didn't even know you were alive.

Still, it was going to be different than I had imagined.

We arrived in San Francisco in late afternoon, and Mr. Matson arranged for us to go to a hotel for the night.

"It's a full day's drive to the ranch," he said, "and we will stay the night here and start first thing in the morning. Your grandfather's carriage and driver will meet us at the hotel. In fact, he's probably there now. He'll drive us out, and one of the supply wagons will bring our luggage along later.''

He had our driver take us to the hotel by way of a hill which overlooked the bay so that I could get a glimpse of the ocean.

I thought I had never seen a sky so blue, or a city so lovely. I could see white houses perched on hills that looked too steep to hold them, and flowers everywhere. There was not a lilac among them, I was delighted to note, but the roses were blooming, there were geraniums in window-boxes, and wisteria vines drooped languidly on porches.

"How do you like our city, Melinda?" Mr. Matson asked. He saw me straining to see as much as I could.

"I think it's the loveliest place I've ever seen," I said. "Is the ranch in a place like this?"

"Not so hilly, actually, although the climate is very like this since the ranch-house is close to the sea. But the ranch is very beautiful in its own way. I think you'll like it."

We stayed the night in a hotel, and, early the next morning, began our journey to the ranch. Our carriage ride took us close to the ocean, and the early morning sun sparkled on the water. We drove through clumps of trees, and the sun shone through a faint morning mist that made the groves seem enchanted. I was enthralled by the loveliness of the area, and commented about it to Mr. Matson.

"You are fortunate to be here when there is no fog. When the fog comes in, it can be so heavy that you can't see past the horse in front of us."

"Is there much fog?"

"Oh, yes, sometimes for days at a time. It can be quite dangerous. But when the breeze comes in and blows it away, there's no place lovelier."

We continued our trip along the coast, sometimes coming close to the edge of cliffs that overlooked great waves crashing on jagged rocks, sometimes making our way through groves of trees so large I could scarcely see their tops.

"Those are the redwoods," Mr. Matson told me. "Your grandfather has a grove of them on his ranch that he refuses to allow cut. He says they can't be replaced, and he's not going to allow anything that old or that beautiful to be destroyed."

My respect for my grandfather rose. I was impressed with the grandeur of those mighty trees, and agreed it would be a shame to level the grove.

By late afternoon, we came to the top of a small rise, and I could see below the white walls and the red-tile roofs of what was to be my home.

I looked and looked again, and Mr. Matson must have noticed my puzzled expression, because he said to me, "There it is, your grandfather's ranch. The— Is something wrong, my dear?"

"Well, no," I answered, "not really. It's just that—it must be the angle or something. It almost looks as if there's a tree growing out of the center of the house."

"Oh, that." Mr. Matson chuckled. "Well, no, it isn't the angle. There is a tree growing out of the center of the house, after a fashion. I will wait and let you see it. It's easier to appreciate first-hand."

As we approached the house, he told me that the ranch was called *Rancho de las Mariposas*—The

Butterfly Ranch.

" 'Butterfly Ranch'? It seems a strange name."

"You won't think so when you've seen the butterflies. In the summer there are thousands of them all over. They are very beautiful. It will seem natural to you then. However, most of the locals don't call it that. It's still referred to primarily as 'the old Montoya place.' The old names die hard."

As we approached the house, my heart was pounding so hard I found it difficult to concentrate.

"Are they expecting us today?" I asked.

"Oh, yes, I wired your grandfather from Boston and told him when to expect us. All the family will be here to see you."

That didn't help any.

We drove through a whitewashed archway into a cobbled courtyard, and a young man ran out to take our horse. Mr. Matson helped me down, and took my arm as we entered the house. Huge oaken doors swung open to admit us to a large foyer. My grandfather, leaning on a cane, was waiting inside to greet us.

I think I would have known him anywhere. He was tall, with snow-white hair and bronzed skin. His eyes were blue, and there were crinkles around them as if he were often out of doors.

We stared at each other for a moment, and at last I said, in little more than a whisper, "Grandfather?"

His face broke into a smile. He opened his arms to me, and I ran to embrace him. I hadn't realized how much I had missed having someone to love, someone to love me, until that moment. My grandfather's love and concern were evident, and I found myself weeping with joy.

My grandfather, his arm around me, turned to Mr. Matson. "You'd have known she was my grandchild, wouldn't you, Steve, with a head of hair like that?"

Mr. Matson nodded, and smiled at me. "It's the same shade, all right."

"Your hair was red, too?" I asked.

"As bright as yours, my dear," he said, hugging me with one arm and leaning on his cane with the other. He was so happy about it that I didn't mention that my father's hair had been red also.

Now he was leading me into a large room where two people stood waiting to meet me. The floor of the room was dark tile, like the entryway, and the walls were whitewashed. The furniture was dark and heavy, and there were brightly colored rugs scattered about the floor. In one corner of the room was a fireplace with an arched opening, plastered, and raised about two feet off the floor. It was very unlike the brick-faced fireplaces I was accustomed to.

There was a piano on one side of the room with a fringed shawl draped across it, and on top a pottery bowl filled with marigolds. It was a pleasant, comfortable room, uncrowded and informal, not at all like any room I had ever seen before.

Against this background, the two formally dressed people who were standing in the center of the room looked as out of place as if they had been dressed for a masquerade.

My grandfather, his arm still around my shoulder,

said, "Melinda, I would like you to meet my wife, Sybil, and her son, Lane Harrington."

I thought Sybil Harrington McCarthy was, at first glance, one of the loveliest women I had ever seen. At second glance, I thought she appeared to be the coldest person I had ever encountered.

Her hair was as white as my grandfather's, although she was obviously some years younger than he. Had it not been for that, she could have passed as her son's sister. She had black eyebrows over the iciest blue eyes I had ever seen. They seemed to pierce straight through me and their coldness was totally uninfluenced by the smile her mouth affected. She was elegantly dressed in a lavender frock, and when she extended her hand to me, I caught a whiff of lilac fragrance.

"We are delighted to have you here at last, Melinda," she said. I had never heard anyone sound less delighted. "Your grandfather most anxiously awaited your arrival."

I thought it ironic to have fled the East to escape the hated scent of summer lilac, only to have it here in a form that would last year-round. I attributed my sudden dislike of Sybil Harrington McCarthy to that hated scent, and inwardly scolded myself for it. That's silly, I told myself. Disliking a woman because of her perfume! You are going to have to overcome this absurd prejudice.

Lane Harrington was quite tall, and blond, with his mother's dark eyebrows and her blue eyes, although his eyes were less piercing and his manner more genial. He was extremely handsome, and flawlessly dressed in a pale gray coat and trousers.

He smiled as he offered his hand. "Welcome to California, Miss Cole. Or may I call you Melinda? Somehow, as your new uncle, I feel formality is a bit unnecessary."

I smiled back at him. "Melinda is definitely preferable. After a year of teaching, I feel that I have heard 'Miss Cole' quite enough."

"My dear," my grandfather said, "I am anxious to sit down and have a long talk with you. We have nineteen years to cover, and I'm in a hurry to get at it."

"James," Sybil said, "you must give the child time to rest first. After all, she's just made that exhausting trip from San Francisco and she was on the train for days before that. At least give her time to have a nap before dinner."

I was about to say that I was so excited that I didn't think I could sleep, but my grandfather said, "Of course, of course. It's rather selfish of me, my child. I'll have Rosa show you to your quarters. After dinner, we'll have a long talk."

A tall slim woman with dark eyes and gray-streaked hair had entered the room, and my grandfather turned to her.

"This is Rosa Dominguez," he said. "She has been with us for many years, and you will find her of great help in answering your questions. Rosa, this is my granddaughter, Melinda Cole. Will you show her to her room, please?"

"Si, Señor McCarthy." Rosa turned to me, her eyes bright with tears. "Your eyes are like your mother's, señorita," she said. "Is it not so, señor?"

My grandfather nodded. "Very like, Rosa."

"She was so beautiful," she said. I dropped my head. I felt that they were disappointed with me. I knew my mother had been very beautiful, and I was not. I was too tall, my nose was too thin, I had an unmanageable mop of rust-colored hair. But when I raised my eyes, Rosa was smiling at me as if she saw only my mother's eyes, and I returned the smile.

"Come with me, señorita. I will show you where you will stay." She led me into the foyer, and I saw that the entryway went straight through into a garden that was in the center of the house.

"This is why it seemed that there was a tree growing through the roof," I exclaimed. "The house is built around a garden."

"We call it a *patio*, señorita. I am told it is like the houses in Spain."

The patio was filled with flowers and flowering vines. There was indeed a large tree which shaded a bench and a table, and further back was an arbor formed by a vine flowering with bright pink blooms. There were roses everywhere, and a profusion of bright blossoms in carefully tended beds. Marigolds, zinnias, petunias, nasturtiums, verbena, and others I had never seen before made patterns of color along the edges of the patio and in beds through which stone paths wandered. In the center, a fountain, mossy with age, trickled water into a small basin. I loved the place at once.

"That's a beautiful vine," I said, indicating the arbor. "I don't think I've ever seen one like it."

"It is called bougainvillea, señorita. It will only grow where the climate is mild."

"What a lovely place this is," I paused to look

59

around me. The house formed a frame for the lovely patio, rising to two stories with long corridors formed by arches running the length of the walls. The rooms opened into the arched corridors. We went up a flight of stairs, covered with the same graceful arches, on steps of brightly colored ceramic tiles. Rosa led me down the corridor to the last door.

The rooms on the corner of the house were furnished much like the large room in which I had been received. There were the same colorful rugs on the tiled floor, the same whitewashed walls, the same dark furniture. There was a large bed with a pale green canopy and a coverlet of the same green material.

The small sitting room adjoining the bedroom had a writing desk and a loveseat. The dressing room had a large mirror, stacks of fluffy towels on wrought-iron shelves, and an ornate porcelain tub which stood on gilt feet and was painted with clusters of pink roses.

It was a beautiful suite, and I said so to Rosa.

"It was your mother's, señorita," she said. "Your grandfather thought you would like it."

I walked to the window and pulled back the draperies. On the outside of the window was an ironwork grill, more delicately shaped than the bars on a jail cell, but as effective, I imagined, in preventing one's escape by that route. I had noticed them on the other windows of the house, and I asked Rosa what they were for.

She shrugged. "Decoration, these days, señorita. In the cities of Spain where the first Montoyas lived, they kept the burglars out, I suppose. Or perhaps," she said, her eyes twinkling, "they kept the young ladies *in*."

I had thought that I was too excited to take a nap, but I lay down and fell asleep almost instantly. It seemed only a few minutes until Rosa knocked on the door and told me that dinner would be servd shortly.

I washed, brushed my hair hurriedly, and went back downstairs the way we had come. In the foyer, with its tile floors and leather settees, I looked right and left to see where to go for dinner. My grandfather was still in the room where I had left him, and he motioned for me to join him. He and Mr. Matson were sipping sherry, and he poured a glass for me.

"Did you have a nice rest, my dear?" he asked.

"Oh, yes," I said. "I would not have thought that I could have slept, but I did."

"Steve and I have been discussing you, and we need to sit down and have a long talk very soon."

"Now, Jim," Mr. Matson said, "I think it can wait a few days until Melinda gets acclimated. After all, you don't know whether she will even want to stay out here."

"May I ask what the talk is to be about?" I inquired.

"Some matters involving the estate, Melinda," Mr. Matson said. "But I think it can wait until you get more settled."

"I'm not sure I've got time for all this hemming and hawing around, Steve," Grandfather grumbled. "I like to get things taken care of right away."

"I would warn against any hasty decisions, Jim," Mr. Matson said. "I think it would be best to settle things in your mind first."

I hadn't the foggiest notion of what they were talking about, but when Mr. Matson mentioned "hasty decisions" Grandfather grunted, nodded, and appeared to accede to his wishes.

A moment later, we were joined by Sybil and Lane, and we all went in to dinner.

The dining room was much like the rest of the house in that it had the same style and decor, but over the table hung a huge crystal chandelier which dominated the room.

"What a beautiful chandelier!" I said. Sybil smiled briefly.

"That came from my home in San Francisco," she told me. "It had been in the family for years, and I couldn't bear to part with it."

"Pretty fancy for a ranch house," Grandfather said.

"I think it's lovely," I replied, and I fancied that Sybil regarded me with a look that was a trifle less frosty than those she had favored me with thus far.

Lane was seated on my right during dinner, and he seemed determined to be as charming and amusing as his mother was distant.

"Do you ride?" he asked as we were finishing dessert.

"No," I shook my head. "I've always wanted to, but I never had a chance to learn."

"It's almost a necessity here on the ranch," he said, "so if you would like, I can give you riding lessons."

"I would love it, but I'm afraid I don't have the proper clothing. I don't own a riding habit."

"I'm sure that should be no problem. We aren't as formal about those things as they are back East, and anyway, I would imagine that one could be found and made to fit until you have an opportunity to have one made for you."

I assured him that if that were the case, I would love to begin riding lessons.

After dinner, Grandfather called me into his study to talk to me. The study also had a fireplace, and was lined with books. It was a small room, but warmly decorated, with a distinctly masculine feel.

"This is my 'hole'," Grandfather winked at me. "Sybil can do what she wants with her elegant doodads in the rest of the house, but this room is mine."

I was looking through the titles of the books, barely able to restrain myself. I had never had access to so many books, and I hoped that Grandfather would allow me to read them.

As if he understood what I was thinking, he said, "The books are yours any time you want them, my dear. Just put them back when you're finished, and don't go rearranging things."

"I wouldn't do that," I smiled. "I don't like people pushing my things about either."

"You're my granddaughter in that," he smiled. "Now, I wanted to talk to you about what Steve and I mentioned earlier. I told him I would wait and make a decision about it later, and I will. He's right about my hasty decisions. I've made some doozies. Your mother's marriage, for one." He paused, and took out a pipe and began filling it, avoiding my eyes. "If I hadn't been so set on that—well, look how much trouble I caused over it.''

"Oh, Grandfather, don't spend any time worrying about that." I pulled up a stool and sat down beside him. "It's over and done. There's no point in worrying about the past."

He looked down at me and smiled. "You're a remarkable girl, Melinda. Some would have been bitter about the life you've led these past years."

I shrugged. "Who knows? Maybe if I'd been raised here I wouldn't have appreciated it as I do seeing it now for the first time."

He nodded. "That may be true. Anyway, my concern—what Steve and I were talking about—was for the inheritance of the ranch."

"The inheritance?"

"Yes. You see, until I became the owner of this ranch, it had been in the hands of the Montoya family. For over a hundred years the Montoyas held this ranch, until Don Diego Montoya, my father-in-law, left it to me. Of course, he left it to me because I was married to his daughter, but he wanted to insure that someone of his blood would keep the property.''

He stopped and looked at me for a long moment. "I don't have to tell you that you are the last of Don Diego's bloodline."

I hadn't thought of that. Somehow all those people had not seemed connected with me. I was plain Melinda Cole, and Don Diego's family seemed remote and exotic, somehow golden in a way I could not be.

I looked up at my grandfather. "I suppose, logically, you are right, Grandfather, but that hardly seems grounds for making this sort of decision."

"It carries more weight than you think, my dear, especially locally. The people here would consider that you'd have the most valid claim to the land, being a direct descendant of Don Diego, if you were a three-headed ape," he chuckled, "which, I'm happy to say, you definitely are not. But you are right in one respect. Bloodlines aside, this ranch must go to someone who cares about it." He was, suddenly, very intense. "I won't have this land sold off and stripped the minute I'm in my grave, if there is anything I can do about it."

"But surely, Grandfather, no one would do that." I was naive enough then to believe that no one could want to lose such a lovely place.

"Oh, yes, child, in some ways this land is more valuable sold than maintained. It is a productive ranch, but there is money to be made in other ways, too, And, you see, while I am worth a lot of money on paper, cash is always in rather short supply here. We have always been fairly self-sufficient and have never made great sums of money. But then, I've always considered the land a trust. I felt that I was just holding it for Don Diego, for his heirs."

He was silent for a moment, then looked at me. "But I feel as he did, that the true heirs to property are those who love it, not those who, by accident or birth or legal manuevering can get their hands on it.

"What I'm saying is that I would like the property to be yours, but I don't want to make any hasty decisions. I've made too many of those. You stay here for a while. See how you like it. After a time, we'll talk about it again."

I left the study in a daze. A month ago, I'd been

concerned about staying alive, feeding myself. Now my grandfather was talking about my inheritance. I couldn't believe it. I was sure the land should go to someone else, someone who knew how to take care of it. What did I know about running a ranch? Surely Grandfather had thought of all that. Surely he knew that I was incompetent to handle such property.

I slowly climbed the stairs. The moonlight shone through the arches on the corridor and lighted my way to my room.

When I entered, I saw that Rosa had turned down my bed and left candles lighted in tall, polished-brass candlesticks. I changed into my nightgown, climbed into bed, and lay for a long time, staring into the darkness.

When I finally went to sleep, I dreamed the same dream I had had before I left Boston. This time the dream was a little clearer. My mother was standing at the end of some sort of tunnel, and I was trying to get to her. She was wearing a long cloak and a hood that covered her face. As I struggled to reach her, I realized that I was up to my knees in water, and my wet skirts were dragging me down, slowing me so I couldn't get to her. As I tried to reach her and make out the warning she was shouting to me, she slowly faded away, and I awakened, sitting straight up in bed and holding myself to keep from shaking.

Why this dream? Why now? It seemed that I had finally come to a home, a place where I could be secure and safe. Why was I having this nightmare? What was she warning me about? It must have been early in the morning before I got back to sleep. The sun was high in the sky when I awakened.

Chapter Five

When I left my room in the morning, I paused on the way out and leaned over the rail of the corridor to look at the patio below. In the early morning light it seemed even more beautiful than before. A jasmine vine twisted around a trellis that reached almost to where I was standing. The fragrance mingled with the scent of the roses below. As I watched, Rosa came along the lower corridor opposite, and I called a greeting to her.

"Good morning, señorita," she called. "I'm afraid breakfast is over, but *El Viejo*—your grandfather—said we were to look after you. Come down with me, and I'll fix you a special meal."

"There's no need, Rosa. I'll be fine."

"Yes, yes, you come down. I will show you more of the house, too."

She waited for me at the foot of the stairs and led me around the patio.

"This is such a beautiful place, Rosa. Have you been here all your life?"

"Oh, yes. And my mother before me. We have always been with the Montoya family. And now with your grandfather."

"What was it you called him just a moment ago?"
I asked.

She smiled a bit sheepishly. *El Viejo*. It means
'the old man,' but it is a term of affection, I assure
you."

"I could tell."

"It is wonderful to have you here, señorita." She
looked into my eyes. "We all love your grandfather,
but it is a blessing to have one of the blood of the
Montoyas here again."

"Thank you, Rosa. I hope I'm not a disappointment to you."

"A disappointment?" She looked puzzled. "In
what way could you be, señorita?"

"Well, I don't speak Spanish, I don't ride, I know
nothing about the ranch, and I feel very much as if a
real Montoya would know all of those things."

"Ahh!" She waved her hand in dismissal. "All
those things you can learn. But the blood—that you
must be born with."

"And even that—I feel I am nothing like my
mother."

"You are your own person, señorita. You need
not wish to be anything else. Your mother would be
proud of you."

"Thank you for that, Rosa." I felt on the verge of
tears. "I would like to talk about her, to learn about
her. I know so little, you see."

"We will have time. Now, come out to the
cocina—the kitchen—and I will fix you a breakfast.
In fact, I will make your mother's favorite. Would
you like that?"

"Oh, yes, please."

I followed her into the kitchen, which I thought was the nicest room I had seen so far. It had a large brick oven in one wall, copper pans hanging from a beamed ceiling, and bright blue curtains at the windows. There were red geraniums in pots on the windowsills. Colorful tile like that on the steps covered the counters and the walls up to the cupboards. There was a well-scrubbed table in the center of the room and Rosa pushed a chair up to it for me.

Two women working the room eyed me curiously. "Señorita," Rosa said, "I would like you to meet our cook, Mrs. Malloy." The cook was short and round, and appeared to enjoy the products of her art a great deal. She extended her hand, a wide grin spread across her plump face.

"I'm delighted to meet you," she said. "We've all been looking forward to it."

"And this," Rosa said, "is my daughter, Antonia." Antonia turned from her work and gave me a sullen, careful appraisal. She was beautiful—small, delicate, with enormous dark eyes and a wealth of black hair that was caught in a braid which fell past her waist.

After a pause which was long enough to be impolite, she muttered, "Nice to meet you," and turned back to her work.

Rosa, obviously embarrassed at her daughter's poor manners, settled me at the table and busied herself with making my breakfast. She served me a dish of poached eggs in a kind of spicy tomato sauce.

"They are called *huevos rancheros—* ranch-style eggs," she explained. "You are not accustomed to the chile spice, which can be very hot, so I didn't put in very much. And here," she turned and removed from the griddle what appeared to be round flat pancakes, and buttered them, *"tortillas,"* she said. "Try them."

I found the food delicious, even though my eyes were watering from the spices. I was glad Rosa hadn't put in much of the chile. I praised her cooking and she glowed.

"Your mother loved this for breakfast," she said, "and so does your grandfather. He prefers tortillas to bread, but the señora—Mrs. McCarthy—doesn't permit us to serve them except at breakfast. She doesn't come down for breakfast." She shrugged. "So we serve them then."

Then she grinned "Ahhh, I know what I forgot. You will like this." A few minutes later she served me a cup of hot chocolate— strong, bittersweet, cinnamon-flavored, and delicious.

"This is very good," I said, sipping the hot drink. "It isn't like any other chocolate I have ever had."

"It is chocolate as it is served in Mexico," she explained. "Not as sweet as you are accustomed to, I would think."

"No, not as sweet, but I like it better."

When I had finished, she showed me around the house. It was different from any house I had ever seen, and she told me that the early Montoyas built it in the style of houses in Spain.

"I am told that, in Spain, there was not much room for gardens, and the cities were crowded, so in order to have privacy, the houses were built very close to the sidewalks and the garden space was kept in the center as a patio."

"That hardly seems necessary here. They had all the space they needed."

"True," she said, "but that was the sort of house they knew, so that was the sort they built."

"It makes a very charming arrangement," I said.

"I think so," she answered, "though there are some who never become accustomed to it."

The house was very large, but its design was simple, and I felt as if I were familiar with it already.

As we turned toward the front of the house, Antonia went past us and did not respond to my greeting.

"Have I done something to offend your daughter, Rosa?" I asked. "I can't imagine why she appears to dislike me so."

Rosa avoided my eyes, embarrassed once more. "It—it is not of your doing, señorita. My daughter—" she sighed. "I have raised her badly, I'm afraid. She has many strange ideas."

Still, I was uncomfortable about Antonia's open antagonism toward me. I wondered what I could have done to have invited it.

I spent the rest of the day wandering around the grounds and the house. I visited the stables and the corrals, where the workers greeted me with polite and friendly interest. I had seen no one from the family all day, but when I returned to the house late in the afternoon, Lane was waiting in the foyer.

"I've been looking for you," he said, offering me his arm, and leading me into the large room we'd met in the night before. "Where have you been keeping yourself all day?"

"I've been exploring," I said. "I've seen the house, the stables, the corrals—it's been very interesting."

"Frankly, it sounds deadly to me," he said, "but I suppose it's all quite different for someone who is new to it."

"Oh, yes," I said. "I've loved it."

He gave me a smile that was faintly condescending, and I felt somehow awkward and provincial. "Would you care for a glass of sherry?" he asked. I nodded, and he poured me a thimbleful from a crystal decanter and handed me the fragile glass.

In an effort to cover my unease, I said, "This is a beautiful wineglass."

"Yes, it is, isn't it? It was my mother's from our home in San Francisco. You will find that most of the more elegant furnishings and accoutrements here were brought by her."

I found this faintly annoying and resented the implied insult to my grandfather's house.

"I find this house a very lovely and comfortable place," I said.

He shrugged. "I suppose it is a style that appeals to *some*," he said. His words seemed to imply that the "some" that it appealed to were hardly worth considering.

I tried to change the subject. "What does one call this room?" I asked. " 'Parlor' hardly seems to suit it."

"The Spanish word is *sala*—similar to the French

salon. And you are right—'parlor' does imply a formality that this room lacks.''

'' 'Formality' wouldn't be the word I would use,'' I said. '' 'Stuffiness' comes a little closer to my meaning.'' I sounded a bit snappish to my own ears, but I was becoming more than a little annoyed with the whole trend of the conversation.

He smiled at me, a warm smile, obviously meant to charm, and seemed to switch personalities before my eyes. ''I believe you're right,'' he said. ''There is nothing stuffy about the Rancho.'' He seated himself beside me on the sofa. ''If you feel sufficiently rested from your trip, perhaps you would like to begin your riding lessons tomorrow. It really is the only way to see the ranch.''

''Oh, yes,'' I said. ''I'd love it. I'm eager to see more of the countryside.''

''Good. When you feel confident enough to try it, we can ride down to the beach and see the smugglers' cave, and over the hill to the old mission.''

''Smugglers' cave? What sort of place is that?''

''Just what the name implies. When California was a Spanish territory, the Spaniards taxed certain imports very heavily, and fortunes could be made smuggling various items past the watchful eyes of the Spanish troops. It is believed that much of the early Montoya fortune was made that way. At any rate, it is known that there was a cave with a tunnel leading from it to the back of the Montoya property.''

''How fascinating! And is it still here?''

''Not the part at this end. That was destroyed by

an earthquake some forty or fifty years ago. The cave at the other end is still visible at low tide. It fills with water at high tide and can't be seen then."

"Can we go into it?"

"Not likely. Jim had an iron gate made to cover the opening some years back, after a would-be explorer stayed too long and was trapped by the high tide. He almost drowned and Jim said it was too much of a temptation. Next time, someone might be killed."

I shuddered. "That sounds frightening."

"Actually, the location is lovely at low tide. We can ride down to see it. It's safe enough from the outside."

At this moment my grandfather and Sybil entered the sala, and my grandfather came over and kissed my cheek.

"Did you have a nice day, my dear?"

"Oh, yes, lovely, Grandfather. Rosa showed me around the house and I did some exploring on my own."

"Good, good. I'm sorry I wasn't able to join you. I've been locked up with Steve Matson all day."

"Lane is going to begin teaching me to ride tomorrow."

Sybil glanced at Lane and favored me with a tiny smile. "Then I'll have Rosa look for a riding habit for you. I'm sure there's one here you can wear."

Lane had risen to pour his mother and Grandfather a glass of sherry, and as he handed the glass to her, he said, "Melinda was admiring the crystal, Mother."

She gave me the same sort of look I had noticed

last night when I had admired her chandelier, a sort of grudging approval.

"It's quite old," she said. "My grandfather had it imported from France."

"It's very lovely," I murmured.

"My dear," my grandfather interrupted, "we are planning a bit of a gala celebration of your arrival. I think you will enjoy one of our local *fiestas*, as we call them. It will give you a chance to meet some of the neighbors."

"It sounds like great fun," I said. "When will it be?"

"A week from tomorrow. You'll find we're less formal about such things out here. We don't spend months getting ready for parties. We just have them."

"By 'out here' he means on the ranches, Melinda," Sybil said. "In the city, the amenities are still observed."

Grandfather gave her an odd look. "By those who can afford the amenities, that is." It seemed an innocuous enough remark to me, but Sybil looked at him almost as if he had offered her an insult, a hostile and almost threatening look. "Yes, of course," she said. "Shall we go in to dinner now?"

Mr. Matson joined us as we were going into the dining room, and after dinner, he and Grandfather shut themselves up in his study again. There was still some light and I wandered into the patio to sit under the tree. I had only been there a few minutes when I saw Sybil, her white gown almost glowing in the dusk, approaching me.

"May I join you?" she asked.

"Yes, of course."

"I felt that we should spend some time getting acquainted since you are going to be with us," she paused, "at least for a while." She sat down and I caught the lilac scent and felt the same unreasonable antagonism toward her. I tried to cover it by smiling, "Yes. This is a lovely place, isn't it?"

"It is one of the more—unique—houses in the area," she said. An oblique answer at best.

I tried a different tack. "Had you lived in San Francisco all your life before you came here?"

"Oh, yes. And my father had been there all of his life. My grandfather settled in San Francisco when it was Spanish territory. We were not among that new lot who came with the Gold Rush," she added with pride and unmistakable snobbery.

"It must have been difficult for you to leave."

"Very," she sighed, "very difficult. I had lived all my life in the same house. I was born there. Lane was born there. I hated to go." There was a mixture of bitterness and wistfulness in her voice.

"I—I'm sorry," I said.

"Sorry?" I was stung by the scorn in that word. "For me?" The light was too dim for me to read the expression in her face, but the contempt in her voice was clear. "My dear," she made a partially successful attempt to cover the fury she had exposed, and withdrew into her customary reserve, "save your sympathy for yourself. After all, you, from what I understand, are the one who has had a difficult life. I am hardly in need of your pity."

"You misunderstood me," I said, hurrying somehow to cover the mistake and trying to repair

76

my inadvertent damage. "It wasn't pity I was expressing. It was simply that, I mean, I know how difficult it is to be one place when you would much rather be somewhere else." How well I knew! "I only meant that if you'd rather be there, it seems unfortunate that you cannot."

She rose, her dignity fully regained. "Of course," she murmured. "And of course these things are often not permanent. I have every hope of returning to my home. Eventually." She left, and I sat puzzling over her last statement.

I decided to go to bed and get a good night's sleep since Lane and I had plans for riding in the morning. I had concluded that my nightmares were the result of fatigue, and I hoped to escape another one by going to bed early. Apparently it worked, because I didn't have a repeat of the previous night's dream, but I was awakened about midnight by some sort of sound. I couldn't decide what it was, so I lay in my bed for a few minutes, waiting for the sound to be repeated. Nothing happened.

Finally, I decided that it had only been some sort of night bird, but by this time I was fully awake and lying in the dark staring at the canopy, pale in the light of the moon that shone through my window.

"This," I told myself, "is silly." I decided to get up and go down to my grandfather's study and find a book to read. I slipped out of bed, groped for my robe and slippers, and reached for a candle. Then I decided not to take a candle with me. The moonlight was bright enough, and I could light a candle in the study. Someone might see the light and think perhaps I was ill. There seemed no point in disturbing someone else.

I stepped out of my door into the corridor. The patio was bright in the light of the moon. I stood and looked at it for a moment, and as I watched, I saw a shadow move in the lower corridor across from my wing.

As she moved into the moonlight, I recognized Antonia. I almost stepped forward to speak to her, when I realized that she was looking around furtively, as if checking to see whether anyone was watching. Then she darted across the patio, and disappeared beneath the corridor where I was standing.

I heard her say something, but I couldn't understand a word, and I heard a man's voice answer. I smiled to myself. She was meeting a lover, I thought, and it must be someone Rosa disapproves of, from the secretiveness of her manner. I debated a moment as to whether to continue on my errand, and decided not to go. I didn't want to interfere, and Antonia seemed to dislike me already. I slipped back into my room and climbed back into bed, leaving the book for another time.

It was a decision I was later to regret.

Chapter Six

Lane and I began my riding lessons the next day. He was an excellent horseman and a good teacher, so within a few days I was feeling confident and becoming competent. The ranch was beautiful, and each day we rode further and saw more of it. I had never been so happy.

One day we rode into a field golden with wildflowers, and Lane told me they were called California poppies. I gathered a bunch and took them home to put in a vase beside my bed.

On the morning before the fiesta, I went out to the stables to meet Lane. He was late, apparently, and there was no one there except one of the ranch-hands. I had never seen this particular man before, but that was not unusual. Every day I saw someone new.

He was inspecting the hoof of one of the horses when I arrived, and he didn't seem to have heard me approach.

"Mr. Harrington and I will be taking the two horses down at the end there," I said, indicating our usual mounts. "Would you saddle them for us, please?"

He looked up at me, a bit surprised, and then smiled, and said, "Sure. Be glad to." He led one of the horses out and dragged the saddle from its place. "You must be Melinda Cole."

"Yes, I am." I thought he seemed a bit forward. Most of the men on the ranch called me "Miss Melinda," or "señorita."

He saddled the horses in silence. I watched for Lane through the stable door.

"Looking forward to the party tonight?"

I frowned. What business was it of his? "Certainly," I said shortly. I regarded him across the saddle. He had dark hair, and blue-green eyes that seemed to sparkle with suppressed laughter. I was becoming more annoyed. What was there about me that he found so amusing?

At this moment, Lane arrived, flawlessly dressed as usual. He stopped and regarded the man across the saddle through narrowed eyes.

"Hello, Allen," he said finally.

"How are you, Harrington?" the man replied.

I looked from one to the other, confused. "Melinda, I see you've met Jarrod Allen," Lane said stiffly.

"No—no," I said, still at a loss. "I thought he was—"

"Miss Cole took me for one of the stable-hands," Jarrod Allen smiled wickedly, "I didn't choose to disillusion her."

"So I see." Lane's manner was definitely hostile. "Then I suppose I should complete the introductions. Melinda Cole, this is Jarrod Allen. He owns the ranch that adjoins Mariposas on the north. Allen, this is Melinda Cole, Jim McCarthy's granddaughter.''

"Miss Cole." He bowed. "I hadn't intended to make your acquaintance until tonight or I'd have dressed more appropriately. This, as you can see," he indicated his rough clothing, "is the attire of the working rancher."

"He means as opposed to the clothing of the non-working rancher," Lane snapped. "Come, Melinda, let's be on our way."

"I owe you an apology, Mr. Allen," I said, with as much dignity as I could salvage from the situation. "I didn't intend to be unkind."

"Just wanted to put the uppity ranch hand in his place, right, Miss Cole? It isn't important. No offense taken."

I blushed and turned and mounted my horse. He was still standing there, watching me. "Was there something else, Mr. Allen?" I asked rather haughtily.

"I came to see your grandfather. Is he in the house?"

"Yes, I believe so. Goodbye, Mr. Allen."

"Goodbye, Miss Cole. You will save me a dance tonight, won't you?" His eyes sparkled with amusement. I didn't answer. I just turned my horse and followed Lane out of the stable.

"What a rude man!" I said when we were out of earshot. "He could have told me who he was without letting me make such a fool of myself."

"Jarrod Allen would never interfere with anyone's making a fool of himself. Indeed, given a choice, he'd rather help him do it."

"Who is he, anyway? Why didn't he just go up to the house and send his horse down like anyone else would have done?"

"He's something of an enigma around here, but he is a great favorite of your grandfather's, though heaven only knows why. He rather has the run of the place. He lives with his mother on a little place north of us, as I said, and has spent a great deal of time ingratiating himself with Jim."

"Well, I can't see what Grandfather sees in him. It certainly isn't his manners."

"Nonetheless, your grandfather does rather like him. There was some talk several years back about the possibility of Jarrod Allen becoming Jim's heir."

"His heir?"

"It was before he and Mother were married, and he didn't know about you, of course. I suppose Allen had reason to hope your grandfather would make him a sort of protégé."

That would explain why he was so rude to me, I thought. And to Lane. Grandfather's marriage must have dashed his hopes and my appearance had written *finis* to them. Serves him right, I thought.

I dressed for the party that night with special care, telling myself that it was because I wanted to make a good impression on Grandfather's friends and neighbors, but I knew inside that I wanted to snub Jarrod Allen and I wanted to look my best when I did it.

Grandfather had asked me to come into his study before the party, so I slipped into the room before any of the guests had arrived.

Grandfather was waiting for me and his eyes lit up when he saw me. I was wearing a dress from what I thought of as the "good days"—the days before my father's death. It was pale gray trimmed with white, the skirt caught up with bunches of tiny pink-satin rosebuds. I thought gray was my best color—it didn't make my hair seem as violently orange as did brighter ones like green and dark blue.

"You look beautiful, Melinda," Grandfather said, rising from his chair to greet me. "You know, in that dress you remind me very much of my mother. She had that same hair, you know."

"No, I didn't. I should tell you, Grandfather, that my father had red hair, too, so I come by it from both sides of the family."

"Ahh," he said, sinking into his chair once more. "I wish I had known your father. He must have been a good man."

"He—he had his faults," I said, looking down at my hands, "but I loved him very much."

"Yes. Well, I don't have to tell you how much your coming here has meant to me. My doctor tells me it could add a year or so to my life." He smiled at me.

"Oh, Grandfather. You have lots of years left yet," I said, but I remembered Stephen Matson's concern for his health.

"No, not so many, Melinda." He sighed. "I wish I did, now that you're here. But my heart—well, I've been living on the proverbial borrowed time for years now. I'm just grateful to have found you before I died."

"I'm glad you did, Grandfather," I said

sincerely. I loved him and hoped he was wrong in his assessment of his health.

He turned to his desk and took from it a square box covered in ruby velvet. "I want you to have this. It is rightfully yours, as you are the last of the Montoya descendants."

"That 'last of the Montoyas' always sounds so ominous to me," I said, trying to sound lighthearted. "As if someone was trying to do us all in."

"Not a chance," he returned my smile. "But this is an heirloom and I want you to wear it tonight."

He handed me the box, and I opened it. Inside, on a bed of ivory satin, lay a golden butterfly on a chain that seemed to be fashioned of gold cobwebs. The butterfly pendant was set with diamonds and topazes, and was so fragile-looking that it hardly seemed substantial enough to support the stones.

I gasped when I saw it, and my grandfather asked, "Do you like it?"

"Oh, Grandfather," I said when I had recovered my voice, "it is the most beautiful thing I have ever seen."

"Traditionally it was passed from mother to daughter on the wedding day of the oldest daughter. I wanted to see you in it, though, and I was afraid I wouldn't last until your wedding day."

"Of course you will," I hugged him, my eyes filled with tears. "And probably you'll be there to see my daughter wear it, too."

He shook his head. "Now," he said, after I had wiped my eyes, "let me fasten this on you, and we'll go out and meet the guests. I heard some of them arriving, I believe."

As he fastened the butterfly around my neck, he said, "I understand you met Jarrod Allen today."

"Well, yes," I said. "Did he tell you that it was under rather embarrassing circumstances?"

"No, all he said was that he'd met you and that he thought you were lovely. I told him he had good taste."

"Actually, I mistook him for a stable-hand."

Grandfather chuckled. "Jarrod is a fine young man, but not one to get dressed up unless he has to. I'm like that myself, so I can understand it, but his mother Evelyn fusses about it. You'll like his mother. They will both be here tonight."

"I'm looking forward to meeting her," I said, carefully avoiding any mention of my instant dislike of Jarrod. There was no point in offending my grandfather, who obviously saw something in him that I had missed.

The Allens were among the first to arrive. Grandfather introduced me to Evelyn Allen, and said to Jarrod, "I believe you two have already met."

"Indeed," he said gravely, but his eyes were dancing with mischief. I felt my face go pink. "How nice to see you again, Miss Cole. Did you enjoy your ride this morning?"

I withdrew my hand from his and answered as icily as I could manage, "Of course. I always do."

Evelyn Allen watched this exchange with amusement. "I understand you thought Jarrod was a stable-hand," she said. "And indeed you had every right. He certainly dresses like one. Perhaps now I can convince him to pay more attention to the way he looks." She smiled at me, and I liked her very much.

"I dress the way I do for the work I do, Mother," he said. "You know that."

"Nonetheless, you could stand some improvement. Melinda," she said, "you come sit down by me for a moment before the others arrive. I'd like to get acquainted with you."

We sat down on the bench in the patio, and she began to ask me questions about myself. She was very easy to talk to, and very soon I felt as if I had known her for a long time. She was a short, plump woman, with Jarrod's blue-green eyes, but her hair had once been fair and was now going gray. She had been widowed for some years, she said, and added, "I tend to talk people to death when I get in company. With no husband and Jarrod out on the ranch so much, I don't get to chatter as much as I like. You will have to come over and visit so we can gossip a bit."

I promised her that I would come at the first opportunity.

"I'm delighted to see you wearing the Montoya butterfly. It becomes you."

"It's lovely, isn't it? Grandfather says it's been in the family for years."

"Oh, it has. It's valuable as a collector's item, in addition to the value of the stones and the gold. It's practically a legend."

"Perhaps I should keep it locked in the safe. Surely it is too valuable to wear every day."

"Does Sybil know you have it?" I looked up at her. She was regarding me intently.

"No, not unless Grandfather told her. I only got it a moment before you arrived, and I haven't seen her since."

"Well, just be prepared when she sees you with it, that's all I'm saying."

"Prepared? For what, Mrs. Allen?"

"I'd guess for fireworks for some sort. You see, Sybil wanted that pendant very badly, and had almost talked your grandfather into giving it to her before your whereabouts were discovered."

"But I thought that the butterfly went to the Montoya descendants."

"It does, and it is right that you should have it. But until you were located, it was assumed that all the Montoyas were dead. So, to whom should it belong? Sybil thought she had as much right to it as anyone. And perhaps she was right."

"I would prefer not to provoke her any more. She doesn't like me very much anyway, I'm afraid. Perhaps I should put it away."

"Nonsense, child. You'd only hurt your grandfather, who has waited years in hopes of seeing it on you. Sybil has her own problems. You don't need to be cowardly because of her."

The music was starting, and in the sala the furniture had been moved to permit dancing. Jarrod Allen approached me and asked me to dance, and I rose after agreeing to visit Evelyn the following week. I had intended to refuse him, but it would have been difficult to do so in front of his mother. I liked her, even if I thought her son something of an oaf, so I went with him to the dance floor.

His arm was very tight around my waist. "You and my mother seemed to be getting along very well."

"I like her. Your mother is a very lovely lady," I

said, looking up at him.

"Unfortunate that her son is no gentleman, is that it?"

"You said that, not I."

"You didn't have to, Miss Cole." The mocking smile was there still. "Subtlety is not one of your virtues."

"And what would you say my virtues *are*, Mr. Allen?"

"Since we are neighbors, I think it would be just as well to dispense with the formality. 'Jarrod' would be fine, Melinda."

I gave him a look that was intended to show my disapproval of this familiarity, and he laughed. "Your virtues . . ." He pretended to be puzzled. "Well, I would say offhand, that they include a certain amount of courage—it took some of that to come all the way out here not knowing what you'd find."

"Perhaps what I had to face there was worse than whatever I could find here."

"You couldn't know that. Most of us would 'rather bear those ills we have than fly to others we know not of.' "

"I wouldn't have suspected that your interests included *Hamlet*, Mr. Allen."

"Jarrod. Quite frankly, Melinda, I doubt if you have given any thought at all to what my interests might include. You've been too busy disliking me."

"You've made that remarkably easy, you know."

"Yes. Well, you might give some thought to the validity of first impressions."

"First impressions are the best, they say."

"I doubt it. They may be the most lasting, but they can be incredibly misleading. And now," he walked me to the edge of the dance floor as the music stopped, "I am afraid I must relinquish you. It would seem there are others who would like to dance with the lovely Miss Cole." He bowed, and left me standing in front of Lane Harrington and his mother. I watched him leave, crossing the floor in the direction of my grandfather.

A maddening man! So remarkably rude! Why then did I feel as if I were almost sorry the dance had ended?

I turned to Lane and started to say, "He really is the most—" but I stopped. Sybil's eyes were fastened on the butterfly, and her mouth was pressed so tightly shut that her lips had gone almost white. Involuntarily I put my hand up to cover the pendant. She didn't say a word, but she turned quickly and stalked away.

I looked at Lane whose face was unreadable. "I—is there something—" He appeared to force a smile and led me onto the dance floor. "I'm afraid my mother was somewhat startled to see you wearing the Montoya butterfly," he said. "She was rather set on having it herself."

"But I understand that it goes to the eldest of the Montoya daughters," I said. "Surely your mother—"

"Isn't a Montoya daughter," he finished for me. "However, until you came, her claim to it was as good as anyone's. If you discount Antonia Dominguez, that is."

"Antonia Dominguez? What does she have to do with it?"

89

"Antonia is supposedly a Montoya descendant, too. Not a legitimate one, of course, but supposedly her father was an illegitimate child of Don Diego Montoya. It can't be proved one way or another, especially since Antonia's grandmother died in childbirth. And Don Diego never acknowledged him. He did pay particular attention to Antonio Dominguez, however."

"What sort of attention?"

"Oh, he took him into his house, saw that he received some education, that sort of thing. There were rumors about the relationship, but there was never any proof. Antonia, however, believes it. And she is convinced that she has a claim to the butterfly."

"Oh, dear," I sighed. "I thought this was the loveliest present I had ever received. Now I'm starting to think it carries a curse, like some of those famous diamonds."

"Don't let it bother you. Mother will get over it, and Antonia doesn't matter. Enjoy it."

But somehow a shadow had fallen on my pleasure, and the evening was less enjoyable than it had promised to be.

We were to have entertainment later in the evening, and I sought a chair beside my grandfather to watch. Antonia Dominguez and a young man were to dance for us.

When they came onto the floor, I thought I had never seen a more handsome couple. Antonia was dressed in a white blouse trimmed with lace which just skimmed her smooth shoulders. She wore a bright flowered skirt, and a red rose tucked behind her ear. She was barefoot, and her wavy hair hung loose.

Her partner wore tight black trousers and a short matching jacket, both trimmed with silver, and a huge sombrero. My grandfather identified the costume as a *charro* outfit, one worn by the early Spaniards.

As they dipped and swirled in the figures of the dance, I had only admiration for them. Antonia, especially, was a superb dancer. She was tiny and graceful, her feet flashing too fast for the eye to follow. She was all fire and passion, and it appeared that her young partner thought so, too. He couldn't take his eyes off her.

As they finished, to much applause, I turned to Grandfather. "Who is the young man?" I asked.

"Raul Marcos," he said, "A nice young man, I believe. He's been in love with Antonia since they were children, but she has refused his proposals. No one can understand why. It would seem to be a perfect match."

That must have been the young man she was meeting that night, I thought.

"Does Rosa oppose the match?" I asked.

Grandfather shook his head. "On the contrary, she has done everything in her power to persuade Antonia to marry Raul, but with no luck. Maybe that's the problem. Antonia wants to make her own choice."

I thought about what he had said. If there was no opposition, why would she be meeting him so furtively? Or perhaps it was not Raul. Perhaps it was someone Rosa didn't know or didn't approve of.

The couple had finished taking their bows, and Grandfather motioned for them to come to where we were sitting.

"Melinda," he said, "this is Raul Marcos. Raul, my granddaughter, Melinda Cole."

Raul bowed. *Mucho gusto*, señorita," he said.

"And," Grandfather continued, "I believe you have met Antonia Dominguez." As I turned from Raul to Antonia, the smile on my face froze. She was regarding me with an expression that could only be termed pure hatred.

"The butterfly," she hissed between clenched teeth. "You have the butterfly. It is mine!" She snapped to my grandfather. "You know it should be mine!"

My grandfather's face darkened. "I know no such thing," he said. "We've gone over this before. You have no more right to this butterfly than my wife does." I was jolted. I had not expected Grandfather to acknowledge the quarrel with Sybil over the pendant, especially not in such a public fashion.

"And your wife has no more right to it than this—this—imposter!" Antonia spat, pointing at me.

People were turning to look at us now. I felt my face flame.

"Imposter!" My grandfather stood up and loomed over the tiny Antonia. "Imposter, indeed! My granddaughter is the true descendant of the Montoyas," he roared, "the legitimate one!"

Antonia's face flushed and she spun to face me. "You will be sorry," she said furiously, leaning close to my face. "You will be very sorry!"

"Leave my house!" Grandfather thundered,

pointing to the door. It was unnecessary. Antonia was storming away with the bewildered Raul in her wake.

Grandfather sat down heavily in his chair, his hand to his chest. "Impudent girl," he muttered. "I shouldn't let her upset me like that."

He looked pale and I forgot my embarrassment in my concern. "Grandfather, are you all right?" I asked. "Shouldn't you go lie down?"

"Thank you, child, I believe I'm all right. I get these twinges from time to time. Especially when I lose my temper."

"Perhaps I could get you a glass of punch," I suggested. "Something cool might make you feel better."

"Yes, you're right, my dear. I think I would like that."

I rose and started for the punch bowl. As I passed Sybil, she gave me a sardonic smile, and said, "How nice of you to be so solicitous. At least until the will is changed."

I stared at her, as shocked as if I'd been slapped. "What do you mean?" I asked.

"Oh, come, my dear," she said with her nasty little smile. "We all understand your great concern for your grandfather. I'm sure you expect to see it well rewarded. If you ingratiate yourself to the proper degree, he's bound to leave you the ranch." She paused. "If he lives long enough."

"I love my grandfather," I said, shaking with anger. "I didn't come here for the ranch or this butterfly or anything else."

"Of course you do. You're very devoted. Why,"

she said with mock innocence, "devotion simply shines in your every deed." Her face altered into a malevolent mask. "And it's easy to be devoted, isn't it, when the rewards are so great?"

I turned and fled from her, but when I reached the refreshment table, my hands were shaking so badly I could hardly pour the punch.

"Allow me."

The cup was lifted from my hands, and I turned to face Jarrod Allen, who filled it and returned it to me.

"Thank you," I murmured. "I was a bit upset."

"I know," he said. "I saw that scene with Antonia. And the one with Sybil."

I didn't know what to say. I had hoped no one had witnessed the exchange with Sybil, and I was chagrined.

"You mustn't take Sybil so seriously," he said. "Your grandfather embarrassed her by exposing a bit of the greed beneath her elegant exterior, and now she's retaliating at the nearest available object. In this case, you."

I was so grateful for his kindness that I smiled at him in relief. "Thank you, Jarrod. I appreciate your consideration." I sighed. "Does everyone here think I'm after my grandfather's money?"

He looked at me intently, for once the mockery gone from his eyes. "*I* don't think you give a tinker's damn about money."

In spite of myself, I felt my heart leap at this. Why did I want this man to think well of me, I asked myself. I didn't even like him. "Thank you again," I murmured, and made my way across the room to my grandfather's chair.

As I lay in bed after the party, my mind raced over what had happened tonight. What had Jarrod meant when he referred to the greed under Sybil's exterior? I had assumed from the things she and Lane had said that she was wealthy in her own right before she married Grandfather.

As I thought of what I had seen between them, though, the relationship puzzled me. If they were both well-to-do, then they must have married for love, or at least for something close enough to be called affection. And yet, I had never seen them exchange an affectionate word or touch, or even a warm glance. They behaved as formally with each other as if they had been mere acquaintances. Indeed, I had seen a certain amount of hostility between them.

I didn't understand it. I didn't understand why, in spite of Sybil's obvious dislike for me, Lane continued to be friendly and helpful. Maybe he simply didn't side with his mother. And yet their relationship was apparently close.

And why, I thought drowsily, do I keep seeing Jarrod Allen's face in my mind? He's an impossible man. He was kind, though, at least once when I needed it. And his eyes . . . I finally dropped off to sleep.

It must have been in the early hours of the morning when I suddenly awakened from a sound sleep, my heart pounding, uncertain of what had awakened me. I sat up in bed, listening. Everything was still. There was no moonlight; the room was dark.

Then I heard the door creak, very faintly: there *was* someone there.

I sat still, clutching the covers in my hands, then thought to myself, "This is silly. You're imagining things." But the door creaked again.

I called out, "Who is it?" in the loudest voice I could manage. Then I heard the sound of footsteps on the other side of the door. I jumped out of bed. The door was ajar. I hadn't imagined it. I looked down the corridors, but there was no one there.

I started to get back into bed, when I remembered the butterfly. I had left it in its box, hastily tucked into one of the drawers of the writing desk. Now I felt my way across the room and groped for it. It was still there.

I would have to find a better hiding place, I thought, until I could have Grandfather put it into the safe in his study. For the time being I shoved it under my pillow. I would take care of it in the morning.

Chapter Seven

In the morning's light I began to wonder if I had been imagining things the night before. I couldn't believe anyone would be stupid enough to come into the room to take the butterfly while I was there. Nonetheless, someone *had* been there. I decided to find a safer hiding place for it until I could have Grandfather lock it up.

I finally decided to slip it inside the pocket of one of my dresses. I thought it would be safe enough there until I was able to take it down to the safe. I dressed in my riding habit and headed for the stables.

I had not expected Lane that morning, since we had not made arrangements to ride, so I had my regular horse saddled and left by myself.

Even though I had been riding only a short time, I felt confident enough to take a short ride alone. The horse was gentle, and I was sure he could find his way around, even if I couldn't.

I decided to take a road that led to the cliffs overlooking the ocean. I had not been there before, but I knew from things Lane had said that this was the road to take, and so I headed toward the sea.

I dismounted at the edge of the cliffs and walked along, the horse trailing behind. I watched the waves crash on the jagged rocks, and thought how wild and dangerous the ocean looked there.

The waves would subside, then rush into the rocks, flinging spray almost to where I stood. I watched, fascinated, for a while, then turned to remount my horse.

I was about to turn toward the house again, when I saw Lane riding toward me down the road. I stopped and waited until he had reached me.

"Good morning," I said. "Isn't it a lovely day?"

He frowned at me. "I was upset when they said you had already left. I thought we were going out together."

"You didn't mention it, and I thought you might be sleeping late after the party."

"I had assumed we were to ride every morning. I didn't realize I had to make a special appointment."

"I think you're being rather rude about this whole thing," I snapped. "It was simply a misunderstanding." I was annoyed at his tone, and perhaps my touchiness about my treatment at the hands of his mother had spilled over to him.

"There's hardly any reason to be so high and mighty, Miss Cole. You're not the heiress to the ranch yet."

"And as far as I'm concerned," I gritted, "I don't care if I never am. I lived nineteen years without hearing of the Mariposas or the marvelous and wonderful Harringtons, and I'm sure I could go another nineteen without seeing either of them again." In my fury, I slashed my horse with my quirt, and he jumped, startled, almost throwing me.

Lane swung his own horse around and grabbed the reins to halt my startled mount.

"If you're going to take your temper out on the horse," he said when he had calmed the animal, "at least wait until you've dismounted. It's safer that way."

"I'm sorry for that," I said. I was shaken and ashamed. I had dismounted and was standing by my horse, my knees weak. "I really don't believe in abusing animals."

Lane shrugged. "Depends on whether there's a purpose. Anyway," he said, turning on me a smile designed to charm, "this has been a bad start to the morning. Let's begin again, shall we?"

I was not quite ready to resume our friendship on the same basis. I had glimpsed something in Lane's remark that showed me that he was not as indifferent to the status of the ranch as he pretended, and not nearly so neutral in his feelings about me as I had assumed. I was not ready to promote an open quarrel; I had enough people angry at me without having done anything except be here. Still, I was wary. I smiled a forgiveness I did not truly feel, and said, "That sounds fine to me. Shall we continue our ride?"

As we rode down the coast, he said to me, "One of the reasons I followed you out was to warn you about standing too close to the edge of the cliffs."

"I'm not afraid of falling," I said.

"You should be. The earth breaks off in great clumps along the edges of the cliffs, and you can be tossed down onto those rocks before you have time to scream.''

I shuddered. The thought of falling onto those jagged rocks was frightening. ''I'll stay well back,'' I said. ''Is the ocean always this wild?''

''This is high tide,'' he answered. ''At low tide there is a place where we can get down the cliffs and ride along the beach. We'll come back when the tide is out some day, and I'll show you the smugglers' cave. Right now, I want to ride up the coast a way and show you something else.''

We rode along the coast a few minutes more, then turned inland. A few miles up the road, we came in sight of what appeared to be a large grove of trees or a small forest.

''That's your grandfather's redwood grove,'' Lane said.

''Oh, yes, Mr. Matson mentioned that there were some trees on the property. Are we going to ride through there?''

''Well, we're going to ride into it. It is actually a much larger grove than it appears from here.''

We rode into the grove for a short distance. It was very quiet inside, and so dim it seemed as if the sun had gone behind a cloud. The trees soared for what seemed like hundreds of feet into the air. The floor of the forest was padded with needles, and our horses' hoofs were almost silent.

Sunlight filtered weakly through the branches to light a spot here and there, but most of the area was dark and cool. I caught a glimpse of blue as a bird flashed among the trees, and I strained my eyes to see deeper into the woods.

Beside the trail was the stump of a redwood that had been felled, and it was as wide across as a small house. I was awed by the size of these enormous trees, and impressed by the quiet and beauty of the grove.

"It's very lovely in here," I said. "These trees are breathtaking."

"And valuable," Lane said. "Your grandfather could realize a small fortune if he sold this for lumber."

"I'm glad he won't," I said, looking around me. "I love them."

"Pity." There was an odd note in that word. "I was hoping you would help me convince him that selling this grove would solve some of the ranch's money problems."

"Money problems?"

"Yes. The income from the ranch has not been as great for the last few years as it used to be. I think that selling the grove would bring in some capital and open up some additional grazing land."

"Does he really need the capital? He sounded as if the problems here were minimal."

"Your grandfather has a great tendency to see only what he wants to see. Consider my mother for instance. She sold her San Francisco property at a loss to move out here, and he has treated her abominably ever since. Take that scene at the party last night."

I preferred not to recall it, but he went on.

"He embarrassed her in front of all those people, implied that she was a grasping woman, and the truth is that all she had asked, for all she did for the ranch, was that one thing: the butterfly."

"I don't think he felt as if the butterfly were his to give to her."

"If not his, whose?" He looked at me, then indicated the grove with a sweep of his arm. "And this grove. She wanted him to sell it and put some of it into improvements for the house. Do you know that parts of that house are over a hundred years old?"

I nodded, but he went on, ignoring me. "And he won't part with his precious grove to do it." He snorted. "Rank sentimentality."

"And when the grove is gone and the money is gone, then what?" I demanded. "There's nothing here but tree-stumps."

He sneered at me. "You sound just like him. If the money were well invested, it wouldn't *be* gone. But neither of you seems to understand that."

We rode on in silence for a few minutes, and then he said, "Of course, that's his problem. And perhaps yours. When I turn thirty and receive my trust, I plan to return to San Francisco and leave this ranch and all its problems."

"Your trust?"

"Yes. My grandfather set it up for me before he died. I come into it when I'm thirty, and I'll have my own money. Two more years. Meanwhile, if it weren't for my mother, this place could rot for all I'd care."

We hardly spoke on the ride back to the ranch. When we reached the stables, he helped me dismount and said, "Don't wait for me in the morning. I've decided to go into San Francisco for a few days. I can only tolerate the country life for so long."

He turned and led the horses away, and I went into the house, discouraged. No matter what I did, I seemed to antagonize someone. It was difficult being in a place where I had no one to talk to.

I wandered through the foyer and out onto the patio, and sat down on one of the benches. How I missed Mavis. No matter how bad things were at Westhaven, I had always been able to confide in her.

As if in response to my thoughts, Rosa came into the patio and said, "Ah, señorita, there you are. I was looking for you."

"Good morning, Rosa, how are you?"

"*Muy bien,* señorita." She stopped and looked at me, a bit hesitant. "Señorita, about last night—Antonia—I wish to apologize for her."

"There's no need, Rosa. I understand, I assure you."

"I feel the need, señorita. It was her father who put all those crazy notions into her head. And now I can't do much with her." She sighed. "I sent her away for a while, to visit her aunt. Maybe when her temper cools a bit—" she shrugged.

"Don't worry about it, Rosa," I said. "I'm sure she didn't mean it."

"Well, it doesn't matter. She's just going to have to get over all those silly ideas, whether she wants to or not. The other thing I wanted to ask you—I don't know how you feel about this—" Again she seemed hesitant to ask me.

"What, Rosa? It's all right to ask me anything."

"Well, your mother always loved to help when we

were making things in the kitchen. We have the strawberries now—they were late this year—and I wondered if you would like to help make the strawberry jam. We are a bit short-handed."

"Oh, yes," I said, genuinely pleased. "I'd love to. But why where you so reluctant to ask me?"

"I didn't know how you would feel about doing kitchen work. In the old days, the *patronas*— the rancher's wives—always supervised the work in the kitchen, but the señora says that ladies do not do such things."

"Don't worry about it, Rosa. I'd love to help. And besides," I gave her a conspiratorial smile, "until now, no one ever accused me of being a lady."

She giggled. I ran upstairs to change my clothes, and then joined her and Mrs. Malloy in the kitchen.

I hulled and washed and crushed and stirred strawberries until I was sure I never wanted to see another one, but when we finished filling the last of the jars with the ruby-colored jam, I was proud of myself. It felt good to do this sort of work.

"I'm tired," I said, stretching. "And hungry. I could eat a seven-course meal tonight."

"I'd bet you'd skip the strawberry jam course," said Mrs. Malloy with a grin.

"You'd bet right on that," I smiled. "I probably won't be ready for strawberry jam until midwinter, when this work will be only a memory. Now," I said, untying my apron, "I have to go get cleaned up for dinner."

As I started out the door, I was met by Sybil, who said, "I've been looking everywhere for you. Your grandfather has had another attack. I've sent for the doctor.''

I was stunned. "Is he all right?" I asked. "Can I see him? Is there anything I can do?"

She shook her head. "No, he's resting now, and I think it's best to leave him alone until after the doctor comes. We won't know much until then.''

"Do you think—does he seem—will he be better, do you think?"

She shrugged. "Who knows? He's survived these attacks before. One wonders, though, how much longer he can continue to do so.''

What was the note I detected in her voice? Complacence? She hardly seemed devastated by the situation. Perhaps it was not as serious as it seemed.

"I'm having dinner sent to my room," she said. "I'd suggest that you might want to do the same." She left. I turned to Rosa.

"I'd rather not go back to my room," I said. "I'd rather wait downstairs so I can see the doctor when he comes.''

"That's just as well, señorita," she said. "Stay here and I will fix your dinner myself.''

"I don't think I'll feel like eating, Rosa," I said. "All of a sudden, I've lost my appetite.''

"You must eat, señorita. You sit down. I'll make you a special dinner.''

When the doctor arrived, I met him in the foyer. He was a small, stout man with a harried air. He had started to rush through the entry when I stopped him.

"Doctor?"

"Yes? What is it?" he asked.

"I'm Melinda Cole, Doctor. James McCarthy's granddaughter."

"Oh, yes, Miss Cole. I'd heard you were here. I must hurry, though. These things are very serious with your grandfather."

"I know, Doctor, and I won't delay you. But please don't leave without talking with me, will you?"

"I promise. Stay here. I'll see you on my way back."

On his way out, I invited him into the sala for a glass of sherry. He accepted gratefully.

"What can you tell me about my grandfather's condition, Doctor?" I asked.

"Well," he sipped the sherry and paused for a moment, as if being careful to choose the right words. "It is grave, Miss—Cole, did you say?"

I nodded.

"As I say, it's grave. But then, he's had these attacks before and survived them, when I'd have thought he couldn't possibly make it. He's a very tough man, your grandfather."

I smiled. "Yes, he is that," I said. "Then you think he has a chance to recover?"

He looked at me. "That depends on what you mean by 'recover,' Miss Cole. It is only a matter of time until your grandfather, tough as he is, becomes so weakened by these attacks that one of them will kill him. Whether this is the one or not, I can't say."

"If I understand you, then, Doctor, what you're saying is that even if he survives this attack, it's only a matter of time until another one."

"That is exactly what I'm saying, Miss Cole. He has massive damage to his heart. How he has lived so long is beyond me. But he may come out of this and survive for a time. We'll see. If he makes it through the night, he may keep going for a while." He set the glass down.

"Meanwhile," he continued, "I am going to stop down the road and send up Mrs. Carrington. She's the best practical nurse I know of locally, and he needs constant care for the next week or two."

"But, Doctor," I said, "his wife and I are both here. Couldn't we give him the help he needs?"

He looked at me briefly and started to say something, then apparently thought better of it and said, instead, "I'm sure that if you have had some experience in nursing, Miss Cole, that Mrs. Carrington would be glad of your help. I'm afraid that   Mrs.   McCarthy is—umm—rather—inexperienced as a nurse and prefers to have—someone more—experienced to take charge."

Suddenly his meaning, though delicately phrased, was quite clear to me. Sybil Harrington McCarthy wouldn't dirty her hands with such a distasteful chore as caring for her own husband. "Ladies" didn't do such things.

I gave him what I'm afraid was a rather cynical smile. "I see," I said. "I have had some experience. Rather limited, but I'm willing to help." Poor little Emmaline! I was all she'd had. "I can relieve Mrs. Carrington when she needs it. Should I go up now?"

"I don't think there's any need. He should be sleeping, and one of the men from the ranch here is

107

sitting with him until Mrs. Carrington comes. You go get a good night's sleep. You'll probably need it to face the next few days."

I returned to my room, and fell into my bed. The events of the day had exhausted me, and I barely had the energy to change into my nightclothes.

The nurse must have arrived during the night, because she was there when I went down the next morning. Alice Carrington was a large, red-faced, hearty woman, and she greeted me as enthusiastically as the circumstances allowed.

"Sure good to have some help, I'll tell you," she said. "When the doctor said you'd offered a hand I'uz real happy to hear it. Lots of folks call me in 'cause there ain't nobody else around. It's real hard, that is, bein' by myself all the time."

"I'm sure it is, Mrs. Carrington. But I'll be glad to relieve you anytime you need it. Would you like to set up a schedule of some sort?"

"You just call me Alice, Miss Melinda. No kin of Jim McCarthy has to be so mannerly with me."

We arranged for me to sit with Grandfather in the afternoons and again in the evenings so that Alice could get away for a while.

Grandfather was in kind of coma, from which he roused occasionally to take a little water and some broth or soup. The doctor said it wasn't a real coma, or he wouldn't have awakened, but more like a kind of sleep. He didn't seem to know any of us, even when he came around, but the doctor said that was natural, too. He said that his body was trying to heal itself, and that the fact that Grandfather had survived that long was a very good sign. I was glad of that.

Meanwhile, Lane was in San Francisco and Sybil, apparently, kept to her rooms. I didn't see either of them for almost two weeks.

Chapter Eight

My days became regulated by Grandfather's illness. In the mornings, I usually went for a ride. Some days, I worked in the kitchen with Rosa. Afternoons I sat with Grandfather, reading or doing needlework. After dinner, I would sit with him again for an hour or so while Alice had her dinner. Sometimes Alice and I would talk quietly after she returned.

"I've known Jim McCarthy for—oh, better than forty years now. Knew him when he first came here."

"Did you know my mother, too, Alice?"

"I should say, Miss Melinda. I was here the night she was born, as a matter of fact. Helped to deliver her."

"Did you really?" It was delightful to hear things about my mother. I was very curious about her.

"I really did. Little thing she was. But pretty—oh, my she was a pretty little thing. She had those big dark eyes, even when she was first born. They weren't that blue color that changes on lots of babies. They were dark from the first. Your grandfather was so tickled with that baby," she sighed, and shook her head. "I don't think I ever saw a man so crazy about a child."

She was quiet for a moment, then she said, "He made a real bad mistake when he tried to get her married to that Durango boy."

"Durango boy?"

"Paul Durango. He was the one she was supposed to marry the day she ran away. He was a no-good. She knew it. Everybody knew it. Everybody except Jim, I guess. He kept thinking it was just high spirits. And your mama loved Jim so much, I guess she would have gone through with it if someone she loved more hadn't come for her."

"What was he like, this Paul Durango?"

"Oh, handsome enough, I guess. Real handsome, in fact. And charming when he wanted to be. But you see, he was the heir to a big ranch. Lots of land. Lots of money. And he'd been raised to think of himself as a sort of prince. His father had this idea that he was like the kings back in Europe in the olden days. And he raised Paul like he was one of those old-time rulers."

"The divine right of kings," I murmured.

"What's that, Miss Melinda?"

"Oh, just an expression, Alice. Paul Durango was raised to think he was something very special, was he?"

"I should say. Miss Maggie wasn't too fond of him, even from the time they were children. She once saw him drown a litter of kittens just for fun, sort of like, and being so tenderhearted herself, she just couldn't stand it. She cried about those kittens for days."

"He sounds like an awful child."

"Didn't improve much with age, neither. About a month or so before they were supposed to be married, he nearly beat a horse to death for some reason or another. Miss Maggie knew about it. All the servants were talking about it."

"You'd think Grandfather wouldn't have been so anxious to have his daughter married to a man like that."

"Oh," she sighed, "your grandfather's changed a lot from those days to the way you know him, Miss Melinda. Back then he was real headstrong hisself, and he had made up his mind that Mariposas was to be joined up with the Eldorado. That was the name of the Durangos' ranch. And he was going to have it that way; nothing could convince him otherwise. He was sure he knew best. And then your mama ran off and married your daddy. Almost broke his heart, but there weren't many folks around here that wasn't glad to see it happen."

"They were glad my mother ran off?"

"Sure. Nobody around here liked Paul Durango, and everybody loved your mama. Nobody wanted to see her married up to the likes of him."

"How did Paul Durango take it?"

"Oh, he threw a fine fit, you can imagine. I mean, never in his life had anything he wanted been kept from him, and now to be made a laughingstock of the whole territory—well, you can see how he'd be about it."

"Yes, I can imagine."

"Anyway, after that, things never went right for Paul Durango again. It was sort of like your mother's going was bad luck for him"

"How was that, Alice?"

"Well, a few months after that, Paul's father died and he inherited the whole property. Trouble was, he didn't know first thing about running it. He'd always been let do whatever he wanted, and work wasn't what he wanted. So things went bad over there. 'Course, he caused most of his own troubles, too."

"Mr. Matson said he died in some sort of brawl."

"Well, he did, but before he did, he lost most of his land by gambling it away."

"He lost it?"

"Sure. He gambled a lot, but he was bad at it, so he'd put up the land for his bad debts. Lost most of it that way. Then he got killed about two years after your mama left, in that place in San Francisco."

"A gambling house, wasn't it?"

Alice gave me a conspiratorial smile. "Well, that was the story they gave out. Gambling house sounds some better than it really was. Lots of the younger men go to those, and it's not considered all that disgraceful. Truth was, it was a bawdy house, and he was killed in a fight over one of the ladies."

"From the way that sounds, it makes me wonder if my mother ran away with my father because she loved him, or because she just didn't want to marry Paul Durango."

"Oh, now," Alice patted my hand, "Don't you go thinking things like that. She loved your father, all right. She'd have had to, to go against her father."

"So you think so?"

"Oh, Miss Melinda, I know so. Your mama was as devoted to your grandfather as ever a child could be. She'd have gone through with that marriage for him, bad as she knew it would be, 'less she had somebody she loved more. Your mama wasn't one of those flighty, light-minded young girls."

"Did Paul Durango have any of the ranch left when he died?"

"Oh, yes, there was a good-sized piece of it left still. Sold for taxes, not long after, since he didn't have anybody to leave it to."

"Who owns it now?"

"Allens have it now. Young Jarrod Allen and his mother Evelyn live in the old Durango house. I expect you'll have met the Allens by now."

I thought about this for quite a while after our conversation. Jarrod Allen's ownership of the Durango ranch opened some interesting possibilities. Perhaps Grandfather had not given up his dream of uniting the two ranches. Perhaps that was why he had such a preference for Jarrod Allen.

Maybe his dream even extended to the possibility of a match between me and Jarrod Allen, I thought. And then I scolded myself. That's perfectly silly, I thought. Grandfather hadn't even hinted at the prospect of such a thing. He said he had made his mistake in that way, and he wouldn't do it again. I'm just dreaming up these things out of thin air, I said to myself. Perhaps I've become a little paranoid.

After a week after my grandfather had been stricken, the doctor seemed to think he was out of immediate danger. Alice and I kept to our schedule, but we were a bit more relaxed about it. When Jarrod· Allen rode over to inquire after my grandfather and bring me an invitation to visit his mother, Alice insisted that I go.

"Lordy, Miss Melinda," she said, "you've done more than your share." She added darkly, "Lots more than some who had more obligation. You just take off and visit with Evelyn Allen. She's a fine lady, and you'll enjoy it." I knew I would. I had enjoyed her company at the party very much.

"Besides," Alice winked, "you'll get to ride over with that handsome Mr. Jarrod. You ought to enjoy that, too."

"I hardly think so, Alice. Jarrod Allen and I could scarcely be said to be friends." And yet I had turned away so that she would not see my face go pink

"That so? Well, it seems a pity." She shrugged. "Still, I guess there's no accounting for taste, is there? I'd have thought Mr. Jarrod would be real taken with a pretty young thing like you."

The ride over to the Eldorado was, indeed, pleasant. I had to admit that Jarrod Allen could be a charming and witty companion when he extended himself.

The road to his ranch skirted the edge of the redwood grove and turned inland over hills covered with scrub oak and wildflowers. It was a lovely ride, and I said so to Jarrod.

"There's a longer road that goes through most of the grove, and the scenery is even more spectacular," he said, "but I promised Mother I'd get you home as soon as possible, and that way takes some time."

"Perhaps I could take that route on my way back," I said.

"Not likely," he answered. "First of all, by the time you return, it's likely that the fog will have rolled in, and that trail can be very tricky to follow in a dense fog. Second, there have been stories of bandits in there recently. You'd be safer on this trail. Besides," he glanced at me, "I have no intention of letting you ride back alone."

"Why not?" I was a bit indignant. "I can find my way. Don't you think I'm competent?"

He smiled at me the mocking smile I had so disliked before. "I have no doubt you are entirely competent, Miss Cole. My mother, however, would skin us both alive if I allowed you to attempt it. She thinks there are certain conventions that proper young ladies have to follow."

I blushed. "And I have just indicated that I'm not a very proper young lady, haven't I?"

"Heaven spare me proper young ladies." The smile was now a broad grin. "I find them quite a nuisance. I won't tell mother the awful truth."

I thought it best to change the subject. "You mentioned bandits. Have there really been bandits recently? I thought that was over years and years ago."

"Not really. The most infamous of the bandits around here is known as Black Bart, but I'm sure you'd be safe from him."

"Oh?"

"He only holds up stagecoaches, for one thing, and he apparently considers it very ungentlemanly to rob ladies. He has never been known to retain ladies' handbags."

"He sounds a rather gallant sort, anyway. Is he considered to be very dangerous?"

"Only to strongboxes and the English language, apparently. His trademark is leaving a bit of absolutely awful poetry with the stage driver after each of his holdups."

I laughed. "A gentleman and a poet. He doesn't sound like a deadly desperado."

"No, but there are some who are. The worst are the ones who hide by the trail and assault lone riders. Some people have been killed by them, although none close by here. Still, you can't be too careful."

As we rode over a hill, I could see in the distance a white house on a small rise. "Is that Eldorado?" I asked.

"Yes," he said, "that's the ranchhouse."

"It isn't built in the same style as Mariposas, is it?" I asked.

"No. You will find, when you have been here for a while, that Mariposas is almost unique. Oh, there are a few houses farther down the coast built in the old Spanish style, or so it's called. It was really the old Moorish style. Eldorado was built about fifty years later than Mariposas, and the builder was copying the houses built by the new settlers."

"It appears to be a lovely place," I said, and it did, indeed. As we grew closer, I could see roses climbing on the veranda and huge trees shading it. There were beautifully trimmed lawns and expansive flower beds.

"Thank you. Quite frankly, I prefer the Mariposas. This house, lovely though it is, is built like houses in the East. The Mariposas seems as if it could only belong here in California.''

He helped me from my horse, and I went up the steps to where Evelyn Allen was waiting for us.

"My dear, it's so good to see you again. How is your grandfather?"

"He seems to be improving, thank you, Mrs. Allen. The doctor feels that he is out of danger—for the moment, anyway.''

"That's good to hear. Come in and sit down." I followed her into the parlor and sat down on the red-plush sofa. The furniture was rather more modern than that at Mariposas, but the room had a cozy, homey feeling. "Now, Jarrod," Evelyn turned to her son, "you must go on about your business. We're going to have a good long gossip, and you'd be bored to death." Jarrod smiled, leaned over and kissed her on the forehead, bowed to me, and left. I watched his broad back retreat down the hall, and suddenly realized his mother had asked me a question I had missed.

"I—I'm sorry, Mrs. Allen, I didn't hear you. What did you say?"

"I asked if Alice Carrington was looking after your grandfather.''

"Yes, she's been staying there. She must be something of a local institution."

"She is, indeed. I don't know what we'd do around here without Alice. She delivers our babies, takes care of our sick, and holds our hands when we have deaths in the family.''

"She seems a very kind woman."

"And loyal. If Alice is your friend, you would

trust her with your life. And we do, actually. If she doesn't like you—well, she's very open about it; she wouldn't give you the time of day.''

She left me for a moment, and I looked about the room. There was a portrait on the wall which looked to be Evelyn Allen at about twenty-five. She had been very beautiful. Another beside it was probably her husband; he looked rather like Jarrod. A small drawing of a young boy attracted my attention. It appeared to be Jarrod as a child, sometime before he acquired his mocking smile. He had been a beautiful child, and I admired the skill of the artist as well as the subject.

Evelyn Allen came in as I was looking at the little picture. ''That's Jarrod when he was five,'' she said.

''I had guessed that it was. He was a beautiful child. And the artist was apparently very skilled.''

''Thank you for both of those very kind compliments,'' she said. ''He was indeed a handsome little boy, and I was the artist.''

''You?'' I was surprised. ''I had no idea you were an artist,'' I said. ''Do you still do any drawing?''

''And painting. It's my hobby, and occasionally I sell a picture or two. I wanted to ask you to sit for me. Your coloring is so lovely that I've been itching to get it on canvas ever since I first laid eyes on you.''

''How kind of you to say so. I would be delighted.'' Then another idea came to me. ''I wonder if perhaps you would be able to copy something for me,'' I said, reaching to remove the miniature of my mother I was wearing. ''This miniature is the only portrait I have of my mother, and I wonder if it would be possible for you to copy it in a regular portrait. Do you think that could be done?"

"I'm sure I could, my dear." She took the picture from me and said, "Of course, you do have that lovely picture of your mother at Mariposas."

"At the ranch?" I must have looked very blank.

"Yes, the one in your grandfather's study." She examined the miniature. "It's the same as this one, in fact. He showed it to me several years ago when we were discussing art. Have you never seen it?"

"I'm sure it isn't there now. I've been in there several times recently, and I'm sure I would have noticed it."

"I would think so." She looked at me speculatively. "Well, all that I can think of is that it has been removed by someone. And I would wager quite a sum that I know who," she murmured to herself, "but there's no point in discussing that now. Here," she said, pouring me a glass of the lemonade she had brought back with her. "I'm sure you must be thirsty after that long ride."

I took the glass of lemonade. "No point in discussing what, Mrs. Allen? Who would care one way or another about a portrait of my mother, except my grandfather or me?"

She looked at me for a long moment. "Sybil Harrington, of course."

"I don't understand why. I know she doesn't like *me*, but why on earth would she remove a picture of my mother? It doesn't make sense to me."

"It would if you knew Sybil Harrington better. She places a great deal of stock in family

120

background and that sort of thing, and you and all the other Montoyas are a constant reminder to her of her failures in that line.''

''But I was under the impression that she came from an old San Francisco family.''

''My dear, if you are an ancestor snob, there are no 'old San Francisco families' in terms of say, the East. And let's face it. All American families are Johnny-come-latelies compared to their European cousins. It's a bit of snobbery Sybil Harrington clings to, and it's the reason she's so deadly jealous of you.''

''Of me?'' I laughed. ''Well, unless you count the Montoyas, I certainly don't have any family name to speak of. I'm sure my father's family were all fine people, but nobody ever heard of them as far as I know.''

''But you see, Melinda, Sybil *does* count the Montoyas. Not only were they a powerful family locally for a hundred years, but they came of Spanish nobility. You may not think that amounts to a great deal, but to a class-conscious woman like Sybil Harrington, it means very much.''

''But even so, didn't she come from a well-to-do family in San Francisco? She surely has nothing to be ashamed of there.''

''Well, her grandfather made a great deal of money, some say by rather devious means. However, that's all water under the bridge. Her father increased the family fortune, and Sybil inherited a great deal of money at a young age.''

''And she invested most of it in the ranch, am I right?''

Evelyn gave me a startled look. "Where on earth did you hear that?"

"Well, Lane said—No, that's wrong." I went over in my mind what he had said, trying to remember where I had got the impression that this was true. "He didn't say that she invested it in the ranch. He said she brought some of the things in the ranch house and—" I tried to remember—"she sold her San Francisco property at a loss to move out here."

"Well, that part's true enough, as far as it goes. What he didn't tell you was that if she hadn't sold it, it was going to be sold by the courts to pay her debts, anyway. It was only thanks to Jim McCarthy that she was able to keep the few doodads she had left."

"But how could that have happened? You said she was very rich. What happened to all the money?"

"I also said she was very snobbish. The snobbery did her in, so to speak."

She paused for a moment. "Sybil's father died when she was eighteen and left her sole heiress to a large fortune. Young women possessed of so much wealth are often prey to fortune-hunters, and she was no exception. Beautiful young women with money are even more sought after. Young men flocked around her, some of them obviously after her money, some of them genuinely attracted to her. Most of them she sent packing."

"But she did marry, finally."

"Oh, yes. There were many young men of good families that she could have had, you know. She was wealthy, she was incredibly lovely, she could have had her pick. And when she was twenty, a young man showed up who could offer something that others could not, however good their families and however rich they were.''

''What was that, Mrs. Allen?''

''A title. He was English: Lord Roderick Harrington. He was heir to a very old estate in England, and plain Sybil Kent could become Lady Harrington. It was the most enticing bait she could have been offered. Their wedding was the social event of the season.''

''I can imagine.''

''At any rate, the elegant Harringtons had a beautiful home in San Francisco, and they began to live in magnificent style. Lavish, one would probably call it.''

''There are some things I don't understand, Mrs. Allen. If Lane's father was a titled Englishman, didn't the title pass to Lane when he died? If so, why hasn't anyone mentioned it? I wouldn't think the reason would be reticence on Sybil's part.''

''Oh, indeed not. You see, it did not seem strange, at first, that the Harringtons would live in San Francisco, but it did begin to seem a bit odd that, after a few years, Lord Harrington had not bothered to return to England to check on his estates. It seemed even odder that Sybil was in no hurry to go to England to play lady of the manor, so to speak.''

''Are you implying that his title was—''

''Absolutely fictitious. It was an elaborate hoax, with forged letters of introduction, the whole thing. It was quite some time before this all came out, but in the end it became obvious that Sybil had been done in by her own snobbery. Duped, as it were.''

"It must have been awful for her.''

"I'm sure it was, but she got very little sympathy from those she had snubbed so thoroughly. And by this time, she had Lane, so there wasn't much chance for an annulment—and a divorce would have been even more scandalous. So she apparently decided to make the best of it and simply ignore the horse laughs.''

"Somehow I find that almost commendable.''

"Oh, Sybil has courage, I'll hand her that. But she set out to make Roderick Harrington's life as miserable as she could.''

"And did she succeed?''

"Not as well as she'd have liked. In the end, he got the last laugh, even if it had to come from the grave.''

I shuddered. "That sounds ominous.''

"Well, perhaps it should. Sybil managed to poison Lane against his father and destroy the man socially, but she couldn't control his spending and gambling, and by the time he died, her fortune was almost gone.''

"How did he die?''

"He fell down a flight of stairs in their house in San Francisco and broke his neck. There were those who said Sybil pushed him, but I don't hold with that.''

"I wouldn't think she would do such a thing, even if she didn't like him.''

"Oh, my dear, I have no doubt that she is capable of such a thing. It's just that if she'd been planning to do it, I'm sure she'd have done it when there was still some of her money left to make it worthwhile. Sybil is an eminently practical woman."

"I can't understand why my grandfather married her. She makes no secret of her dislike for the ranch, and she certainly is not attached to him. Nor is he to her, as far as I can tell."

Evelyn sighed and gazed out the window for a moment. "You have no idea how charming Sybil can be when she chooses to. She had no doubt that once she and your grandfather were married, she could convince him to buy her San Francisco house back for her and let her live there part of the year."

"He would not be willing to agree to that if I know him."

"Of course he wouldn't. But you see, selfish people are so busy with their own schemes that they seldom see others accurately. They think only of what they want. If Sybil had looked at your grandfather realistically, she'd have known that he had no interest in her house in San Francisco, and even less interest in parting with some of his own beloved ranch to pay for it."

"Like the redwood grove, for instance."

"Like the redwood grove, specifically. You've already heard about that one, have you?"

"Yes. Lane wanted me to convince Grandfather to sell it. He said we need to make improvements in the ranch-house at Mariposas."

"What did you say to that?"

"I refused. I like that redwood grove. I think Grandfather's right to keep it."

"Good for you. Because you can bet on it, my dear, not one cent of that money would ever see its

125

way into the Mariposas. It would go to setting Sybil up in San Francisco in the style she loves.''

I was silent for a moment, and then I looked at her. ''Does she hate me because she is afraid I might inherit the ranch?''

''Of course. You must know that. Jim McCarthy's had a bad heart for years now. All she had to do was marry him and let time do its worst—the ranch would be hers. Then you came into the picture.'' She gave me a wicked little smile. ''I'd have loved to have seen her face when Jim got the telegram saying you'd been found. I'll bet she had a fit.''

''You know, there's another thing. Lane said something about a trust—that he comes into money in two years, when he's thirty. Can't they use that to buy back the property?''

''Hmm. That must be from Sybil's father. I'm surprised he had the foresight to set aside some money Sybil couldn't get her hands on. Well, yes, I suppose they could use it for the property in San Francisco, depending on how much it is.''

''Lane seems to think it's a great deal.''

''Of course. He would. I'm sure I don't know. They may turn out to be wealthy again. It will have been collecting interest for thirty-five years now. It should be a tidy sum.''

She rose from her chair. ''Well, we've gossiped about the wicked Sybil long enough, my dear. Come with me. I want to show you around.''

She showed me the gardens in the back of her house, both flower and vegetable gardens. Her flowers were lovely. I was especially impressed by one beautiful white rose she showed me.

"That's my favorite," she said. "It's called the Snowflake Rose, and I love it. I've always fancied that Jarrod's bride might have those roses for her wedding bouquet."

"They would be lovely," I murmured.

"Yes, they would, and I hope the bush lives until that day," she said with some asperity. "I should like to live to see my grandchildren, you know."

I muttered something to the effect that of course she would, and she shook her head.

"I'm beginning to wonder," she said. "Jarrod's going on thirty now, and I've had hopes for years that he would settle down with some nice girl. He's been seeing Constance Robinson for nearly a year now, and so far, nothing's come of that."

Why did I suddenly find that distressing? I didn't even like the man, I told myself. Why should I care whom he married? But nonetheless, something like a sharp pain pierced me, and I could say nothing to Jarrod's mother for a moment. I pretended to be smelling the roses, and when I had collected my thoughts and was in control of myself again, I said, "I don't believe I've met Constance Robinson. She wasn't at the party, was she?"

"No, she's been gone for a month, visiting relatives. She should be back soon, and I'll have you over to meet her. She's a lovely girl. Besides, you'll enjoy having someone near your own age to talk to, I should think."

Why did I think I'd hate Constance Robinson, no matter what sort of lovely girl she was? You're being unreasonable, I told myself. One would think *you* were in love with Jarrod Allen. Ninny, I scolded myself. He's a rude, impossible man. And furthermore, he doesn't even like you. Don't be silly.

When I left in the late afternoon, Evelyn loaded me down with delicacies to take to my grandfather, and armloads of flowers for myself. Jarrod helped me onto my horse and handed me the flowers, their stems wrapped in damp paper to keep them fresh.

As we rode toward the coast, I could see the fog beginning to roll in over the hills.

"Looks as if it's going to be a foggy ride home," he said. "Keep your horse close to mine so you don't get lost."

"Is it safe?" I asked. "We won't lose our way, will we?"

"I won't. You might by yourself. I've found my way over this road in all sorts of weather and at all times of day. We won't have any trouble."

I was glad to be with him, because the fog closing in around us made me feel lost and disoriented. I found myself listening to every sound, trying to sense where I was. How easy it would be for me to get lost, I thought. The fog seemed somehow sinister, as though it was seeking me out and cutting me off from the rest of the world. I shuddered, and Jarrod turned toward me.

"Are you cold?" he asked. "I have a blanket we can wrap around you."

"No," I said, "I'm not cold. In fact, it's been so warm that the cool air feels good. I just find the fog a bit spooky, that's all."

"You surprise me, Miss Cole," he said in the faintly mocking tone I found so irritating. "I wouldn't have thought you'd be spooked by anything."

"You are an impossible and irritating man," I flared. "No wonder you haven't married. Who'd put up with you?" And then I blushed, realizing what I had said, and he laughed.

"My mother must have been off on her favorite subject again," he said. "Namely, when is her wayward son going to get married and provide her with grandchildren to comfort her in her old age?"

I said nothing.

"Well," he continued, "my mother may not have much longer to wait. I've found the woman I want to marry, and if I can convince her, my mother could be a grandmother by this time next year."

"Poor girl," I snapped. "I certainly hope she knows what she's getting into." I sounded brave enough to my own ears, but inside I felt the same sharp pain I'd felt at the mention of Constance Robinson. So he did intend to marry her. Why should that bother me? And yet it did. I felt angry and dismayed.

"I'm sure she does," he said, looking at me with that same irritating smile. "But she can take care of herself, count on that."

We rode for a while in silence, then as we came to a fork in the road, he said to me, "That way leads up to the old mission. Have you been up there?"

"No, but I've heard it mentioned. It's quite old, isn't it?"

"By American standards it is. Something over a hundred years, or thereabouts."

"Is it still in use?"

"Yes, although it's badly in need of care. It was damaged by an earthquake some years back, and has never been completely repaired. Your mother would have been married there if she hadn't eloped."

"I'd love to see it."

"It's quite beautiful, even in its current condition. I'll take you up and show it to you sometime."

"I'm sure I can find it by myself," I said as coolly as I could manage.

"I'm sure you could, too," he said, smiling, "but I would like to take you just the same."

"I can't imagine why, and besides, won't your intended be jealous?"

"Oh, no. How could she be? She doesn't know she's my intended yet."

"When do you plan to let the poor thing in on the secret?"

"In due time. Anyway, you needn't keep referring to her as the 'poor thing.' She's quite lovely, you know."

"All the more reason she should be warned as soon as possible so she can make her plans to flee."

"I'm sure she won't choose to."

"You certainly have a wonderful opinion of yourself."

"I'm·a wonderful person. Just ask my mother."

I couldn't help laughing in spite of myself, and we reached the ranch before I realized we were there. He had certainly managed to lighten my spirits in spite of the gloom and fog, and as I went up to my room, I found myself wondering whether that had been precisely his intention.

I took the bouquet of flowers down to the kitchen to put them into water, and found Rosa deep in conversation with Raul Marcos. Her face was creased with concern, and though she waved to me, she seemed preoccupied. I waited a moment or two to see if there was a problem, and when Raul left, she came over to me.

"You look worried, Rosa. Is there something wrong?"

"I hope not, señorita. It's my daughter Antonia. She's missing."

"Missing? I thought she was at your sister's."

"So did I. I sent her there the day after the party, but Raul went over to see her today, and my sister says she has never been there."

It did indeed sound strange. "Is there somewhere else she might have gone, Rosa? To a friend's house, perhaps, or to another relative's?"

"I've sent Raul to see everyone I could think of. He should be back tomorrow morning to let us know whether he has located her."

"If there's anything I can do to help you, Rosa, let me know. I'm going up to see Grandfather now."

I stopped by Grandfather's room and checked on him. He was awake, and he gave me a smile and I stayed by his bed for a few minutes. Then I went back down to the kitchen and fixed myself some supper. By the time I was finished, I had decided to get a book from the study and go read in bed for a while.

I climbed into bed and settled back to read, when suddenly I remembered the pendant. I hadn't

131

checked on it since I had hidden it away in the pocket of a dress, intending to have Grandfather put it in the safe. In my concern over his illness, I had forgotten it.

Now I got out of bed and took one of the candlesticks to the closet. I groped in the pocket of the dress. Nothing was in it.

I tried the other pocket. Empty. I sat down on the floor, puzzled. Perhaps I put it in another dress, I thought. I went through all of the pockets in my clothes, but to no avail. The butterfly was definitely gone. Someone had taken it.

Stunned, I sat down on the edge of the bed. Who could have stolen it? I turned over all the possibilities in my mind.

Antonia? I wouldn't have put it past her, but hadn't she been gone at the very moment I put the pendant in the dress?

Sybil? She wanted it, but I hardly thought she'd steal it. She wanted it to wear, and she certainly wouldn't be able to do that.

One of the servants? Perhaps. And yet, I couldn't believe that any of them would have done it.

And what was I to do about it? Whom could I tell? Grandfather was still too ill; I couldn't very well go to Sybil. I decided to wait until Lane returned from San Francisco and discuss the matter with him. He usually had a sensible solution to problems.

I blew out the candle and climbed into bed. I couldn't sleep for a long time, and when I did get to sleep, I was back in the same nightmare I had had before.

Each time I had the dream, details of it became clearer to me. I was in a long stone tunnel, and it seemed to be filling with water. My skirts were wet and dragging, and I was floundering, trying to reach the end of the tunnel. My mother was there, waiting for me at the opening, holding out her arms to me, shouting a warning that was covered by the sound of wind or rushing water. The closer I came to her, the farther she receded. Then the warning shout became a scream that went on and on, and I awakened suddenly, shaking, to realize that the noise was real. Outside, in the patio, there was great deal of bustling about, and someone was screaming.

I jumped out of bed and grabbed my wrapper and rushed to the rail. The patio was lighted, and a number of people were milling about. Standing in the center of the group, being comforted by Mrs. Malloy, was Rosa, who was screaming and sobbing. I ran down the stairs and was met by Jarrod Allen, who put a hand on my shoulder and led me into the sala.

"What's happening?" I asked, turning to try to look over my shoulder. "Why is Rosa screaming?" I looked into his face, which, for once, was solemn. He looked at me for a long moment.

"We found Antonia," he said.

"Found her?" I looked at him blankly. "Where? Was she hurt? Was she—" Suddenly the meaning of his set jaw, of Rosa's screams, became clear to me. "Oh, dear God," I whispered, pressing my fist to my mouth. "Was she—"

He nodded. "She's been dead for several days, apparently."

"How? Where?"

"Down by the cliffs. She had apparently fallen over."

"But I don't understand. How on earth could you find her in this fog?"

"Coastal fog is tricky. I met Raul as he was riding to the home of one of her relatives up the coast a bit. He told me what he was doing, and I rode along with him for a way. Up the coast the fog had been blown away by a breeze, and that stretch of rock was clear."

He stopped for a moment. "And she was there?" I asked.

"Down on the rocks. Although to be honest, our finding her was almost an accident. I stopped to check on one of the shoes on my horse, and when I stopped, I caught sight of something white wedged between the rocks. It was a bit of cloth, and when I pulled it loose, I happened to glance down and see her."

"Do you think the cliffs broke off with her? I've heard that happens."

"Frankly, I don't know what to think. There were no clumps of earth around to indicate that."

"She wouldn't have jumped, would she?"

"I don't know."

Somehow I had the feeling that there was something he was keeping from me. I looked at him, and he appeared to be watching me, waiting for something. What?

"Is there something you're not telling me?" I asked. "I have the feeling that there's something else."

He didn't answer for a moment. He appeared to be trying to decide whether to say something else.

"Look," I said impatiently. "If there's something more I should know, please tell me. I'm not going to faint. I've been through a number of things in my life, and I can handle knowing about this."

He continued to regard me silently for a moment, and then he said, "There appeared to be signs of a struggle on the edge of the cliff. There was grass torn up, rocks were dislodged, that sort of thing. And Antonia appeared to have scratches on her face and neck, the sort that are made by fingernails."

I felt the color drain from my face. "Are you saying that someone murdered her?"

"I'd almost bet that she was pushed."

"But who would do such a thing? Why would anyone want to kill her?"

He didn't answer me. He reached into his pocket and pulled out something and laid it gently into my hand.

It was the Montoya butterfly.

Chapter Nine

I was so stunned I had to sit down. For a moment, I could only stare at the thing in my hand.

Slowly the implications began to sink in. I looked up at him. "But you don't think that I—this was stolen from my room," I said, suddenly frightened and defensive. "I don't know how long it's been gone. You don't think that I would kill—" I stopped. It was impossible that he could believe such a thing of me.

"I don't have any idea what to think," he said. "I found that lying beside her body."

"Why did you bring it to me?" I asked, my voice harsh. "Surely the sheriff will want it for evidence."

"I'm sure he would," he said. "I didn't choose to give it to him."

"I suppose I ought to thank you," I looked up at him, "for protecting me. Although I can't see why, if you believe me to be a murderess, that you would bother."

"Haven't you stopped to think that it is not necessarily you I am protecting?" His eyes, when he looked at me, seemed distant. "Have you thought what it would do to your grandfather if his beloved only granddaughter should be accused of murder? His health is fragile enough already. This would probably finish him.''

Of course. I should have known. It would not be for my own sake he would do such a thing. After all, what was I to him?

''I am not guilty,'' I whispered. ''I did not kill her. What possible motive could I have?''

''I can think of several. There were many people who witnessed the scene between you and Antonia at the party. She stole the butterfly. You tried to take it back. There was a fight, and you pushed her.''

''But it just didn't happen.''

''Or perhaps it's true that her claim to the butterfly is better than yours.''

''How could it be? Even if her father was a Montoya, a claim which can't be proved, I am the legitimate descendant.''

''Are you? Have you proof of that? Antonia accused you of being an imposter. Suppose that turned out to be true? It would be a powerful motive.''

''But—'' I felt the weight of the accusations and I had little defense against them. Except that I was innocent. ''I'm just not guilty. I'm not, I tell you. I didn't do it.'' My frustration had turned to anger, and I was furious that he could believe that of me, that he could think those things. I stood up and faced him. ''If you think I'm a murderess, give this to the sheriff, and let them try me.'' I raised my arm to fling the butterfly at him, but he grabbed my wrist in a grip of iron, and for a moment we stood there, staring at each other, his eyes hard, my heart pounding fiercely.

And then, before I could move, he had swept me into his arms and his lips were on mine, hard and longing. My legs felt weak and for a moment my body melted against his. I felt his hands in my hair, and his lips moved over my eyes and my face.

Then I gathered my strength and pushed him away from me as hard as I could. This was the man, who, five minutes before, had practically accused me of murder. Did he think his silence could buy me?

I scooped the butterfly from where it had fallen on the floor and rushed toward the door, clutching my wrapper around me. Standing in the doorway, her face set in a cynical smile, stood Sybil Harrington.

I felt my face go red as I pushed past her and ran up the stairs.

I didn't sleep much for the rest of the night. I kept going over in my mind the events of the evening, Antonia's death, the butterfly, and coming back always, inevitably, to that kiss.

I felt shamed by that kiss and by my response to it, because, I had, for one long moment, responded completely. It was foolish, I thought, utterly foolish. What had Sybil thought? What *could* she have thought? Me, in my wrapper, in the arms of that man? I knew him to be a rude and cynical person, but I had never guessed that he would so take advantage of my shock and fear. But did he, Melinda? asked a cynical voice in my head.

Obviously, I thought, I had underestimated his capabilities. I should have listened to Lane. Lane had said that he'd go to great lengths to make someone appear a fool, and he'd been right.

But I kept going back to that kiss and hating myself for the knowledge that I had liked it, had wanted it to go on, and had not wanted to push him away.

You are a fool, Melinda Cole, I told myself. He's already told you he's in love with somebody else. You know him to be an unscrupulous oaf. You're a fool.

And with those harsh words to myself, I finally got back to sleep.

The atmosphere at the ranch was subdued for the next few days. Rosa was away making arrangements for the funeral. The sheriff came by and asked all of us whether we knew anything about Antonia's death.

I answered the questions which were put to me as a matter of routine. It was obvious that he didn't consider my information to be of much importance. I hadn't been at the ranch long enough to be considered a suspect.

I felt guilty at concealing the matter of the pendant from him, but I didn't really see what purpose would be served by revealing it. I knew I wasn't guilty. If Antonia had stolen the butterfly, I could only bring shame to Rosa by letting it be known. I was truthful in all my answers, but then, the sheriff didn't ask about the pendant.

We were told an autopsy was being held to

determine the exact cause of death.

The funeral was to be conducted at the old mission. Grandfather couldn't attend, of course, and Sybil declined to go. Mrs. Malloy said that Sybil had said that she "hardly felt it necessary to attend the funeral of the daughter of one of the servants." That sounded typical.

It was left, then, for Lane and me to go. Lane had seemed cool to me since his return from San Francisco. I wondered if he had not forgiven me for the quarrel we had before he left, or if Sybil had reported having seen me in Jarrod Allen's arms.

I chose not to ask.

The road around the mission was crowded with mourners' carriages and buggies. Lane helped me out of ours and escorted me through the archway into the mission courtyard. The arch led to a garden in front of the chapel. A very old, moss-covered fountain played there, its water running into a pool filled with waterlilies and goldfish. Cobbled walkways wound among beds of flowers and herbs. Large trees shaded the mission itself.

In places the whitewashed plaster had broken away so that the adobe bricks of which the buildings were constructed were visible. The walls around the mission had fallen down in spots and the bricks lay in crumbling heaps where they had fallen. The worn steps we climbed to the chapel were chipped in places, and the elaborate facade around the chapel door was cracked.

Still, the herbs and flowers gave evidence that someone cared about the place, at least enough to give it what attention they could.

"This is such a beautiful place," I murmured to Lane as we entered. "It's too bad it's so badly in need of repair."

He shrugged. "Most of the local parishioners are quite poor," he said, "and most of the people who have money aren't Catholic."

Since we were inside, I said nothing, but it seemed a shame to me, anyhow. I didn't see what religion had to do with it. The place was old and beautiful. Surely, for those reasons, it should have been preserved, regardless of what denomination was involved.

The inside of the church was unlit except for the banks of candles on one side and those around the huge golden altar that reached to the ceiling. It was very elaborate, with intricately carved cherubs surrounding a blue-robed statue of the Virgin Mary. Huge candles in enormous brass candlesticks showed walls and ceilings covered with paintings. The murals were crumbling in places and blurred with smoke in others, and it appeared that water had leaked through the roof and run down the walls in other spots.

I had never before attended a Catholic service and found it difficult to follow. I concentrated on the prayers, trying to remember my schoolgirl Latin, but with little success. Still, concentrating on the mysteries of the service helped me keep my mind from its purpose—putting to rest poor Antonia.

I looked around the chapel and recognized a few people I had met at the party. I saw the Allens across the room, and shifted my gaze quickly so that I would not catch Jarrod's eye.

I could see Rosa among the group of friends and relatives who surrounded her, but I could not see her face through her heavy veil. She appeared composed, though weak, and when we stood, she leaned on the arm of a pale Raul Marcos, seeming barely able to stand alone. My heart went out to her. Poor Rosa; now she had no one.

As we left, I turned to Lane, who had barely been able to stifle his boredom during the service, and asked if he would wait for me for a few moments. I wanted to see more of the mission, and I was sure that he was not interested in poking about with me.

He agreed to wait in the shade of the courtyard, and I wandered off along a path through the flowers.

I walked around to the side of the chapel, and saw a vegetable garden behind the building. The building itself appeared to be much larger than I had thought at first. It stretched back for some distance. It was obvious to me that there was more to the mission than the chapel I had entered.

As I returned to the courtyard where Lane was waiting, a black-robed priest came around the corner. He was not the priest who had conducted the service and who had gone with the other mourners to the cemetery. He was younger, I observed, and taller.

"Hello!" he said, startled. "I thought everyone had gone."

"Almost everyone has," I said. "I wanted to look around a bit, though. I haven't been here before."

"I didn't think you looked familiar," he said, extending his hand. "I'm Father Murphy."

142

"It's very nice to meet you, Father," I said. "I'm Melinda Cole."

"Ah, yes, Jim McCarthy's granddaughter." He smiled. "It's very nice to meet you, Miss Cole."

"I am surprised you have heard of me," I said. "Is my reputation that bad?"

He laughed. "On the contrary. Everything I've heard has been quite complimentary. I've been looking forward to meeting you."

"I've been looking forward to seeing your mission. It has special meaning to me."

"Oh?" He raised his eyebrows.

"Yes, you see, my parents met here the night they eloped. This was their trysting place, so to speak. I have wanted to see it for some time."

"Then you must let me show you the grounds and the rest of the mission buildings."

"I'd love to, but I'm afraid it will have to be another time. Lane—Mr. Harrington—is waiting for me, rather impatiently, I'm afraid."

"That's too bad. But do come back soon. And of course, we would be delighted to have you attend mass on Sundays."

"Thank you for inviting me, Father, but I'm not Catholic, you know."

"For that matter," he smiled, "neither was Our Lord. You are invited just the same, and do come back to the mission at any time. I think you will find it most interesting."

I thanked him for the invitation and returned to the garden where Lane was waiting for me, tapping his foot. We climbed into the buggy and rode in silence for a time.

I was considering the fact of my religion, or lack of it. I hadn't been raised in any sort of church, but I knew that my mother was Catholic, and I wondered whether my grandfather was. One would think so, with his Irish heritage. It had never come up in our talks. I'd have to remember to ask him.

In the middle of my meditations, Lane turned to me and said, "The sheriff seems to suspect foul play in Antonia's death. Is that right?"

"It appears so. From the fact that they're doing an autopsy and from some of the things Jarrod Allen said about the body, it would seem that they have reason to believe her death was not accidental."

"What did Allen say about it?"

"He said there were signs of a struggle and that there were scratches on her face and neck."

"Hmm. If you ask me, the first person they ought to talk to about any possible suspicions is Allen."

I frowned. "Why would you say that?"

"Well, hasn't it occurred to you that the way he found the body was something more than mere coincidence?"

"I'm not sure I know what you mean."

"Consider it this way. He finds a body which was lying on rocks beneath a cliff, hidden from the view of the road, and he does it in a dense fog, and he arranges to have a witness along to verify his story. Doesn't any of that seem a bit odd to you?"

"Since you put it that way, perhaps—but he said the cliffs were clear of fog when he was there."

"Even so, that story sounds totally fabricated to me, and it wouldn't surprise me if the sheriff thought so, too."

"What do you mean?"

"I mean it wouldn't surprise me if Jarrod Allen knew exactly where the body was for a very good reason—he put it there."

I was astounded at his statement. I had thought of Jarrod Allen as many things—a rude, inconsiderate oaf among them—but never as a murderer. For a moment I was too surprised to think. Then I turned to Lane.

"What possible motive could he have for killing that poor girl?"

Lane shrugged. "I can think of several possibilities. For one thing, Rosa was almost sure Antonia was seeing someone secretly. Raul wanted to marry her, and she had refused him. That was common knowledge. The mystery was why. Now, suppose the man she was seeing was Jarrod Allen."

"But why would he keep it a secret? Neither of them was married."

"Perhaps his mother didn't approve. One would think she'd want better things for her son than marriage to a hired girl."

"Somehow I can't imagine Evelyn Allen being such a snob."

He glanced at me with an odd, unfathomable look. "Perhaps Jarrod just wanted to have his little fling without taking any responsibility for it. Maybe he was the one with an eye to better things."

"Somehow it just doesn't seem logical to me."

"Then how to explain his coincidentally 'finding' the body? And besides, who else might have done it?"

"I don't know. Maybe no one did. Maybe it was just an accident."

"And maybe you just don't like the idea of Jarrod

Allen's being implicated."

"Don't be absurd," I said, but I knew my face was red. "I don't even like the man. It's just that fair is fair, and I don't see any real evidence that points to him or anyone else. The fact that *you* don't like him doesn't make him a murderer."

He smiled cynically, but added nothing.

When we returned to the ranch, no one was around, so I went up to my room to change and then went in to see my grandfather. He was sitting up in bed when I arrived, and I went over and gave him a hug.

He had improved greatly during the past week, and was well enough to spend part of the day reading or talking with an occasional visitor. The doctor appeared amazed but delighted with his progress, and I was happy and relieved.

"How are you feeling today?"

"Improved, my dear, much improved. How was the funeral?"

"Very subdued, Grandfather. Rosa seemed weak, but remarkably composed. I'm sure that, under the circumstances, I'd have been quite hysterical."

"I doubt it," he said. "You aren't the hysterical type. But you're right. If ever an occasion was grounds for hysteria, this would have been one such occasion. Were the Allens there?"

"I caught a glimpse of them. We didn't get a chance to talk. Lane and I didn't go out to the cemetery."

"Just as well. Rosa's remarkable composure probably didn't hold up out there." He stopped, then looked at me for a long moment.

"My dear," he said, "I need to contact Steve Matson. I want to get him out here."

"Of course, Grandfather. How do I go about contacting him?"

"Just write him a note. I'll give you the address. Have one of the men take it to him when he goes in for supplies. I don't think there's any real urgency, but I would like to talk to him. I have a few—"

At this moment Alice Carrington came into the room, bringing Grandfather's tray. She greeted me and set about arranging the meal so that Grandfather could eat. I noticed that she seemed a bit preoccupied—she was not her usual jovial self—but I attributed this to the fact that she was busy with Grandfather and had had more work to do since Rosa had been gone.

When she was finished, she turned to me, an odd expression on her face, and said, "May I see you outside for a moment, Miss Melinda?"

"Of course," I murmured, and Grandfather grumbled, "That's right, go outside and talk about the invalid. Makes me feel such a bloody fool."

"Now, Grandfather," I soothed as best I could, "it's probably only about tonight's dinner. You'd just be bored, anyway. I'll be right back."

I slipped outside with Alice, who led me down the corridor away from Grandfather's room.

"There's been some terrible news, Miss Melinda, and I didn't want to just blab right in front of your grandfather. Wouldn't do getting him all upset."

"No, you did just right, Alice."

"You know how scared we was to tell him about Antonia, him so sick and all."

"Yes, yes, I know, Alice." I was impatient with her. "What is the problem now?"

"The sheriff arrested somebody for murdering that poor girl."

My heart almost stopped. "They did? Who was it?"

"Raul Marcos."

"Raul?" My fear changed to astonishment. "They arrested Raul Marcos?"

Alice was enjoying her role as the bearer of news. "They did. The sheriff come down to the cemetery where they was burying poor Antonia and took him off."

"Why? Do you know if they found more evidence?"

"Well," she said, drawing the story out as long as she could, "you know how they was doing an auto—an ata—"

"An autopsy, yes."

"Yes. Whatever you call it. Well, anyway, they did. They found out that poor child was going to have a baby."

"A baby!"

"Yes'm, she was. And somebody sent the sheriff a letter saying Raul Marcos killed her out of jealousy and that he was the last one what saw her alive."

"Who sent the letter?"

"Don't nobody know. I heard it wasn't signed."

"There must be more to it than that. They can't convict a man on an anonymous letter."

"Well, there may be. That's all I heard. But I didn't think it would do to say it in front of your grandfather."

"No. You did exactly right, Alice. I'll figure out a way to tell him. He will need to know, otherwise one of the servants might let it slip. I'm glad you came to me."

She nodded, and went back to Grandfather's room. I went into the patio and sat down to try to think about what to do. Surely there must be more to the sheriff's case than Alice knew. How I wished now that I had gone down to the patio that night I heard Antonia talking to her lover! If I knew who that was, I'd know who had a motive to kill her.

I went back to Grandfather's room, after making an effort to compose myself. We chatted for a few minutes, and he wrote down the address of Mr. Matson's law firm. I took the address back to my room and wrote a short note, asking Mr. Matson to come out to talk to my grandfather, and explaining the situation to him. I sealed and addressed the letter and went out to look for someone to take it to him.

Lane was in the sala when I went through the foyer.

"Lane," I said, approaching him, "who goes into San Francisco with the supply wagon?"

"I don't know who will be going this week," he said. "Was there something you needed?"

"Yes, as a matter of fact, I have a note to be delivered to Mr. Matson. Grandfather wants to see him, and I've written asking him to come out."

"I see." He paused and looked at me a moment as if considering something. Then he said, "Look, why don't you give the note to me? I'll be going in myself, and I can see to it."

"I'd appreciate it if you would, but I don't want to cause you any problems about it."

"Not at all," he said, and smiled at me. "I'm a more reliable messenger than the ranch hands."

I gave him the note and returned to my room to

try to figure out a gentle way to let Grandfather know about the arrest.

After the recent tragedy, I was glad when life at the ranch settled into a more normal routine. The weather was warm and lovely during the day, and in the evenings the fog that rolled in off the coast was a cool contrast.

I worked in the kitchen with Rosa and Mrs. Malloy, making apricot jam and canning vegetables. Rosa was still feeling her loss deeply, as was to be expected, and the problem had been complicated by Raul's arrest.

"He swears he's not guilty, señorita," she said to me, "and I believe him. Raul loved Antonia all her life. He was like my own son. I cannot believe—"

"Nor can I, Rosa," I soothed, putting my arm around her shoulder. "I'm sure it will be all right. I don't see how they can possibly have the evidence to hold him."

"They say—the sheriff says—that there is more they haven't said, some things they know that they haven't told. It could be bad, señorita."

I comforted her as best I could, but secretly I thought she might be right. It was hard to know how Raul would fare.

Lane returned from San Francisco with word that Steve Matson was out of town for a month and would call when he returned. I told Grandfather, who was not happy about it, but was forced to accept the wait.

I continued to ride in the mornings. Grandfather was now up and about for a limited time during the day, and Mrs. Carrington had gone back home. I had more time to myself, and so I rode farther away from the ranch, exploring places I had not seen.

Some mornings Lane rode with me. Our relationship, which had been strained for a time, was becoming more cordial. He seemed to be making an effort to charm and entertain me, in contrast to his mother. She avoided me consistently and spoke to me only when it was absolutely necessary.

Since I was alone so much, I came to value Lane's company, and we spent more and more time together. One morning, he wanted to show me the smugglers' cave we had talked about, and so he suggested an early morning ride down to the beach.

We took a steep trail down the cliff to get to the ocean, and then we galloped across a strip of sand, firm where the low tide had left it damp. The sea gulls swooped around us, their raucous cries echoing off the cliffs. It was lovely to be on the beach in the early morning.

"How beautiful it is here," I said.

"It is a nice place," Lane said. He was making every effort to be agreeable. "You must be careful about coming down here, though. If the tide is wrong, you could get trapped."

"Can that happen?"

"It can and it has. The tide can come in very quickly here, and the way the beach is shaped, you could get cut off from the trail before you had even seen it coming. Look." He pointed back down the way we had come. "See how the beach is narrower there?"

I did.

"When the water comes in, it fills that stretch of beach first. If you wait too long you can look around and find the trail behind you blocked. And there's no other way out. It's best to come with someone who knows the area."

We rode on down the beach to the cave. I could see that it would have been a perfect location for smugglers to ply their trade. The opening was situated among the rocks in such a manner that it was only visible when one was directly in front of it. From the cliff overhead, it would not be seen at all, and from the sides, projecting rocks made it invisible. On a dark night, one man watching from above could spot anyone approaching from any direction.

We left our horses and walked to the mouth of the cave. As Lane had said, we were unable to enter because of the iron gate that was fastened into place over the opening.

"I should think it would be interesting to explore," I said, trying to peer through the darkness.

"Not likely," Lane said. "It would be wet, mostly. It fills with water at the high tide, and any romantic relics the smugglers might have left would have been washed out years ago."

"There might be some interesting rock formations, though," I said, still curious.

"Not interesting enough to tempt me in there, I can assure you. When that cave starts to fill up with water, there's no place to go."

I shuddered at the thought. I strained my eyes to

see into the cave, but it was hard to see past the grate. The whole area was still in shadow, and I could only see a few feet into the entrance. Bits of seaweed hung from the bars. The grate-like door was fastened to the rock in such a way as to make it impossible to open without the key to the large padlock that held it shut.

"Too bad the tunnel from the house is blocked," I said. "We could get in that way."

"I suppose, if those things interest you," Lane shrugged. "I'm not much for exploring damp holes, myself."

We returned to our horses and rode back up the beach. I looked behind us as we started up the cliff trail. The water had already begun to fill the tracks our horses had left. The tide had begun to turn.

Chapter Ten

The Allens were planning a gala party for the Fourth of July and I was pondering what to wear. I had worn the gray-and-white dress to the last party, and of course could wear it again, but I would have loved to have something new. Still, I didn't like to bother Grandfather about such things.

He thought of it himself, though, and suggested that I might like to take a trip to San Francisco to see a dressmaker.

"I'm sure Sybil will be ordering a new one," he said. "She never misses a chance to get a new dress. Ask her—no, better tell her—you're going with her to pick out a new dress."

"I hardly think she would take kindly to that thought, Grandfather. She's not the sort who takes to telling very much, and she doesn't like me as it is."

"Humph. Doesn't matter if she likes you or not. Doesn't like me too much, for that matter, but as long as I pay her bills, she'll do what I say. Now, you go along and plan to go to San Francisco. I'll take care of Sybil."

I don't know what he said to her, but when she came to ask me to go to the dressmaker, Sybil was almost friendly.

Lane drove us to San Francisco. We spent the night in a hotel, and in the morning, we visited the dressmaker. Lane drove us there, up streets that seemed so steep I thought the horses would not be able to climb them; then we went down the other side and I was sure we would topple over and roll to the bottom.

The dressmaker greeted Sybil as if they were old friends, and glanced at me curiously. "This is my husband's granddaughter, Melinda Cole, Mrs. Lewis," Sybil introduced me. "She will need a dress for the party, also."

"Of course," murmured Mrs. Lewis. "If you will both come with me, I'd like you to look at some new fabric you might like. Mrs. McCarthy, I believe those things on that table might be to your taste. And Miss Cole," she turned and looked me over, assessing me carefully, "I have several things you might like."

She began to search through some bolts of fabric. "We'll need to be careful because of your brilliant coloring," she said. "We don't want to choose a shade that will fight it. What colors do you prefer?"

I gave her a small, rueful smile. "Quite frankly, pink is my very favorite, but I'm sure you know what a disaster that would be with this hair."

"Miss Cole, I have found that one can wear any color if it is the right shade. Even red with that hair, believe it or not." She smiled at me, and I liked her. She didn't make me feel as if red hair were a handicap, just a minor problem to be dealt with.

"Here," she said, pulling out a length of material. "This is a shade of pink I think you might like." It was beautiful fabric, very pale, and almost lavender, but it was indeed still pink, a dusty pink, and held up to my face it made my hair look more like polished copper than raw carrots. I was delighted.

Her assistant took my measurements, and we chose a style and trim, and she assured us that the dresses would be finished in time for the party, and that she would send them to the ranch with the supply wagons.

Sybil, who had chosen a mauve fabric for her gown, assured her that would not be necessary. "Lane will pick them up himself," she told Mrs. Lewis. "I wouldn't trust them to anyone else."

As we started to leave Mrs. Lewis's shop, Sybil turned back to discuss some of the final details with her, and I wandered out by myself to look at a bit of the city. Across the street from me was an old lady selling flowers. She had buckets full of roses, and I saw daisies and gladiolas, and some I didn't recognize. I stepped out into the street, intending to go across and ask her the names of the ones I didn't know. As I stepped off the curb, I heard a series of retorts—small explosions like pistol shots—and then loud whinnies from a frightened horse. As I turned toward the source of the sound, I realized I was directly in the path of a runaway horse and carriage.

It seemed an eternity before I could move, and when I did, I felt as heavy as if I were under water. It appeared to me that the horse was almost on me before I could gather the strength to jump. I could see his eyes, rolled back so that they were almost white; his hooves seemed to flash almost over my head. Then I leaped—almost rolled, in fact—toward the opposite side of the street. The rear carriage wheels rolled over my skirt as it dashed past me.

I lay there a moment or two, trying to catch my breath, as people dashed from everywhere, it seemed, to come to my aid.

"Young lady, young lady, are you all right?" A large man with a very red face, whom I judged to be the owner or driver of the rig, had his arm around my shoulders and was helping me to a sitting position.

"I think so," I said, when I could get my breath. "I think I may have turned my ankle."

"Stand back, let her get some air." A policeman shouldered his way into the crowd that had gathered around me. "What happened, Miss?"

"I—I'm not really sure," I said, trying to get to my feet, embarrassed now that the danger was over. "I started across the street, and then I heard something like gunshots, and when I looked up, the horse was almost on top of me."

"I'll say almost on top of her," the old woman at the flower-stand said vehemently. "If the little lady hadn't been near as quick as a cat, she'd of been a dead 'un."

The officer looked around at the crowd. "Anybody know who fired those shots?" he asked.

"Weren't shots, officer," someone volunteered. "Was firecrackers. Some Chinese kids tossed 'em right under the horse's nose. Scared that animal silly."

"Firecrackers!" the officer snorted. "Wish they'd outlaw those blasted things. They cause more trouble than—well, anyway, miss, can you stand up?"

"Yes—yes, I think so," I said, attempting once more to get to my feet.

By this time Sybil had crossed the street and was coming through the crowd. "Melinda, what on earth happened?"

"She 'bout got trampled to death, that's what happened, lady," the flower seller said. "Runaway horse nearly got her."

"I'm all right, Sybil, I just turned my ankle, that's all."

The officer was supporting me, the red-faced man having gone to see what damage his horse had done. He turned to Sybil. "Is she with you, ma'am?" he asked her.

"Yes, officer, we have a carriage here somewhere." She looked around for Lane, who was nowhere to be seen. "Melinda, how unfortunate for you. But thank goodness you weren't hurt. At least not badly."

She had the officer help me back into the dress shop, where Mrs. Lewis gave me a chair and rushed to fix me some tea. I found, now that it was all over, I was shaking very badly. I was grateful for Mrs. Lewis and her ministrations. Sybil went outside to look for Lane, and returned with him a few minutes later.

He appeared to be very concerned, and helped me into the carriage and drove me back to our hotel. I was tucked into bed, and a doctor was called to examine my ankle. He pronounced it badly sprained, but said it would be fine if I stayed off it for a few days.

He left me some medication in case I had pain and was unable to sleep. By this time, I was feeling more than a little silly about all the attention I was getting.

"This is perfect nonsense," I told Lane when he came to see me after the doctor had gone. "I feel fine. In fact, I feel a perfect fool lying here in bed."

"Don't be silly, Melinda. You had a rather violent shock and you need the rest. Besides, we have that ride back to the ranch tomorrow, and you'll need to be ready for it." He took one of the tablets the doctor had left for me and handed it to me with a glass of water. "Now take this like a good girl, and get some sleep."

I glared at him, but I took the pill, and soon felt my body begin to relax, and my eyes begin to droop. As I began to drop off, I heard Sybil come into the sitting room that connected our rooms. She and Lane were talking in low voices, and Sybil seemed angry with him about something.

"Unfortunate . . ." I heard her say. Was she concerned about me? That would be a surprise. ". . . another way. Something more certain . . ." Lane said. What did that mean? My mind was getting foggy. ". . . more careful next time . . ." said Sybil. She was right about me. I would have to be more careful, I thought. And then I dropped off into a sound sleep.

Chapter Eleven

The ride back to the ranch the next day was notable only for the fact that I was miserably uncomfortable every bit of the way. My ankle ached, and my whole body was sore.

When I got home, Grandfather had to hear all about the accident, so he insisted on getting up and going to the sala where I had been propped up, my foot on a stool, my every need anticipated by Rosa.

I minimized the fright I had had for his benefit. "Really, it was a rather silly accident, Grandfather," I said. "I was so wrapped up in the flowers across the street from the dress shop that I stepped right out in front of a horse. Likely scared the poor thing to death."

"Humph. You'd better take care of yourself, young lady. You don't want to take this thing about being the last of the Montoyas seriously."

"Not likely, Grandfather. It doesn't strike me as a good idea."

"Besides," he said, his eyes twinkling, "if that ankle doesn't get any better, you won't be able to dance with Jarrod Allen at the Fourth of July party."

160

"Oh, Grandfather," I tried to scoff, but I know my face was pink, "Jarrod Allen is not particularly fond of me, that I have noticed. Besides," I said, "I think I'd rather spend the time sitting out the dances with you and Mrs. Allen."

"Nonsense, girl," he frowned at me. "You need to be spending your time with people your own age, not with old fogies like me. I think you might meet young Constance Robinson at this dance. She's about your age and you might just hit it off."

"Perhaps," I agreed. Why did I dislike Constance Robinson without even having laid eyes on her? I had no reason to believe that she was other than perfectly lovely, but I didn't like her already. I didn't say that to Grandfather, though, who was talking to me about Jarrod Allen.

"I had hoped, you know, that you and young Allen might hit it off, too." He sighed. "It would be a joy to me if I could see this ranch in good hands before I go. Jarrod is a fine young man." He looked at me intently. Then he spread his hands in a gesture that indicated his refusal to involve himself. "But I meddled in what was not mine to meddle in before, and made a mess of it. This is your life, Melinda, and it's yours to choose. I won't interfere." Then he smiled suddenly, the sparkle back in his eyes, and said, "But I will give you my opinion. Every chance I get."

I laughed and leaned over to pat his hand. "I hope so, Grandfather. I do value your opinions, you know."

"Humph." He gave a small sort of snort, but I could tell he was pleased. "By the way, when is

Steven Matson going to be back?"

"Well, the month is up the week after the Fourth. I'll send another note to him if we haven't heard within a week after he's due back."

"Good. Not like him to take off so long. He usually takes a week, maybe two, but a month seems long. I'm anxious to get him out here."

My ankle was improved enough in a few days that I decided to ride over to the mission and visit with Father Murphy. The ride was lovely, and the mission itself was beautiful in the early morning, with the mist in the trees and the flowers blooming even more profusely than they had been when I had been there last.

I tied my horse outside the arched gateway. No one was in the garden, and I wandered among the pathways, stopping to trail my fingers in the water of the fountain and watch the goldfish for a moment.

"Ah, Miss Cole." Father Murphy came out the chapel door and greeted me. "How nice to see you here. Did you come back for your guided tour of our old mission?"

"I did indeed, Father. It took me longer to get back than I had hoped." I told him about my accident in San Francisco.

"You must be careful around here on the Fourth of July. I'm afraid firecrackers are not only popular with San Francisco's Chinese residents on that day."

"I'll watch out for runaway horses. Have you been here long, Father?" I asked as we went into the mission through a door adjacent to the chapel.

"About five years. I have learned to love this area in that time. Come through here and I'll show you some of the rooms back this way."

We went through a small, dimly lighted room into a kind of patio, similar to the one at Mariposas except that it was much larger. The walls on three sides had arched corridors running the length and width of the building, but the fourth, opposite me, was a high wall which rose above the red-tiled roofs of the mission in graceful curves. Arched openings in the wall held five bells, two large ones near the bottom, two smaller ones in the center, and a single small one in the rounded top of the wall.

There were rough, worn benches here, and trees and flowers with cobbled walkways winding among them. The columns along the arcades were made of plastered brick which showed through along the bases where the plaster had chipped away. Moss grew between the tiles that formed the floors. The whole place had a serenity that not even the neglect of the years could destroy. It was green and shady and very lovely.

"It's so beautiful here, Father, and much larger than I had thought. What are all those rooms used for?" I asked, indicating the doors that opened off the long corridors.

"We—Father Sherwood and I—live in some of them. Some are used for storage. Some aren't used for anything nowadays. The Franciscans who started these missions used to live here, and the rooms had various purposes. Some of them were used for lodging travelers, for instance."

"The Franciscans?"

"The order which founded these missions. You see, the missions originally numbered twenty-one in all, and they began at San Diego and went all the way to Sonoma. They varied in size. This mission was one of the largest at one time."

"And the bells, do they still ring?"

"Oh, yes. I'm surprised you haven't heard them on a Sunday. That's our *campanario*—the campanile."

"I can't understand, Father, why this lovely place has been allowed to fall into such disrepair."

He sighed. "Actually, most of the missions have been given up by the church, secularized and sold. We began using this one, after it had been deserted for some years, because we needed a chapel. We've done more work on it than shows, you know."

We had walked the length of the corridor on one side. As we passed through a wicket in the campanario, I could see other buildings in the back, most of them fallen into ruin.

"What were those buildings used for, Father?"

"Various things. You see, this mission was almost like a little city in its busiest time. It was virtually self-sufficient. There was a tannery, a mill, a wine press—everything they needed, actually."

We wandered among the old buildings and I looked at the ruins of what had once been a thriving small community. In one room I saw huge cast-iron caldrons which had been used in making candles, in another, the wine press Father Murphy had mentioned. And out past the buildings, we walked among the poppy-covered graves of the old cemetery. It was no longer used, and many of the gravestones were broken or overturned.

"It's sad, don't you think?" I asked him.

"That it's fallen into such disrepair, you mean?"

"Well, yes, it's so lovely, you know. It seems a pity that so few people care for it anymore."

We were standing beneath an arbor which was covered with grapevines. Unripened clusters of grapes hung over our heads.

"In a way you're right, I suppose. And there has been talk of a group organizing to protect all the old missions. It should be done. It's part of California's heritage."

"Precisely. Religion actually has little to do with it."

"Well-l-l, I wouldn't go that far, you know." He smiled at me. "This and a few of the other missions still hold regular services. That does have something to do with religion."

"But you do understand what I'm saying?"

"Yes, and you're right. Of course, there is no longer any real need for much of what the missions provided in the way of goods and services, but—well, hello, Mr. Allen. We weren't expecting you until tomorrow."

I spun around to face Jarrod Allen, who was walking through the arbor toward us.

"Miss Cole, you do know Mr. Allen, don't you?"

"Indeed, Father, Mr. Allen and I are acquainted," I said coolly.

Jarrod smiled at me, that same mocking smile, and said, "How nice to see you, Miss Cole. It seems you didn't wait for me to bring you to the mission after all."

"I wasn't sure the invitation was still in force, Mr. Allen." Father Murphy looked from me to Jarrod and back, as if puzzled or amused by the conversation, then said to me, "Mr. Allen is our most generous benefactor, Miss Cole. He sees that we are supplied with certain foodstuffs from his ranch."

I looked up at Jarrod and I could feel a small frown between my eyebrows. "Oh?" I said. "Are you Catholic, Mr. Allen?"

"No," he said smiling. "Presbyterian. Why, Miss Cole? Do you think Catholics have a monopoly on Christian charity?"

I blushed, and Father Murphy laughed. "We'd like to think we invented it," he said, "but at this moment I'm afraid a bit of graceful Christian gratitude is more in order. Now," he said, putting an arm around each of us and turning toward the mission, "let's go back for a cup of tea, shall we?"

We had tea in what appeared to be a small sitting room near the chapel. The room was very plainly decorated. The walls were unadorned except for a beautifully carved wooden crucifix on one wall. There were no rugs on the tile floor, and the furniture was dark and heavy, and appeared to have been hand made.

When we were settled with our tea, Jarrod said to Father Murphy, "We're having a Fourth of July party at the ranch, Father, and we'd like to have you come."

"I'd be delighted," he said. "We don't get many such invitations and I'm not going to let one go by."

"Bring Father Sherwood, too," Jarrod

166

continued. "I'll send a driver for you early in the evening."

Father Murphy turned to me. "Will you be there, too, Miss Cole?"

Before I could answer, Jarrod said, "Of course she will. She's promised me most of her dances."

"I've done no such thing," I snapped, and was embarrassed when they laughed. In an effort to recover my composure, I said, "We're hoping my grandfather will be well enough to attend, also."

"And Sybil and Lane will be coming, am I right?" Jarrod asked.

"Of course. In fact, Sybil and I made a special trip to San Francisco to order dresses."

"And almost got herself killed in the process," Father Murphy added.

"How?" Jarrod asked. "What happened?"

"It was hardly as dramatic as all that," I said, and explained about the accident.

He frowned. "Sounds as if you'd better stay away from the big city," he said. "It's no place for a dreamer."

"I didn't have any trouble in Boston," I said coldly. "Perhaps people know how to keep their horses under control there."

"Or maybe," he said, "they have their women under better control."

I rose abruptly, refusing to give in to my rage in front of Father Murphy. "I think I'd better go, Father, before I say something terribly unladylike. I did appreciate the tour and the tea very much."

He rose, smiling. "Do come back, Miss Cole, any time. I have enjoyed your visit."

167

Jarrod Allen stood up and said, "I'll walk you to your horse, Miss Cole."

"I'm sure that won't be necessary, Mr. Allen," I said, still struggling to keep my temper in check. "I believe I can find my own horse."

He said nothing, but smiled and took my arm and escorted me from the room. Once outside, I jerked my arm from his grasp and walked rapidly away from him toward my horse.

"Melinda," he called after me. I said nothing but continued on my way. He caught up with me and turned me to face him. "Melinda, I wanted to apologize for my behavior the last time I saw you." I stared past his shoulder and said nothing.

"Listen to me," he said softly. "I know my timing was terrible. It wasn't the time or the place. I am asking you to forgive me."

I looked at him, my face as expressionless as I could make it. "I'm sure no apology is needed, Mr. Allen. I can't think why you would consider my forgiveness necessary."

He dropped his arms and looked at me, his face as blank as my own. "Very well," he murmured. He spun around and started to walk away. Suddenly I felt very small and petty.

"Mr. Allen," I called after him. He turned to me, his face wary and closed. "I'm being unnecessarily rude. It's my turn to apologize. I've never thanked you for returning my butterfly or for not mentioning to the sheriff that you found it. I am grateful to you for that."

"You don't owe me any thanks. After Raul was arrested, I wasn't sure I'd done right."

"Then you must still have some suspicions about me."

"About you? No. In spite of what I said, I've never suspected you." Relief flooded me. "It's just that the butterfly might help the sheriff determine the real killer. I can't believe it could be Raul. Not after seeing his face when we found the body."

Perhaps something in what Lane had said about Jarrod had begun to stir in the back of my mind. Perhaps I just wanted to shock him. For whatever reason, the question just seemed to pop out of my mouth, almost of its own accord.

"Did you know that Antonia was going to have a baby?"

He stared at me. "A baby?" he said blankly.

"Yes," I said, and I watched him carefully. "I wondered if you knew about it."

"No," he said, regaining his composure. "I hadn't heard."

I shrugged, and mounted my horse. "Perhaps I shouldn't have mentioned it," I said.

"It's an interesting bit of information," he said, and turned and walked away from me.

I don't know what I had expected. I don't even know why I said it. If there had been any truth in Lane's accusations, what could I have found out from Jarrod's reaction, anyway? At any rate, I had learned nothing, and I turned toward the ranch.

Lane was bringing the dresses from San Francisco two days before the party, and I could hardly wait to see mine. I had wanted to have a pink dress for as long as I could remember, and had

169

always been told, "Not with that hair. You simply *can't* wear pink." And now I was going to be able to. It was a small pleasure, but I was excited and looking forward to his return.

When he arrived at the ranch, I was waiting in the sala to greet him. He carried a large box under his arm, and I begged him to let me see it.

"Not yet," he said. "Mother would never forgive me if I opened it before she arrived."

"I may never forgive you if you don't," I said, frowning in an attempt to appear angry. At this moment, Sybil arrived and took the box from Lane.

"Only one box?" she asked. Lane shrugged. "That's the only one she gave me."

"Mrs. Lewis is ordinarily more careful about her packing," she said. "But since she knew they were coming to the same house, perhaps she thought one would suffice."

She unfastened the ties on the box and opened it. She lifted out the lovely mauve dress she had ordered and spread it on the sofa. Then she turned back to the box, lifted out the tissue, and said to Lane, "There's only one dress here. Are you sure there isn't another box?"

"Mother, I am quite capable of counting to two. I was only given one box. I brought it. That's all I know."

My disappointment must have been plain on my face. I had wanted that dress so badly, and now I was not to be able to wear it.

"Really, Lane, I can't think why you didn't check the box," Sybil was saying. "This is very disappointing for Melinda."

170

I tried to muster some understanding, forgiving words, but the smile I attempted turned into a grimace.

"I really am sorry, Melinda," Lane said, and he did appear to be sincere. "It's a devil of a thing to have happen. I could kick myself for not having checked."

"It couldn't be helped," I murmured. "It must have been some sort of mixup." But I couldn't help thinking that it was very easy for him to be contrite. It hadn't happened to him. And it was all very well for Sybil to be apologetic. She had her dress.

"I'd offer to let you have this one, Melinda," Sybil said, "but of course we are such different sizes." How easy to make a gesture that was sure to be refused! Sybil was a full head shorter than I was, and very slim. I'd never fit into her dress.

I muttered something about having something to do elsewhere, and left the sala. I felt as if I were going to cry, and I didn't want anyone to see me crying over something as silly as a dress. I wondered if a mistake had truly been made or if—I put the thought from me. That, I told myself, is positively silly. Of course it was an accident. The thought of anything else was merely ridiculous.

I climbed the stairs to my room slowly, and lay down on my bed. Well, it is fortunate, I thought, that I have the gray-and-white dress. I can wear it again. After all, I've only worn it to one party, and it will be fine for the Fourth of July celebration.

I heard a knock on my door, and opened it to find Rosa standing there. Since Antonia's death, Rosa had grown even closer to me, mothering me, as if, since I had no mother and she had lost her daughter, we could replace those lost ones for each other.

Now she had heard that Lane had returned, and she had come up to see my new dress. "Where is it, señorita? I can hardly wait to see it on you."

I sighed. "There was some mistake, Rosa. Apparently the dressmaker neglected to put it in the box she gave to Lane. I won't have a new dress to wear to this party." I managed a small smile. "I'm sure it will be ready for the next one, though."

Rosa frowned. "Your beautiful new dress didn't come?"

I shook my head. "Some sort of accident, I suppose."

She snorted angrily. "Accident. The señora does not have accidents," she muttered, her voice filled with contempt.

"But, Rosa," I said, "surely you don't think anyone would do such a thing on purpose."

"I do think so," she said. "I think she would do almost anything." She paused, then leaned toward me. "There were stories that she murdered her husband in San Francisco," she said softly.

"You don't believe that, do you?"

Rosa shrugged. "Some people do. She is the sort of woman of whom such things might be believed."

"Even so, that hardly constitutes proof. No," I shook my head, "I'm sure the whole thing was an accident."

"And I am sure it was not. But even so, you are without a dress, and that is a problem. I think I can help you with that, señorita."

"How, Rosa? The party is tomorrow night. There's no time to make a new dress."

"No, not a new one, but there is time to change an old one."

"An old one? Are you suggesting that we remake my gray dress?"

"No, not your dress. You wait here. I have something to show you."

She left the room and soon returned with a dress that she spread on my bed. It was made of layers and layers of ecru lace with a sash of pale green silk, and pale green around the neck and sleeves. It was old-fashioned, but it was beautiful and beautifully kept.

"Do you like it?" she asked.

"It is gorgeous," I said sincerely. "Was it my mother's?"

"It was your grandmother's," she said. "She was tall, like you. Your mother was very small."

"Do you think we can do anything to it to make it look good for the party?"

"Of course. You leave it to me. I am very good at sewing. I will do the neckline like this—" She showed me her ideas, and I thought that if everything worked, she was right about the dress. The style was simple, and it could be brought up to date with a few alterations.

"I will take care of it, señorita," she said. "I will not let her make you appear disgraced at the party."

"I hardly think wearing the same dress twice would disgrace me, Rosa," I smiled.

"When everyone knew you ordered a new one?"

Her eyes narrowed. "I will not let her make you ashamed," she hissed. She turned and left the room, taking the dress with her. I stared after her for a few moments. I was surprised at the intensity of her dislike for Sybil. Rosa had always seemed to be so calm, taking events in stride. It was apparent that there was more to her than met the eye. I was certainly glad that Rosa didn't dislike me. She was not the sort of person I would like to have for an enemy.

Rosa did wonders with the dress. I had not realized that she was so accomplished a seamstress. She had widened the neckline and put a large lace flounce around it so that the lace skimmed my shoulders. The arms were bare otherwise, for she had removed the sleeves. She had reshaped the skirt so that the lines were now fashionable. The dress looked new, and when I put it on, I was delighted.

The color was perfect with my hair and it made my skin look creamy. I had heard that lace was very flattering, and now I believed it.

Rosa was delighted with my appearance. "You look perfect, señorita," she said. "This dress is the perfect color to show off the butterfly."

I had almost forgotten about the butterfly, now safely locked up in Grandfather's safe. "Do you suppose I should wear it, Rosa? The last time—"

We were both remembering the scenes that had occurred the last time I had worn the butterfly.

"This time, nothing will happen, señorita. You must wear it. Señora Susana had this dress made to wear with the butterfly. Wait until you see it."

She was right. The color of the dress was a

perfect foil for the flashing gold of the butterfly. I looked at myself in the mirror in Grandfather's study, and the image there did not look at all like the picture of myself I carried in my mind.

My skin was creamy against the lace, and my hair, done by Rosa in elaborate curls, looked shiny and polished. I was surprised and pleased at the image. I turned to smile at my grandfather.

"My dear, you look beautiful," he said. "But I am surprised to see you in that dress. I had understood that your new dress didn't arrive from San Francisco. Gave Lane a pretty severe tongue-lashing about it, in fact."

"It didn't, Grandfather. This is one that Rosa and I—altered a bit for the occasion."

"Well, whatever you did, you look fine. Seems to me," he said, peering closely at the dress, "my wife, Susana, once had a dress something like that. Shows off that butterfly, too."

I smiled and said nothing.

When Sybil and Lane joined us, Lane's eyes widened when he saw me. Sybil's face betrayed nothing, if indeed she felt any surprise about the dress I wore. She commented that I looked lovely, and Lane agreed.

"You're wearing the butterfly," he said.

"Yes," I answered. "Shouldn't I be? It looks well against the dress, don't you think?"

"Yes, yes, of course," he said. He seemed slightly confused. I attributed it to his surprise that I had managed to acquire the dress on such short notice.

We were among the first guests to arrive at the

Allens', and Jarrod helped Sybil and me from the surrey.

He took my arm and led me toward the house, leaving Lane, who had been in the act of offering me his arm, standing by the rig.

"That was a bit rude," I said. "Lane was waiting to walk me into the house."

"I am not, as you have so often pointed out, a very nice person." He smiled down at me. "But since you knew it already, you couldn't have been shocked at my behavior. Besides, my mother is waiting to see you. She has been looking forward to having a bit of a chat with you before the other guests arrive."

He led me across the veranda into the parlor where his mother was waiting to see us.

"Melinda, how good to see you again." She kissed my cheek. "I've been waiting to talk to you ever since your last visit, but with all the trouble and all, I haven't had a chance to get Jarrod to take me over. Come in here with me." She led me into a small room just off the parlor.

"I'll have to go out and be a good hostess in a moment, but I wanted to ask you. Did you ever find the portrait of your mother?"

"No," I said. "Frankly, I hadn't thought to ask about it or look for it. Things have been rather in an upheaval at the ranch lately, and it slipped my mind."

"I was going to suggest that you look in the cellars."

"The cellars?" I asked. "I didn't know there were any."

"Oh, yes. There were wine cellars dug out of the rock the house sits on. The smugglers' cave led into one of them."

"I know about the smugglers' cave," I said. "Lane showed me the entrance to it from the beach one day. But no one mentioned the cellars. I suppose, if I'd thought, I'd have known the tunnel had to come out somewhere."

"I suppose they don't use them any more, except for storage. But frankly, if I wanted to hide something in that house, that's where I'd put it." She paused and looked at me a moment. "You see, Melinda, that house is very different than it appears to be. It has secrets."

"Secrets? Well, I suppose. All old houses do, don't they? And parts of the Mariposas are very old, I understand."

"It's a different sort of house. It appears to be a warm and comfortable place, and I suppose it is, to those who love it. But it has its secrets, and you must never forget that houses have personalities, like people. They can be friendly, or—" She made a gesture, spreading her palms and raising her eyebrows.

I smiled. Evidently Evelyn Allen had a gift for the mysterious. "You make it sound as if the house had ghosts or something."

"I haven't heard stories about ghosts at the Mariposas, although it wouldn't surprise me to. Heaven knows, it has housed enough strange characters to have produced a couple. No," she shook her head, "it isn't that. It's as if that house gets wrapped around the people who live there and does things to them."

"What sort of things?" I was intrigued.

"I'm not sure. But I do know that those who want it will do almost anything to have it. Or to keep it, once they've got it. I sometimes think that Jim McCarthy loved that house more than he loved his wife and child, and goodness knows, he loved them to distraction." She gazed into space for a second, then shook her head as if coming back from far away, and smiled at me.

"Now, I didn't bring you in here to go all strange and mysterious on you. I wanted to tell you that the portrait might be there. Ask Rosa to help you look. Have you asked your grandfather? No one could take that picture without his knowledge."

"No, I haven't," I answered. "But I will."

She stood up. "I hear more people arriving, so let's go meet them. You look incredibly lovely, my dear. Is that the dress you got in San Francisco?"

"Well, no. Not exactly. I'll explain what happened to you another time. It's a long story."

She looked at me with some curiosity, but didn't ask anything else, and we went out to meet the other guests.

Father Murphy had arrived, and I was happy to see him. He brought me a glass of punch, and as I took it from him, I saw a young woman whom I did not recognize enter the room.

"Father," I said touching his arm. "Who is the girl who just came in?"

He turned and followed my gaze to where the young woman was standing.

"Ah, that would be Constance Robinson. Lovely

178

young woman, isn't she?"

She was indeed, and Father Murphy's face wore the same look of rapt admiration that I saw on the faces of most of the men present. I think Constance Robinson was the most beautiful girl I had ever seen. Her hair was golden blond, and her eyes were clear blue. Her eyebrows were dark and her eyelashes were thick and black. Her blue gown set off her coloring to perfection, and her figure was slim and flawless.

As I watched, she laid a slender white hand on Jarrod's arm and said something to him, and they both laughed. Then he took her hand, tucked it under his arm, and led her toward Father Murphy and me.

"Miss Cole," he said when they came up to us. "This is someone I have wanted you to meet. Melinda Cole, Constance Robinson. Or should I have said it the other way? My mother would be appalled at my lack of good manners, but at least you know who you are. And you know Father Murphy, of course."

"Of course," she murmured. "I am delighted to meet you, Melinda," she said, but the tone of her voice and the coolness of her manner did not indicate to me that she was particularly delighted at all.

"And I, you," I said. "I've heard many nice things about you."

"Oh?" she said, raising an eyebrow. "From Jarrod, I hope," and she looked up at him and smiled, placing her other hand on his arm.

"No," I said, feeling like an intruder. "From

Jarrod's mother, actually."

"How nice," she said, her eyes never leaving Jarrod's face.

I felt at a loss as to what to say. She was obviously not interested in me; she had eyes only for Jarrod. I was rescued from the awkward silence by Father Murphy, who said, "Miss Robinson has been in the East, visiting relatives. Baltimore, wasn't it, Miss Robinson?"

"Yes," she smiled at him, revealing perfect teeth. "My mother's family. I hadn't seen them since I was a child, you know."

"Melinda is from Boston, I believe," he said, making an attempt to draw us together in conversation.

"Yes," I said, "I lived there all my life until I came here."

"Boston?" she said. "Did you know the Ruperts? Marilyn? Todd?"

"No," I said, smiling. "I'm afraid not."

"Oh? I'm surprised. They're very social. Simply the nicest people. One of the best families."

"I'm afraid I'm not very well acquainted with most of the best families," I said, my discomfort turning to anger. "We simply moved in different circles."

"Oh," she said, and I was dismissed from her awareness with that syllable. "Oh, there are the Manfords. I must go say hello. Come with me, Jarrod."

She turned and led him away to another group of people. Father Murphy watched as they walked away. "There has been talk that Jarrod and Connie might get married, but so far none of the talk has come from them."

"One might wonder why not," I said. "It is obvious that she would not object to the idea."

"Perhaps the objections are not on her part." I looked at him quickly, but his face was impassive.

"Surely, Father, Jarrod wouldn't have any objections to marrying someone as lovely as Constance Robinson."

"She is indeed very beautiful," he said, "but it may be that beauty is not sufficient in and of itself."

I didn't quite agree. Men as arrogant as Jarrod Allen hardly needed anything more in a woman to consider marriage. Beauty was, in and of itself, quite sufficient for those who were interested primarily in themselves, but I didn't tell Father Murphy I thought so.

Still, what I felt about Constance Robinson could only be described as jealousy. Pure, unadulterated jealousy. Probably normal, I told myself. Probably every woman in the room is a little jealous of Constance Robinson. If I knew that my jealousy went much deeper than envy of her beauty, I refused to admit it to myself.

There was music for dancing, and the wide veranda had been cleared to accommodate those couples who wanted to do so. Lane asked for the first dance, and while we were dancing, I mentioned to him that I had met Constance Robinson.

"She's very lovely, isn't she?" I asked him.

"Yes, she is rather pretty," he said.

"Rather pretty? I thought she was gorgeous."

"I suppose if you like the type. I rather prefer redheads, myself."

"I thank you, my dear uncle, that was gallantry beyond the call of duty." I smiled up at him.

He stopped and made a small bow to me. "Gallantry to order, any time, day or night. I am at your service, mademoiselle."

He resumed the dance, and I laughed. Lane could indeed be charming when he chose to be, and tonight he was at his best.

"In fact," he said as we waltzed the length of the porch, "my preference for redheads is so definite that I am considering the possibility of marrying one."

I looked up at him, and my dazed expression must have amused him because he burst into laughter.

"Oh, Melinda, you are funny." He smiled down at me. "And why not? Why shouldn't we get married? It would be, practically speaking, the perfect match."

I had a difficult time finding my voice, but when I did, I said, "You *do* mean me. You *are* proposing to me."

"Of course. Do you have such a difficult time featuring that?"

I shook my head. "No. I mean yes. I mean, it simply never occurred to me that you had thought of me—well—in quite that way."

"And why not? You are quite beautiful, especially tonight. You are very intelligent. You have everything a man could want in a wife. I beg you to consider what I have said."

"I will consider it, Lane, I promise. But you will forgive me if I appear rather stunned. I hadn't considered the possibility of marriage to anyone.

You must give me some time to think it over."

"Of course. Though I did consider that it might be amusing to announce our engagement tonight. Imagine how surprised everyone would be."

Surprised was hardly the word for it, I thought. Shocked would be more likely. The temptation to jolt Jarrod Allen out of his smug arrogance was almost irresistible, but I had better sense than to be so impetuous, even for the effect it might have. A voice in my head warned me. And besides, Melinda, what makes you think he'd care, one way or another? And why is it that now, in considering another man's proposal, your first thought is of Jarrod Allen? Why not of your grandfather, or Sybil?

I found myself unable to think about anything else. I finished the dance with Lane, and excused myself to be alone with my thoughts. How I wished I had someone to talk to! I missed Mavis at times like these. Much as I loved my grandfather, he was hardly a dispassionate observer where I was concerned.

I slipped away into the little study where I had sat with Evelyn earlier in the evening, and closed the door behind me to think about what this proposal could mean.

Was Lane Harrington in love with me? Somehow I didn't think that was possible. Lane didn't seem the sort to love anyone, and yet, perhaps that was just his way. Perhaps he actually loved me as much as he was capable of loving anyone. He was certainly charming and attractive; at least he was charming when he chose to be.

But why me? Lane was raised in San Francisco society, and I certainly couldn't compete in that social setting.

Was it the ranch? Perhaps I was getting cynical. I could see Lane considering marriage to me to insure that he could not lose control of the ranch, he and Sybil. But if that were the case, why did Sybil not at least pretend friendship?

I was confused, but as I sat there, my answers became clear in my mind. If I had to ponder all the possibilities in this fashion, I clearly was not ready for marriage. I would not be ready for marriage until I knew instantly, in my heart, that it was right. As long as I had to sort things out logically, it was only my mind that was involved, not my emotions.

I realized I must say no to Lane, and strangely, I didn't think he would be too upset by that. Somehow I had the feeling that the proposal was one of calculation on his part, too, not an impetuous, head-over-heels-in-love proposal. And *that* was the sort I wanted; logic in such matters did not appeal to me, no matter how good the match looked on paper.

I went back to join the party, and was approached by Jarrod as soon as I entered the room.

"I've been looking for you," he said. "I believe it's my turn for a dance."

I preceded him to the veranda, where he swept me into his arms, and we whirled the length of the porch. I felt my body pressed close to his, and I leaned against his arm to try to loosen the iron grip in which he held me, but he only smiled at me in his mocking way and pressed me closer to him.

"Mr. Allen," I hissed through clenched teeth.

"I'm finding it increasingly difficult to breathe. Do you think you could loosen your grip enough to prevent my fainting right here?"

"But certainly, Miss Cole. I had no idea you were so short of breath these days." He smiled at me, his head tilted to one side. "I wouldn't want you to faint. People might think you were overcome with the joy of the moment, and we wouldn't want them to get the wrong idea, would we?"

He loosened his arm, and I glared at him. "We certainly wouldn't want Miss Robinson to get any wrong ideas, would we, Mr. Allen?"

"Or Mr. Harrington. Am I right, Miss Cole?"

"I'm sure Mr. Harrington wouldn't get any wrong ideas. He knows what—" I stopped before I said, "what a boor I think you are." That seemed a bit much, even under the circumstances.

"What you think of me?" He finished my sentence. "But let us not forget the witness to the one romantic scene you have allowed me, Miss Cole. I'm sure the elegant Sybil has filled her son's ears with that story."

I bit my lip and stared past his mocking face, over his shoulder. "If she's honest with him," I said at length, "she'll tell him the whole truth—that it was not my choice and that I pushed you away."

He leaned close to my ear and said to me, softly, "But only after you realized that you were beginning to enjoy it. Lie to me if you like, Melinda, but don't lie to yourself. You liked my kiss."

I wrenched myself from his arms and ran down the steps into the darkness, my face burning. I hated him! I hated him! I ran, spurred on by my anger, until the lights of the house were no longer visible, until I was hidden in the mists that swirled around the trees.

Why did he insist on doing this to me? Why didn't he just marry that Constance Robinson and leave me alone? As I stood in the darkness, my anger cooled, and slowly turned to embarrassment. I was certain I had made a spectacle of myself, running away from the party like that. How humiliating to have to return now, and behave as if nothing had happened.

I stepped away from the tree I had been leaning against, and started back to the house. The mist had thickened in the few minutes I had been standing there, and now I looked around to try to determine the direction from which I had come.

I went a few steps in the direction I believed I had come from, and I realized I was going the wrong way. I turned back in the opposite direction, and when I had gone a short distance, I could hear the music and I knew this was the way I had come.

I walked slowly back toward the house, and marveled at how quickly the fog had come up and how rapidly I had lost my sense of direction. I had always considered myself good at finding my way, even in strange places, but I had been swiftly disoriented by the approach of the fog. I was shaken by the discovery that I could so quickly be turned around.

As I approached the veranda where the guests were dancing and laughing, I smoothed my hair back into place and tried to assume an air of composure. I hoped few people had noticed the incident, and if questioned, I was prepared to say that I had merely gone for a short walk.

I went back to the veranda and climbed the steps slowly. No one seemed to notice my approach, and no one seemed to think anything was wrong.

As I went into the parlor, I saw Jarrod Allen in a corner with Constance Robinson. He was bending over her, smiling, and she was hanging on his arm, chattering into his ear. She turned toward me as I entered and gave me a look of utter disdain, then turned back to Jarrod. I smiled wryly. So much for the possibility of friendship from that quarter, I thought.

My grandfather and Evelyn Allen were sitting on a sofa together, and my grandfather motioned for me to join them.

"You look a bit flushed, my dear," Evelyn Allen said as I sat down with them. "Is it too warm in here?"

"Oh, no," I assured her. "I just went for a bit of a walk and got turned around. I probably hurried on my way back."

"Oh, dear," she shook her head at me, "you must be very careful in the fog. Even people who know the countryside well get lost in it. Especially in the dark."

"I'm starting to realize that," I said. "I was quite confused for a few moments."

"Are you enjoying yourself, young lady?" Grandfather asked.

"Of course," I assured him. "It's a lovely party."

At this moment Lane approached and asked me to join him, and I rose and walked with him to the punch bowl.

"Are you having some difficulty with Jarrod Allen?" he asked. So someone *had* noticed, I thought.

"No," I said, "not really. I just find the man insufferably rude, that's all."

"I still think he knew more about Antonia's death than he let on," Lane said darkly. "If you ask me, there was just a bit too much coincidence there. Did you know she was going to have a baby?"

"Yes, I'd heard."

"Raul insisted that he knew nothing about it. I think Jarrod Allen might."

"You think one of them is responsible?"

"Raul swears he never touched her, and I believe him. Antonia made no secret of the fact that she was not interested in him."

"If not Raul, then . . ."

"We know she was seeing someone. And Jarrod Allen was at the ranch quite often before you came. What other reason might he have had for putting off his engagement to Constance Robinson? They are obviously quite interested in each other."

I glanced across the room to where the two of them were standing, his dark head very close to her blond one. Perhaps Lane was right. There didn't seem to be any reason for postponing the engagement that everyone assumed would be forthcoming.

I sighed and turned to Lane. "I'm really feeling quite tired, Lane. Do you think we could leave?"

He raised his eyebrows a bit, but he nodded. "I think I can arrange that, if you're sure that you want to."

"I'm quite sure."

"Then I'll borrow a buggy from the Allens. I'm sure that can be done, and we can return it tomorrow. We'll leave the surrey for your grandfather and my mother to drive back."

During the carriage ride back to the ranch, I became even more aware of the treachery of the fog. Twice Lane had to stop and get out of the carriage to check our location. Then, on one or two occasions, the fog cleared, so that we were able to see quite clearly.

We arrived home in due course, and I went to my room immediately to hide the butterfly and go to bed. I sensed that Lane wanted to talk to me, but I was not in a frame of mind to discuss anything at the moment, so I climbed the stairs to my room slowly, and wandered down the corridor to my bedroom.

I looked into the patio as I went, and was overcome by a sense of the strangeness of the place. In the dark foggy night the patio, usually so warm and friendly in the daylight, appeared filled with strange shapes and dark shadows. The tree loomed out of the fog, shapeless and sinister, and the arches of the corridor seemed to frame grotesque scenes, each different, all of them changing as I watched. I shivered, and quickly closed the door to my room behind me. Letting my imagination run away with me would accomplish nothing, I thought, but I did feel better after I had lighted the candles and turned down my bed. I slipped out of my dress and looked for a place to hide the pendant. I decided to put it under my pillow where I was sure it would be safe for the night.

I got into bed and blew out the candles. I lay in bed for a long time, staring at the ceiling, and thinking about the events of the evening. I thought I would never fall asleep, and when I finally did, it was only to slip into the strange nightmare that I had been having since I first heard about Rancho de las Mariposas.

Chapter Twelve

This dream was again slightly different from the others. It was even clearer and more frightening, and I was filled with a terror that was stronger than I had ever experienced.

I was in the tunnel again, and the walls were wet stone. I was wading in water that became deeper as I tried to walk in it. My mother was there again, her arms stretched out to me, and I struggled to reach her, held back by the water and some force I could not overcome. The water rose higher, and as I struggled to reach my mother, she pushed back the hood on her cloak, and suddenly she was not my mother at all. She was Antonia, and she was laughing at me, her head thrown back to reveal the golden butterfly at her throat.

I awakened, screaming out, and thrashing at my bed. When I realized where I was, I sat up in bed, breathing heavily and holding my hands to my face. I didn't hear a sound. I listened to see whether I had awakened anyone with my screams, but there was silence. I sat shivering in bed for a few minutes, and then got up to light a candle. Suddenly the dark was frightening and I didn't want to be alone.

I thought that I must have been turning into a coward. There had been a time when the darkness was not frightening to me, when lying alone in the night was not to be contemplated with fear. Now, since the nightmares had come, I wanted to banish the shadows, throw light into the corners for fear of what might lie there. And what could lie there? I asked myself. Whatever might possibly be there? There could hardly be anything too frightening, I scolded myself. There's nothing there at night that isn't there in the daytime, and in the daytime, you aren't frightened. Why now?

But I couldn't answer that. I only knew that at night I had become afraid, afraid of the dream, of something I could not see or name, that seemed to be coming closer, pressing in on me.

I fell asleep when the room was light enough to see without the candle, and when I awakened again, the sun was high. I went down to breakfast, and then to the stables. I realized as I entered the stables that the Allens' horse and buggy was still there, so I decided to return it myself, as I had nothing else to do that day. That, I told myself, is probably part of the problem. You don't have enough to keep you busy. You, who were used to working all the time, are idle, and you probably feel guilty about it. And, I told myself, you know what to do about that.

I determined that I would return the buggy, driving over with my horse tied on behind, and then I'd ride back and find some work for myself. There was always plenty to do in the kitchen; Rosa could use another pair of hands now that Antonia— the thought of Antonia made me shiver, and I put her out of my thoughts. The dream was too recent.

I had the buggy hitched and my horse saddled, and I started off down the road. I left word for my grandfather that I was going to the Allens' and I set out.

The sun had cleared away most of the night's fog, but some mist still hung in the trees, and the early morning sun slanted through it. A grasshopper flew up as I passed and landed in the dust in front of me. Blackberry vines grew in the ditches beside the road and the berries were starting to turn red. In a few weeks they would all be heavy and black, and ready to pick for jam.

I was enjoying my early morning outing, happy to wash the night's fears out of my mind with the clarity of the day. I was approaching the Allen ranch when I saw a rider coming toward me from its direction.

I clenched my teeth. It could only be Jarrod Allen, and after last night's scene, I had no desire to see him again. I had hoped that by being early, I could return the buggy, and simply leave without encountering him.

He stopped when he saw me, and dismounted.

"Good morning, Miss Cole. You're up very early this morning."

"I wanted to return the buggy," I said.

"There was no hurry." He walked over to where I had stopped the horses. "Besides, you didn't need to do it yourself, after all. You could have seen to it that someone else returned it."

"Since I was responsible for borrowing it, I

hardly thought it would be fair to make someone else return it."

"You left rather abruptly last night. Were you feeling ill?"

"As a matter of fact, I was," I said, knowing that I lied. "I'm surprised you noticed."

He looked at me and sighed and said, "Melinda, can we call a truce? I'm getting very tired of sparring with you every time we meet."

I was surprised. For once, he seemed serious, the mocking smile gone from his face.

"I suppose so," I said. "After all, I wasn't the one who started it."

"I would almost be willing to argue that point, but I promise, no more battles. In fact, I wanted to ask you to come with me on a picnic."

"A picnic?"

"Yes. I had my mother pack a lunch, and I thought we might ride back up into the hills to a place I know that is perfect for a picnic. I think you'll enjoy it."

"Well, I really don't know . . ."

"I promise to be on my best behavior, and I think you'll love the place."

I said yes. Perhaps I had been hoping he would ask me to go with him. Perhaps I had gone there secretly hoping to see him. I know now that I had been lying to myself all along about my feelings for Jarrod, refusing to allow my mind to own what my heart knew from the first time I had seen him. Whatever the truth of it, by the end of that day, I was forced to admit to myself that I was hopelessly in love with him.

We took the buggy back to the ranch and left it. Then we rode back into the hills for a way, along a dusty road that curled along the floor of a small valley, and then wound its way over a ridge that rose in front of us. The hills were golden brown this time of year, and the scrub oak showed against them in dark green patches.

When we came to the top of the ridge, I could see below us a strip of green that lay like a ribbon at the foot of the hills that rose on either side. The trail dropped down toward it, angling its way down the side of the slope.

As we rode toward the strip of green, I could see sunlight glinting from the water of the creek that was the source of that strip of green. Jarrod pointed to a large tree that hung over the stream.

"See that old oak?" he asked. I nodded. "That's where we're going," he said. "Best place around for a picnic."

As we approached the tree, I could see under it a great slab of rock that stretched from the trunk of the tree to the edge of the creek and against which the water swirled and lapped. It was to this rock that Jarrod carried the hampers that he had slung over the horse behind his saddle.

I dismounted and helped him spread the picnic cloth his mother had packed in one of the baskets.

"Now," he said, rummaging in one of the hampers, "I'm sure she said she had packed—ah, here it is." He drew out a large container of what appeared to be lemonade and popped it into the stream to cool.

Then he turned and looked at me inquiringly. "I

don't suppose a city girl like you has ever done any fishing. Am I right?''

"You are indeed correct, I'm sorry to say."

"Well, Miss Cole of the Boston Coles, you are about to have your first lesson." He went back to his saddle bags and unloaded a number of strange-looking items, then reached under some brush and pulled out two poles.

"I keep these here for the times I get down this way," he explained. "This is my own secret fishing hole, and I like to be prepared. Now," he picked up a small tin and opened it, taking out what were unmistakably worms.

I looked at the wriggly little creatures and grimaced. "Yick," I shuddered. "Is it *absolutely* necessary to use those?"

He glanced up at me, frowning for all the world like a small boy who has just encountered a sissy. "Girls!" he grumbled disgustedly. "Worms can't possibly hurt you, but if you are unable to overcome your female squeamishness, you might try some cheese I brought with that very thought in mind."

"Very considerate of you, I'm sure," I said. "I think I'd prefer the cheese."

"Suit yourself," he said, handing me the pole, "because once you have been duly instructed in the delicate art of angling, you are on your own."

"Do you really think that fishing is a necessary part of a young woman's education?"

He smiled at me, a warm and happy smile, and my heart turned over. "Very definitely. All young women should know how to fish. You never know when you might be stranded in the wilderness and

196

have to live by your wits."

"In that case, I suppose I'd best give it my full attention."

He showed me how to cast my line out and told me about the best places to fish. I watched him, did my best to imitate his practiced movements, and managed to place my bait in a place he said was not half bad. As I repeated the maneuvers, I became better at it, but as time passed, he had managed to catch two fish and pull them, shining all silver and slippery, from the water, while I hadn't had a nibble on my line.

"I doubt that they're biting on the cheese today," he grinned. "You might have to switch to worms if you are going to have any luck."

I shook my head, but after he caught his third, I gritted my teeth and approached the container of worms. "I give up," I sighed. "Show me how to use the nasty little things."

He showed me, baiting his own hook again, and laughed as I struggled to attach the crawly little creature to my hook. I finally succeeded, determined to do it just to show him that I could, and was rewarded for my efforts by a tug on my line within a few minutes of having cast it out again.

"Oh. OH!" I shouted, and I jumped back, yanking the fish from the water and swinging it in toward me so suddenly that I hardly had time to duck as it swung, twisting and dripping, straight at my head. It sailed just past my ear, and Jarrod, coming up behind me, barely managed to grab the line in time to keep from being slapped in the face by it.

"Miss Cole, you swing a vicious fish," he said, as he struggled to release the hook from my catch.

"I know! I mean, I'm sorry. I'm just so excited. I never caught a fish before!" I was happy and delighted with my success and my newly-acquired skill, and I was all but jumping up and down with excitement.

He smiled up at me. "I know," he said, "it's obvious. But you managed to land a dandy for your first time out. This one's the biggest one of the bunch. Now," he said, rising to his feet, "I'm going to fix a fire so we can have these with our picnic."

He put my fish with the others and set about making a small fire. He arranged some rocks, gathered some brush and twigs, and had it going in short order. Then he cleaned the fish and arranged them to roast over the fire.

I unloaded the picnic hampers his mother had packed and spread the food out on the cloth. She had made deviled eggs and a chocolate cake and fresh bread. There were pickles and sandwiches and coleslaw.

"Jarrod, your mother packed enough food in here for six people," I said.

"My mother doesn't understand people with delicate appetites," he said. "She cooked for my father and me too long."

"Well," I said, helping myself to a crisp pickle, "she seems to understand me very well. I do love to eat, too. How long 'til the fish is done?"

"A few minutes more. Why don't you pour us a glass of that lemonade? It should be cool by now."

I poured the lemonade and handed him a glass,

and sat on the rock and sipped one myself. When the fish was done, he served it on the tin plates his mother had packed, and we sat on the cloth and ate what seemed to me enormous amounts of food.

When I had finished I leaned back against the tree-trunk and sighed. "I can't remember when I have eaten so much," I said. "Does fishing always have this effect on one's appetite?"

"It does on mine. More cake?"

"Ohh, noo," I groaned, "I couldn't possibly eat another bite. I think I had three slices. It was delicious."

"So?" he grinned at me. "I had four, but I won't tell if you don't."

I shook my head and smiled at him. I had never seen him the way I saw him at this moment. He was relaxed and obviously attempting to be charming, and, just as obviously, succeeding. Unlike the Jarrod Allen I had seen heretofore, this one was not bitter or contemptuous or arrogant. This one made me think of a little boy, off on a holiday, and I could visualize the child he must have been.

We were silent for a time, and I looked up at the sunlight slanting through the leaves overhead and making patterns of light and shadow on the rock and the water. Last night seemed far away with its nightmares and unpleasantness. Jarrod Allen seemed a different person from the man I had run from at the dance the previous evening. The thought of the dance reminded me of Constance Robinson and I felt the twinge of envy that the thought of her called up. I wondered if Jarrod brought her here, if they had picnics, and I was instantly sorry for the thought. I didn't want to know that he had brought anyone else here. I didn't want to think about him and Constance Robinson.

Suddenly I hated the idea of his marrying her, and as much as I hated it, just that much was I certain that he was going to. I had seen them together, and had seen her air of possession, the way she looked at him. Father Murphy's comments to the contrary, I was quite certain that beauty like that was enough to acquire for its owner anything her heart desired, and it was apparent that Constance Robinson's heart desired Jarrod Allen.

Jarrod had been lying on the rock and now he raised himself on one elbow and looked at me. "You're frowning. What brought that on? Too much chocolate cake? Or are you having bad daydreams?"

I forced myself to answer lightly. "Too much chocolate cake. I've definitely started to feel the effects of my gluttony. Serves me right for making such a pig of myself."

"Serves us both right," he said, lying down and covering his eyes with his hat. "I may not be able to move for hours. My father used to say that eating too much ought to be as socially disgraceful as drinking too much. Fortunately for me, at this moment, it isn't."

"Was your father strict about things like that?"

"Like what? Overeating and getting drunk?"

"Yes."

"Not really." He chuckled a bit. "He had been known to do both on occasion, and he usually said that right after he'd had four slices of Mother's chocolate cake."

"How long ago did your father die, Jarrod?"

"About ten years ago."

"You know," I said, "this may sound strange to you, but it would have seemed more natural to me if my grandfather had married your mother instead of Sybil. They seem more alike, and quite honestly, Grandfather appears to enjoy your mother's company much more than he does his wife's."

"I know. The truth is," he sat up and looked at me, a hint of a grin on his face, "he did ask her."

"He did? Really?" I was shocked. "And she refused him? But why?"

"It wasn't long after my father died, and I suspect she wasn't ready. It took her a long time to get over my father, you know, and by the time she might have considered Jim's—your grandfather's—proposal, his interests were elsewhere."

"That's too bad," I said, my mind busy with the implications. "Things might have been so different if . . ." I sighed. "No point thinking about what might have been. It just seems unfortunate, that's all."

We packed up the picnic gear and headed back to the ranch. I thought, as we rode in silence, of the light Jarrod's information threw on the situation around me. If Jarrod had indeed been my grandfather's stepson, he would have stood to inherit the ranch. It must have been a disappointment for him. And it would explain much of his mother's animosity toward Sybil. By the time she changed her mind and realized what she had given up in my grandfather, he was married to someone else. It was indeed interesting, and I wondered whether any of it meant anything.

When we reached the ranch, he helped me from my horse and I went in to say hello to Evelyn.

She met us at the door and ushered me into the parlor.

"Did you have a good time, my dear?" she asked.

"A splendid time," I answered. "I even caught a fish."

"My goodness, that sounds like fun. I haven't been fishing in years. And did Jarrod behave himself?" She cast a glance at her son, who was lounging in the doorway.

"I was a perfect gentleman," he said, his face all innocence. "Wasn't I, Melinda?"

"He was," I answered, "except that he made me bait my own hook. Otherwise, I have no complaints."

"It's a good thing. I warned him, you know." She sighed. "My dear, if you knew the trouble I went to to teach that boy some manners, and he simply never learned. I've no idea what to do with him at his age."

I laughed. "I've a feeling it's much too late to do anything by now," I said. "Probably he's just incorrigible."

"I'm not sure I like listening to you two discuss my shortcomings right here in front of me," he grumbled, crossing the room and flopping into a chair. "Besides, Mother, speaking of manners, your own are slipping a bit. Aren't you going to ask Melinda to stay for supper?"

"Of course I am. Will you, dear?"

I shook my head and stood up. "I really can't," I

said, "though I'd love to. I left the ranch early this morning intending to be back early, and I don't want to worry my grandfather. I'd best be back in time for dinner."

"I'll ride back with you," he said, rising from his chair.

"No, there's really no need," I said. "I'm fine by myself now, and there's no fog. Besides, it won't be dark for hours yet."

He walked me to my horse and helped me up. "It was a lovely day," I said, and I meant it. I didn't know when I had enjoyed myself more.

"I'm glad you had a good time," he said. "We'll have to do it again."

I almost said I doubted that we would have a chance if he followed through on his plan to marry Constance soon. But I didn't. I murmured something polite and began to pull on my riding gloves. As I did so, I dropped one of them, and it landed at his feet. He stooped to pick it up, and as I reached for it, he took my hand and held it for a moment, looking into my eyes as if he meant to say something. But he didn't. Instead, he bent over my hand, kissed it gently, and looked up at me, the mockery back in his eyes.

"Until later, Miss Cole," he said, and turned back toward his house. I swung the horse around and raced toward the gates, my vision blurred with sudden tears, my mind muddled with confused and painful thoughts. Why did he mock me now? We'd had such a good day. Why did he have to spoil it?

Out of sight of the house, I slowed the horse to a walk and tried to calm my thoughts to match.

Melinda Cole, you're a fool, I told myself. The man who wants to marry you, you don't want. The man you want is in love with someone else. You're an idiot, I said to myself. But there it was, finally past all denying. I loved Jarrod Allen. And I'd have nothing to show for it but pain. For the first time, I was almost sorry I'd come to California.

Chapter Thirteen

When I arrived at the ranch, I was met in the sala by an angry Lane.

"Where have you been all day?" he demanded. "The boy in the stable said you left in the Allen's buggy early this morning. You could have delivered it and been back by noon."

My eyebrows shot up in surprise. "What difference does it make where I was?" I asked. "I'm not under any restrictions that I know of. I'm allowed to come and go where I want. Or am I wrong?"

"Well, no, I'm not—I mean, dammit, Melinda, I was worried about you. You've been gone all day. I wanted to see you this morning to discuss—after all, I did make you a proposal last night. You might consider my feelings, you know."

I was embarrassed and a bit ashamed of snapping at him. After all, there was no point in taking out my anger on Lane, when it was Jarrod Allen I really wanted to scream at.

"I'm sorry, Lane. I didn't mean to worry you. I took the buggy back to the Allens and spent the day there. You know Evelyn and I are friendly." I knew I was, if not lying, avoiding the truth. Why couldn't I say I had been with Jarrod Allen all day? Somehow I felt wary of telling Lane that. There was something in his manner that was threatening in a way I had not been aware of before, and I hesitated to let him know. Let him think I'd spent the day with Evelyn.

He appeared to make an effort to control his anger and to regain the facade of charm he usually cultivated.

"Well," he said, smiling at me and taking my arm, "there's no harm done, is there? I was concerned, that's all." He led me toward the patio and the bench beneath the tree. "Did you have a nice day?"

"I did, yes," I said. "It was very pleasant."

"I still think you should avoid seeing too much of the Allens, Melinda. Especially Jarrod."

"Oh, Lane," I said. "Are you going to raise your accusations about Jarrod Allen again? I think you're being unduly suspicious of him. I don't think there's a shred of evidence to connect him with Antonia's death."

He looked at me, his face curiously blank, his eyes leaving my face to focus on something just past my shoulder. A muscle twitched in his jaw. He was silent for a moment, and there was something in that silence that I found more ominous than his anger.

"There are a few things you don't know about Antonia's death, Melinda," he said in a strangely soft voice. "You knew she was going to have a baby."

I nodded and mumbled, "Yes." His eyes were still

focused somewhere beyond me.

"You did not know that she was married, though, did you?"

"Married?" I gasped. 'To whom?"

He shook his head. "No one knows, apparently. Raul told the sheriff that Antonia had told him the last time he asked her to marry him that she could not. She was already married, she said, and she was going to have the Mariposas. But she wouldn't tell him her husband's name. She said it had to be secret." He turned his head to look at me. I stared at him.

"When did Raul say this?" I was having a hard time grasping what he was saying.

"A few days ago, according to the sheriff. He was here today. He thought someone might know something else." He paused. "No one here knew anything. But you see the point of his search, don't you, Melinda?"

"I think—I mean—if she were married—secretly—then her husband—"

"Is undoubtedly the killer," he finished my sentence.

"But why would she keep it secret?" I asked. "What difference would it make if others knew?"

"Raul said they had to keep it a secret because his mother would not approve."

"His mother? He said the husband's mother would not approve?"

"Those were his words. Consider if you will to whom they might apply."

"Frankly," I said, looking at him straight on, "they could apply to two eligible men I know, and

207

probably to several dozen I don't. But I'm speaking of Jarrod Allen and yourself.''

''True,'' he said, shrugging, ''but frankly, Melinda, can you see me married to the daughter of a maid?'' He said the word ''maid'' in the same tone he might have used for ''worm.'' ''And for what purpose?'' He looked at me and smiled, a twisted smile with no humor in it. ''No, I'm afraid you'll have to admit that the only person who fits into this puzzle is Jarrod Allen.''

It couldn't be true, I thought, my mind scrambling to make sense of what I had heard. It simply couldn't be Jarrod. I could see no purpose to it. Why would he have married Antonia—or anyone—and kept the marriage a secret? Surely Evelyn Allen was not the sort of woman to quibble about her son's preferences. Or perhaps I did not know her as well as I thought I did.

She had indeed kept from me the fact that she had at one time considered marrying my grandfather. Perhaps she was capable of disapproving of her son's choice of a wife to such an extent that he would keep it from her. But somehow it still didn't make sense. I didn't see Jarrod doing that, and I said so.

''Honestly, Lane, it still doesn't make sense to me. Why would he marry Antonia in the first place, unless he was in love with her? And if he was in love with her, why kill her?''

''Because Jarrod Allen was not in love with Antonia, my dear naive Melinda,'' he said, cynicism dripping from each word. ''He was in love with Mariposas, and it seemed a way to get it.''

"But Antonia was not the heiress to Mariposas."

"No, but she might have been, you know. She was considered to be descended from the Montoyas and she said she had proof of her lineage. No one I know has seen the proof, but if she did, she might have shown it to someone she knew would be interested. Very interested."

"You're saying that she showed this—proof—to Jarrod Allen and he married her, thinking that it would put him in a better position to inherit the Mariposas when my grandfather died."

"Precisely. Your grandfather has never made any secret of the fact that he considered himself only a sort of caretaker of the ranch in the place of the real heirs, the Montoya descendants. If Antonia could prove that she was the last of that family, she stood to convince your grandfather that the ranch should be hers. And if it were hers, it would be his. And Allen covets this ranch, make no mistake."

"If Antonia could prove her lineage, why didn't she do so before now, before I came?"

He shrugged. "Perhaps she was bluffing. Or perhaps she did, and your grandfather wouldn't accept it. The point is not, probably, whether the proof existed, but whether Allen—or whoever her husband was—believed that it did."

"Still, Lane, it sounds rather farfetched to me."

"And it may be." He smiled at me, seemingly conciliatory. "It's all guesswork, of course." He paused, and spread his hands and stared down at the open palms. "Still, it would explain a number of things."

"Such as?"

"Such as why he hasn't announced his engagement to Constance Robinson, for one thing. Before you came, it was considered almost a sure thing. But so far, nothing. It would also explain," he gave me a sidelong glance and stared across the patio, "his recent attentions to you."

"To me?" I must have looked blank, because he said to me, "Don't pretend innocence, my dear Melinda. You must know that my mother saw the scene between you on the night Antonia's body was discovered. I must say, he doesn't waste any time."

I knew that I was blushing, giving truth to his words in a way I hated myself for. "But you must know I had nothing to do with that. If your mother had been honest with you, she'd have told you that."

"Don't be upset, my dear. She did tell me. I know Jarrod Allen's character. I wouldn't dream of accusing you of an impropriety. Other than the obvious one, perhaps, of being in the sala in déshabille, a fact more than accounted for by the untimely occasion."

I wanted very much to make some cutting retort, but I found myself unable to do so. Nothing he had said had been wrong, factually, but the slight sneer with which he spoke seemed to put a totally different light on the whole issue. I felt, somehow, guilty, although I had nothing that I could think of to feel guilty about.

"At any rate, I suppose there would be only one way to prove my point," he continued, "and if you are as unfriendly towards him as you say—" was there a bit of emphasis on the word "say"? I couldn't tell—"it would be most unlikely."

"What would be unlikely?"

"His proposing to you."

"Proposing to me?"

"Of course. If his stratagem is the acquisition of the ranch, it would be an obvious move, don't you think?"

"Is it so obvious? You proposed to me. Would it be an obvious move for you?"

"Hardly, my dear Melinda. Your grandfather hasn't changed his will yet, you know. As of this moment, my mother and I are the heirs. You would stand to gain more than I from our marriage. Or hadn't you thought of that?"

"No," I said, "I hadn't thought of it. But then, I wasn't really thinking of gain, one way or another, yours or mine. I was thinking more in terms of love, actually. Or lack of it. Do you really think marriage should be contemplated in terms of a business merger?"

"Of course. It's really the only sensible way to approach it. Not," he said, taking my hand and smiling at me as if trying to make the words seem less calculating, "that there should not be some attraction. I wouldn't have asked you if I didn't believe we would enjoy each other's company. We would have a delightful time, Melinda. San Francisco is a lovely city, and you would like living there."

"San Francisco? We would live in San Francisco?"

"Of course. You don't think I'd want to spend my life on this ranch, do you? Not that it isn't a lovely place, of course," he said hastily, "but I am really a city person at heart, and the ranch life is not the sort I can tolerate for very long."

"I see," I murmured, drawing my hand from his. I had hoped not to have to go through this so soon, and I especially disliked the thought of telling him I would not marry him right at this moment. My head was filled with his accusations regarding Jarrod, and I wanted to be alone to sort out my thoughts.

Still, his reference to the "sensible" approach to marriage strengthened my conviction that he would not be at all brokenhearted at my refusal. I didn't want to be "sensible" about marriage; on the contrary, I wanted to be in love—giddy and senseless. I found his "business merger" less than attractive.

"Lane," I said, searching for words with which to refuse him, "I don't think marriage for us would be a good idea. We have very different philosophies about it, and I'm sure they would conflict in a very short time."

"In other words," he said with a sardonic smile, "you are refusing my proposal."

"I feel I must," I said. "We simply don't see things in a similar fashion. For instance, I love the life here on the ranch, and I'm not sure I would be a suitable companion and hostess for you in the sophisticated circles in which you move in San Francisco."

"Perhaps you are right," he said, his smile, I thought, a trifle set. "Perhaps there are too many differences between us. Perhaps you would prefer someone like Jarrod Allen. But you must be careful, my lovely Melinda, that you don't come to the same unhappy end as his first wife."

He turned and stalked away from me, and I felt that, while he was angry, he was hardly heartbroken and probably not even surprised. Why did I feel that I had given him the answer he had expected?

I left the patio and went up to my room to dress for dinner. I walked slowly, my mind racing with thoughts of Jarrod Allen and Antonia. I didn't believe the version of the story that Lane had proposed. Did I? Surely it simply did not make sense. But I kept coming back to the fact that all the pieces fit, all the ends were accounted for. Except that there wasn't a shred of proof, I reminded myself. It's all pure speculation.

I stood in the upper corridor in the gathering dusk, staring aimlessly down at the patio. The house was different after dark, I thought. Already shadows were gathering in the patio, and the plants and bushes, the arches and corridors were taking on an appearance they did not have in daytime. Then the house was open, light, pleasant; after dark it was a house with secrets, a place where there were deep shadows and unspoken thoughts.

Pure nonsense, I scolded myself, shaking my mind out of the momentary gloom that had overtaken me. You're getting carried away with your own imagination. Still, I did feel better when I closed the door to my room and lighted the candles.

Lane was gone the next day, and Sybil said he had gone to San Francisco for a short time. She appeared to avoid me, and when we met at dinner or at other times, accidentally, she spoke to me only to answer questions. At times I would catch her watching me, but when I looked at her, she turned her head quickly. I felt I was being observed, but for what purpose, I had no idea.

I shrugged it off, and put it from my mind. I spent the afternoons with my grandfather, and about a week after Lane had gone, he reminded me that Stephen Matson had not yet answered his letter.

"He ought to be back by now," he grumbled. "It's not like him not to come out or even send a message. Why don't you write him another note, Melinda? See if we can't get him out here."

I assured him that I would, and then, remembering what Evelyn Allen had said about the portrait, I asked, "Mrs. Allen said there used to be a portrait of my mother in your study. Whatever happened to it, Grandfather?"

He frowned. "Darned if I know. Sybil said she was sending it into San Francisco to have it reframed just before you came. Said you'd like to see it looking better. I haven't seen it since. I better ask her about it."

He looked over at me. "I miss it, but I hadn't had much of a chance to think about it since you've been here, you know. I'll have to see what we can do about getting it back. You'd like to see it, I guess."

"Yes," I agreed, "I would."

"Well, if I could ever get Steve Matson out here, I'd have him check on it. He's a good man to do things for me." He paused and looked past me to the window of his study, then banged his fist on the arm of his chair. "Damn, Melinda, I hate feeling like an invalid. I used to be able to do the work of three men around here. And that's not bragging, either," he said, giving me a stern look as if I might doubt his word. "It's a fact. And now—" He sighed, and slumped in his chair. "You're the only good thing about my life these days, child."

I moved from my chair to put my arms around him and kiss his cheek. "I know it must be hard on you, Grandfather, being confined in this way, but if it keeps you with me—" I stopped and groped for words. "I mean I'd rather have you here, even as you are, than not at all." I thought the words sounded awkward, but my grandfather patted my arm and smiled.

"You're a blessing to me, child. I want to get Matson out here so that I can get that will changed. You know that, don't you?"

I shook my head. "No. Are you sure that's what you want to do, Grandfather?"

"Very sure, my dear. The way it is now—well, it's a will I made some years back, and it isn't the way I want it to be. Things have changed now, you know. I know better now what I want."

I didn't want to question him about the will. I didn't know how to ask about it without sounding greedy or insensitive, so I decided to change the subject.

"Where are the cellars, Grandfather?"

He turned to look at me. "The cellars? They're down under the old part of the house, the wing where the kitchen is. Why do you ask?"

"Evelyn Allen mentioned them and I was curious. I'd been meaning to ask if I could see them."

He chuckled. "You and Evelyn must do a lot of

talking about this place. Well, that's all right. She's a fine woman.'' He looked into the distance again, a strange look on his face. ''Sometimes I wish . . . well, no matter. Anyway, ask Rosa to show you where the cellars are. You'd better take a lantern if you want to do any exploring down there, and don't go poking around too far in that tunnel. You know about the tunnel?''

''Is that the one that leads down to the smugglers' cave?'' I asked.

He nodded. ''That's right. It still leads about halfway down to the beach, but an earthquake blocked it off sometime back and you can't get through. Besides, it isn't safe down there. I don't want you getting hit on the head with falling rocks or whatever, so be careful about it.''

I promised I would be cautious in my explorations, and set out to find Rosa to show me the way into the cellars.

''The cellars, señorita?'' she asked when I had told her my intention. ''But why? There isn't much down there to see.''

''I suppose not, Rosa, but I'm just curious, you know. I didn't even know the cellars existed until recently, and I'd like to see them.''

She shrugged. ''As you wish, señorita. My Antonia used to love to go down there, too. Even after she was grown. I, myself, do not like underground places, but I'll show you the stairway down and you can see what's there.''

''Are they used for anything besides storage now?''

''No, not really,'' she said. ''We use the first

room, as you will see, for food storage. Carrots, potatoes, apples, that sort of thing. And the canned goods go on the shelves. But the rooms in the back are not used anymore, and of course, the tunnel has been closed off since the big earthquake. Not that it was used before, actually, for years and years."

"Smuggling is not as profitable as it used to be, is that it?"

She smiled as she led me into the kitchen and into one of the large pantries. "Not any more, señorita. There were stories that the tunnel was used by young lovers as a way to meet, out from under the watchful eyes of their parents, but nobody would tell about that."

She opened a door revealing stone steps leading down into what appeared to be a large room. She reached up over her head and took down a lantern, lighted it, and handed it to me.

"You will need this. I will leave this door open, too, so you can follow the light back this way. The cellars run the length of the wing. You will know when you see the old tunnel. It is located about the middle of the wing, and it will be on your left, like this." She made a T with her hands to show how the tunnel joined the cellars.

"Be careful going down the steps," she cautioned, and I took the lantern and started down.

The rooms were much larger than I had thought they would be. I suppose that I had thought that they would be something like the little root cellars I had seen in New England houses, but this was nothing at all like I had imagined.

The first room was as Rosa had said, a storage

room for food. There were shelves lining the walls, and free-standing shelves in the center of the room, containing jars of canned goods, jams and jellies, bags of flour and sugar, racks of spices, and boxes of salt and other staples. Large bins on one side held the carrots and potatoes she had mentioned. There seemed to be enough food there to keep us for a year, if needed.

Further back, however, the rooms were different. They connected with stone archways, and beside each arched entry were brackets where torches had apparently been placed in earlier times. The walls were smoke-stained above the brackets, I noticed as I held my lantern up to get a closer look.

The food storage area was swept clean and the cobwebs brushed out of the cor ners, but as I went farther back, the rooms were hung with webs in the corners, and the dust was thick on the floor. It was not, however, totally undisturbed. Ahead of me as I held the lantern high, I could see sets of footprints in the dust leading back into the dark recesses of the cellars.

In fact, there were enough footprints of fairly recent origin to make a pathway back into the darkness. Antonia must have used these cellars recently, I thought, and more often than I would have gathered from what her mother said.

The rooms in which I now found myself were filled with huge empty wineracks and odds and ends of furniture stored there over the years. In the far corner of one room, I saw something which attracted my attention, and I moved past some of the wineracks to have a better look. It was a cradle, I saw as I approached, an old-fashioned, elaborately carved cradle for a baby. I pushed it with one finger and it rocked gently back and forth.

I held the lantern closer and saw, carved in the foot, a letter "M," entwined with flowers. Montoya? McCarthy? I wondered if this had been my mother's cradle. It was beautiful, and certainly sturdy enough to be used again.

I left the cradle and went on back to the next room. I caught an odor like the sea, and raising my lantern, turned toward the wall where the tunnel entrance would be located. I could see it there, a large archway leading back into the darkness. As I moved closer to it, I could feel a bit of air on my face, and could smell the ocean even more strongly. Even if the earthquake had blocked the passage, I thought, it must not have sealed it too tightly for air to come through.

I stepped into the mouth of the tunnel and held the lantern up, trying to peer into the darkness beyond. The tunnel floor sloped downward, gently at first, but as I moved into the passageway further, more sharply. I went a few feet into the tunnel, then remembered what I had promised my grandfather, and turned back toward the cellars.

As I came out of the mouth of the tunnel, I was startled to see in front of me something I had missed on my way in. I had turned toward the tunnel without looking to my right, and so missed the scene before me now.

Pushed back against the wall in the alcove formed by the archway on each end of the room was a sofa, two chairs, and tables with kerosene lamps on them.

It was, in fact, a small parlor, complete with a desk against one wall. This area was clean—none of the furniture was dust-covered—and had been used, I was sure, quite recently. As recently, I was certain, as Antonia's last visit.

I set my lantern down on the desk and surveyed the little parlor. An eerie feeling crept over me, as if I were intruding in someone's home. This must have been where Antonia met her lover, I thought. And then, I amended mentally, her husband. The furniture was old and unfashionable, but it was clean and had been polished. She must have chosen the pieces from among the cast-off items stored in the cellars.

I was touched by the little room. Poor Antonia, I thought. Her only home with her husband was a hidden little cellar parlor, furnished with odds and ends no one else wanted. Her pathetic attempt to make a place for them to share told me more about her than I would ever have guessed from the few times I had seen her. I could no longer think of her as just a mean-tempered girl who had been hostile to me. She had loved her husband, and had made an effort to make a place they could share, only to be cruelly betrayed by him. I found myself disliking Antonia's killer with a more personal feeling than I had before I knew this about her. It would be a wicked man who could do such a callous and cold-blooded thing.

A crime of passion, an accident, a violent fight—I suppose I had thought that Antonia's death was a result of something like that, and suddenly, chillingly, the knowledge came to me that it was none of those things. It had been more intricately calculated than that.

I shuddered, and reached for my lantern. I picked it up, and as I did, I noticed that one of the desk drawers was open a crack. On impulse I pulled it open, and in the back of the drawer, pushed almost out of sight, was a small notebook. I pulled it out and opened it. It was a sort of diary, a journal that Antonia kept.

I thumbed through and saw from the dates that the entries were random and irregular. The first entry was dated almost three years ago, and the last one was two days before her death.

I felt a sense of excitement as I clutched the little book. Surely, if she had been married, her husband would be named here, and if so, that would be evidence as to her murderer. My first impulse was to sit down at the little desk and read the book by the light of the lantern. I thought better of this, though, and decided to take it back to my room, where I would be able to read it more clearly. The lantern light was difficult to read by, and Antonia's fine script hard to see. I slipped it into my pocket and hurried down the passageway back toward the kitchen.

As I climbed back toward the pantry, Rosa appeared at the top of the stairs.

"Ah, señorita, I was just coming to call you," she said. "There is someone here to see you."

"To see me? Who is it, Rosa?"

"Father Murphy," she said, "he is waiting in the sala for you."

"Oh, my, Rosa! Could you tell him I'll be just a

minute?" I shook my skirts on the stairs before I reentered the kitchen, blew out the lantern, and hung it on its peg. "I'm a mess from poking around in that dusty cellar. I need to run up to my room and clean up a bit, then I'll join him."

"Of course, señorita," she said. "I'll take him some tea and cookies."

I thanked her and ran out the door, back along the corridor, and up the steps to my room. I did need to freshen up; I was dusty from my explorations. But I also wanted to hide the little diary until I got a chance to read it. I didn't think it necessary to mention it to anyone until I had a chance to glance at it myself. No point in getting anyone excited over something that might turn out to be nothing.

I slipped the book into a drawer of my dressing table and washed my face and hands. I straightened my clothes and my hair and rushed back down to the sala, where Father Murphy was waiting for me.

Chapter Fourteen

"I'm sorry to keep you waiting, Father Murphy," I apologized as I rushed into the room. "I was poking around in the cellars and I'm afraid I wasn't very presentable."

"My dear, I can't imagine your not being presentable," he smiled at me, "not even after poking around in the cellars."

"Father, your Irishness is showing," I laughed. "That sounds exactly like a bit of blarney to me."

"Not a bit," he said, his face carefully innocent. "I was never more sincere. Now, come over here and sit down and share some of this tea and these cookies. I want to talk to you a bit."

I poured myself a cup of tea and sat down in a chair opposite him. "Now," I said, "to what do I owe the pleasure of this delightful visit?"

He raised an eyebrow. "It's obvious you've Irish blood, too, Miss Cole. You aren't so bad with the blarney yourself."

"It's probably contagious, Father. But it is good to see you."

"Thank you, my dear. I've come begging favors,

so I thought I'd best be on my good behavior."

"It will probably work, too," I said lightly. "What sort of favor did you have in mind?"

"Well, Evelyn Allen told me that you used to be a teacher back in Boston. Is that right?"

"Dear Mrs. Allen. I think she knows just about everything about everybody around here," I said. "But yes. I was for a time."

He nodded. "Good. I was hoping to talk you into helping us at the church school up at the mission. We could certainly use an experienced teacher up there."

"I didn't even know you had a school up at the mission, Father," I said. "I didn't see it when I was there."

He smiled a bit sheepishly. "Well, actually, we don't exactly have a school—yet. Father Sherwood and I have wanted to start one for some time for the children of the local workers, but we haven't been able. We needed a good teacher, as a matter of fact, and now that you're here, we thought, perhaps . . ."

I laughed. "Father Murphy, are you telling me that you want to start a school, and have me teach it?"

"As a matter of fact," he said, his face hopeful, "that is just what we had in mind. Do you think you could help us?"

"I'd be glad to," I answered. "In fact, I was thinking just recently that I needed a project of some sort. I'm a bit at loose ends here on the ranch."

His face brightened. "That would be wonderful.

Miss Cole. Do you think we could start next week?"

I assured him that I could, and so I became a teacher once again. This time it would be very different, however. Father Murphy left the choice of teaching materials and subject matter up to me, and I thought I could do better than the dry stuff we were forced to teach at Westhaven. I was excited about my new job.

When he left, I hurried back up to my room, eager to get to the diary. I removed it from the drawer and sat down at my desk to read it.

Antonia had apparently used the diary as an outlet for experiences and feelings she could not talk to her mother about, and she had, evidently, no one else to talk to. The picture I got of her from the book was that of a proud and lonely girl, who felt that she was meant for better things than serving as a maid, and who believed that only an accident of birth had kept her from the place she deserved. The entries in the book were spaced at odd intervals; she had, seemingly, written in it only when her life became confused and she needed to sort it out on paper, or when she had a need for making confidences and had no one else in whom to confide.

The first entry, made nearly three years ago, had been written after Raul had asked her to marry him for the first time.

I knew for some time now that Raul was trying to get up the courage to ask me to marry him, but I have offered him no encouragement, and have tried to keep away from him as much as I could so he wouldn't get the chance.

But tonight he came after dinner, and Mama sent me out to see him and he asked me. I said no, I said I wasn't ready for marriage, I said anything I could think of except yes. Raul was my friend. Why won't he leave it at that? I cannot marry him. The thought of spending my life with him in that miserable little house is more than I can stand. I want something more. His is not the life I want!

I didn't tell my mother. She would urge me to say yes, to marry Raul. It's too bad she's too old for him. They'd make the perfect pair, my mother and Raul. They'll both settle for whatever they can get and be grateful for it. Not me. I don't plan to spend my life as a maid at the Mariposas. I should be mistress here! My father knew I should. But my mother, forever with her speeches about remembering my place, and my father's grand ideas, and being grateful—bahh!

My father knew who he was. I know who I am. Let my mother slave for El Viejo if she likes. He's no Montoya. He doesn't even belong here. But I do, and I know another who wants the ranch as I do. Between us, we shall have it, I think. I must make him believe the truth—that I should be the one to have the Mariposas.

There was a space of several months before the next entry. The tone of this one was excited, as if she could see some way to achieve her ambitions, to finally accomplish the goal she had carried with her all her life.

I believe that I have finally managed to interest him in my plans. I have not said to him directly that I have proof of my birth, but I have indicated that perhaps such proof exists. He is interested. We have talked about it. And indeed I do have the letter, but I have no intention of letting him see it yet.

He talks to me, and he watches me when he thinks I am not looking, but I know. And I know what he is thinking. We are much alike, he and I. We both want better things than we have. We both deserve more. And we both want the ranch.

I know it would be easier without his mother. He must be careful of her. She would not approve of his association with me, and we both know that. But I think it can be arranged. If she doesn't know, then she cannot object. And we will see that she does not know.

But in all of her entries, there were no names. Why would she never mention a single name? Only Raul had been mentioned by name, no one else. I wondered about it. Perhaps she had been concerned that the diary would be found. And yet, she said other things that she surely would not want known. If only she had once mentioned a name, given a clue!

I plowed through more of the thin little volume. Apparently, the plan went better than she had hoped, because she related on two more occasions the growing interest of the other person, and at last, wrote, triumphantly, that she had succeeded in bringing her plan to partial fulfillment.

It is arranged. We are to be married in two days' time. I do not fool myself that he loves me, but I know that he loves what we can have together, and it is enough. I will not have to serve as a maid here. It will be mine, and I have the proof that will bring it to me. I know that is why he is marrying me, but I don't care. I can hardly wait to see the look on his mother's face when she learns. She talks of his getting married, pretends that she has hopes for it, but the truth is that she does not. And when she learns that I am to be her daughter-in-law—hah!

I know that he wants me, whether he loves me or not, but I am not fool enough to give him what he wants for nothing. I have a trade to make.

There was a lapse here of some time. Her next entries dealt with a new frustration: her husband insisted on keeping their marriage secret for some time, for some reason.

I cannot see why he insists on going on this way. We are married. Why can we not live as husband and wife? I want to go to El Viejo and tell him. I want to tell his smug mother and wipe that look off her face when she knows. But he says no. He says that we must wait. I do not know why, but I have told him I will not wait much longer.

And finally, among the most recent entries, came the first reference to myself.

They say that they have found her, that granddaughter of El Viejo. He knew they were looking. He said that is why he has been waiting. If she is really his granddaughter, our plans will have been for nothing, he says, and we will have to think of something else. I did not know there was a granddaughter. I hate her. I hope she dies. I hope she is not real, She is an imposter, she must be. She knows about the ranch and she wants it for her own. She will not have it; I will see that she does not. It should belong to me. It should have belonged to my father.

228

But even if she comes, at least I have married him,
so I have managed part of my plan, anyway. I will
find some other way to get the ranch, and with the
ranch, the butterfly. I will think of something for
the ranch, but he, at least, is mine. We will have
what is already his, at any rate, and the child I carry
will not grow up to be the servant his mother was.
We still have something. It is good, at least, that I
arranged that. But we must tell him soon. Soon it
will be seen that I am to have the baby.

And finally, the last entry:

She has come. She is beautiful. She has red hair, but
the eyes are the eyes from the picture. Montoya eyes.
She is the granddaughter. He wishes he had waited for
her now, I can see it. If he had known, I know he
would have. Then he could have had all of it. He
thinks of the mistake his mother made that has now
probably cost him the ranch, and he thinks of the
mistake he made in marrying me, and I think he may
hate me. Thank God for our child. When I see him
tonight, I will tell him about it, and maybe he will be
glad. Maybe he will not hate me when he knows. And
if he does, I will simply tell everyone the truth. He
would not dare to leave me then, if they all knew. And
she would not think much of him if she knew.

I sat still for a long time and thought about what I
had read. *The mistake his mother made that has*
now probably cost him the ranch. His mother had
refused to marry Jim McCarthy. And her son had
married Antonia on the strength of her so-called
proof of her birth. It must have been that way. It
was all that seemed to fit the facts that I knew.
Jarrod Allen had married and murdered Antonia
Dominguez.

Chapter Fifteen

I sat in my room for a long time, thinking over everything I knew. Antonia had gone to meet her husband that night to tell him about her pregnancy, and his response to it had been to throw her off the cliff.

I leaned my head on my hands. I felt sick and confused and incredibly bewildered. The phrase *the mistake his mother made* stuck in my mind and seemed to swim before my eyes. What could it be but Evelyn's refusal to marry my grandfather?

And so it seemed that Lane was right. And where did that leave me? I had fallen in love with a murderer, a man who had killed his pregnant wife, the woman he had only married to get control of a ranch he coveted.

I stood up slowly and put the book back in the drawer. I would take it tomorrow and show it to the sheriff, although I knew that there was nothing in it to convict anyone. It would hardly hold up as evidence in a court of law, but it might help to free Raul. It would seem conclusive evidence that Antonia had been murdered by her husband, not by Raul.

I started to lie down on my bed for a moment, and then I remembered that my grandfather wanted me to write a note to Steve Matson. I decided to go down to his study to write the note, and I let myself out of my room, and wandered down the stairs to the study.

It was a bit too early for my grandfather to be there yet, but his custom was to sit in his study for a while before dinner and read or look over correspondence about the ranch. I thought I would go into the study and write the note for him, then wait until he came down and have a chat with him before dinner.

I let myself into the study and crossed to my grandfather's desk. I opened the drawer and took out some paper and a pen, then, placing them on the desk, I sat down to write.

Until I sat down at the desk, I had not glanced at the chair opposite me, and as I did so now, I jumped so that I almost overturned the inkwell on the desk. Across from me, placed so that it faced the desk squarely, was the portrait of my mother. It must have been a lovely portrait at one time, but now it had been slashed almost to ribbons, hacked and torn so that the canvas hung in strips from its frame.

I rose from the desk, went to the picture and stood before it for a moment, touching it gently with my fingertips. It had been shredded so that I wouldn't have recognized it had I not known some of the details that were visible around the edges. They were the same as on the miniature I wore.

I had been in this room earlier in the day and it had not been here then. I had sat in the chair on which it rested. I was certain that my grandfather had not seen it. And then the thought occurred to me that my grandfather was meant to see it, that it had been placed there precisely so that he would see it.

And when he saw it—I could imagine his fury. I could not conceive of anything that would make him angrier. And slowly, the truth began to break in my mind. Of course it would make him angry. That was exactly what it was intended to do. The last time he had been provoked into unreasoning anger, he had had an attack that had been nearly fatal. And another one, coming so soon after his recovery, might very well kill him.

As it was intended to do. My grandfather was supposed to be here soon. Everyone in the house knew that was his custom. He would come in, see the picture, go into a towering rage, and very probably die from it.

I grabbed the frame and hurried with it back to my room and hid it in the closet. I wanted to remove it before my grandfather saw it, and he would be down any minute. I stuffed it back behind some clothes and sat down a moment to think.

Who would have put it there? There was almost no mystery to that. Sybil had had the picture removed—"for reframing," my grandfather said. Reframing, indeed. The elegant Sybil had destroyed the picture in a fit of temper and had set it in place to anger my grandfather into a heart attack.

I knew she didn't like him, but it had not occurred to me that she would make an active effort to provoke him in such a way. I made up my mind to confront her with the picture as soon as possible.

Now I was confused to the point of frustration. Sybil had set up the picture to anger my grandfather, I was sure of that. If he died now, she and Lane stood to inherit the ranch. And Jarrod—Jarrod Allen had killed Antonia.

Was there a connection? Or was I caught in the middle of a murderous struggle for my grandfather's money? Perhaps if I sat down and told him what I suspected—but no, I couldn't do that. I would be as guilty as Sybil if I did. My conclusions would anger him to the point of unreason, and have the same effect on him. No, I thought, I cannot talk to Grandfather.

Father Murphy, I thought, perhaps I could talk to him. And, I sighed to myself, perhaps not. He thinks Jarrod is a saint. I'm not sure he would be the most objective listener I could approach.

Suddenly it was imperative that I get a note off to Stephen Matson. He was the only person I knew who would be both objective and capable of taking any action needed.

It was too late to write the note before dinner, so I decided to wait until after dinner to go back to the study and write the note. This time I would place it in the hands of the messenger myself. Lane had probably not emphasized the importance of it when he left the first one.

But then, I thought, why should he? Why should he be in a hurry to deliver a note that might very well do him out of an inheritance?

Melinda, I said to myself, you are becoming paranoid. You see enemies in everyone. Lane is the man who asked you to marry him, remember? And even if it was a rather calculating proposal, at least he cared enough to ask.

No, no point in getting obsessed about this, I thought. I'll get the note off to Mr. Matson and then when he comes, I'm sure he'll take care of everything.

I went down to dinner, determined to appear calm, despite the strange events of the day. I sat down at my place, and Sybil joined me. We made polite conversation, waiting for my grandfather to appear.

He was late. We waited, and I observed Sybil, who appeared calm and unruffled. A few moments slipped away. Was she really wearing an air of expectation, or was it merely my overworked imagination? I watched her, as unobtrusively as I could, and then we heard the door to the study close, and Grandfather came out to join us.

His air was quite normal as he bid us both good evening. I glanced at Sybil, and was forced to admire her self-control. A look of something, a slight expression, a narrowing of the eyes, passed across her face and was gone as quickly as it appeared.

A wicked woman, I thought, but she has the control of an actress.

I don't know what we ate or what we said or how I made it through the meal. As soon as I was able, I excused myself and went into grandfather's study to write the letter to Steve Matson.

I stressed the necessity that he hurry to see my grandfather, and sealed the letter, and took it with me to my room. I'd go to the stables in the morning and see that it was placed in the hands of the man who was going into San Francisco on the weekly supply trip.

I went to bed early and dropped off to sleep, but I didn't sleep well. I woke up several times, and in the middle of the night, I awakened and was unable to get back to sleep for a long time. The occurrences of the day were scrambled in my mind like a jigsaw puzzle whose pieces wouldn't fit. Had Jarrod killed Antonia? It seemed so to me. And had Sybil put the picture in Grandfather's study? I thought she must have.

And were the two things connected? Nothing made sense to me any more, especially the fact that the thought of Jarrod Allen made my heart race in spite of my belief in his guilt, and in spite of my certainty he was in love with another woman.

I drifted off to sleep eventually and was awake at the first light.

I dressed quickly and went down to the stables to look for the driver. One of the stable hands, a man I knew only as Lou, was entering the stable as I approached.

"Lou," I called to him, "wait a minute."

He stopped and turned to me, a look of some surprise on his face.

"Howdy, Miss Melinda," he said, touching his hat. "Pretty early for you to be out, ain't it?"

"Well, yes," I answered, "but I have an errand of some importance, and I need to know who's taking the next supply wagon into San Francisco."

"Well, that'd be Ben, Miss Melinda, but it'll be a

week before he's going. The supply wagon gets back today."

My disappointment must have been plain on my face, because he said to me, "If it's real important, Miss Melinda, I could take it in for you. That is, if it's all right with your grandpaw."

"Oh, I'm sure it will be, Lou. It's his message, and he wanted me to get it out today. Or at least as soon as possible."

"Why don't you just give me the message then, and I'll check with your grandpaw and if he says go, then I'll be off. And if he says no, then I'll just bring it back to you."

"That sounds fine," I said, handing him the message. "It's to go to Stephen Matson. I wrote his address in San Francisco here on the outside of the letter."

He took the letter and headed off toward the house to check with my grandfather. I watched him until he had rounded the corner of the building, and then decided that as long as I was up so early, I might as well go for a ride while it was cool and clear.

I rode off in the direction of the mission, hoping to be able to see Father Murphy, and talk to him some more about the mission school. After I had talked with him yesterday, all thoughts of the school had vanished from my mind, but now I thought of a hundred things I wanted to ask about.

Father Murphy appeared delighted to see me, and invited me in to share his breakfast. "I know you can't have eaten," he said, "you'd have left too early to be here by this time of day. So come in and have breakfast with me. I hate to eat alone, anyway, and Father Sherwood was called away earlier to see one of our sick parishioners.''

I was delighted to join him. We shared a breakfast of oatmeal in cream, sweetened with honey, hot tea, and fresh peaches. It was remarkably good.

"This is delicious, Father Murphy. I don't think I've ever eaten sweeter peaches.''

"Nor I. The Allens sent them over. Evelyn Allen has a tree she insists produces the best peaches on the West Coast, and I'm inclined to agree with her.''

At the mention of the Allens, a chill seemed to fall over me. I thought I had been right when I decided to go elsewhere with my suspicions about Jarrod Allen, and I decided to test my theory.

"You think very highly of Jarrod Allen, don't you, Father?'' I said, pouring myself another cup of tea.

"Oh, I do indeed, Melinda. He is a fine young man. In fact, I venture to say that you'd have to go a long way to find a finer.''

"You don't think he'd ever be guilty of something—malicious? Or criminal?'' I lowered my eyes over my tea.

"Jarrod Allen?'' Father Murphy was clearly shocked at the idea. "I'd stake my life on his reputation, Melinda. Has someone been spreading stories about Jarrod?''

"No, not really, Father.'' I searched through my mind for a way to explain away the question. "I'd just heard a bit of gossip, that, it seems, isn't even worth repeating.'' I stood up and smiled at him in an effort to give truth to what I had said. "Now. I'd

237

like you to show me around the rooms you had in mind to use for the school."

We spent the morning going through the rooms he had in mind for me to use, and discussing the materials I would need. He told me about some books one of his parishioners was donating, and his plans for getting donations from other members of his parish.

His enthusiasm was contagious, and by the time I was ready to leave, I had caught some of it from him. I was looking forward to the teaching, and to being able to try my own ideas and plans in the classroom. It was late in the morning when we finished, and I began my return trip to the ranch.

As I approached the ranch house, I realized that I was riding slower and slower, and it suddenly occurred to me that I was not looking forward to returning to the Mariposas. I had loved being there until recently, but now I wasn't sure I wanted to go back. When the house came into view, I stopped and looked at it.

It was beautiful, there was no doubt of that. The white walls gleamed in the sunlight, and the red-tile roofs looked like flame in the heat of the summer sun. But Evelyn Allen was right. There was something about that place that was no longer lovely to me. It did have secrets and I felt as though that lovely white shell held some ugly and unpleasant things, things I was not sure that I wanted to know.

I rode into the courtyard and dismounted. I knew I was going to have to face Sybil about the portrait, and I was sure I was not going to enjoy the confrontation. I didn't like the idea of those pale, cold eyes staring through me as I questioned her about the picture, but I had to do it. If I did not, I was afraid that something of a similar nature would happen again. I had to let her know that I knew what she had done, and make her aware that I would do everything in my power to protect my grandfather.

I went into my room and removed the portrait from my closet. The frame was large and finely carved, and to my eye, not in need of repair. I suspected that the excuse that Sybil had used was a ruse that permitted her to take the portrait out of the study.

I picked it up and took it down the hall, down the stairs to Sybil's room. My knock was answered by a "Come in," from inside the room, and I opened the door and entered.

It was the first time I had been in Sybil's room and I would not have guessed that a room like this existed in the house. The furniture, all fragile and French-appearing to my untrained eye, was white, with gilt trim. The headboard of the bed rose halfway up the bedroom wall, and was trimmed with garlands of gold flowers. The draperies, the coverlet, and the carpet were all the same pale shade of lavender.

The scent of lilac perfume filled the air. Sybil was seated in front of a large dressing table whose mirrored surface was covered with a myriad of small bottles, pots, jars, and containers. As I entered, she turned to greet me with a frosty smile.

"To what," she taunted, "do I owe the honor of this unexpected visit?"

I ignored the sarcasm. "There was no honor intended," I said. "I came to show you what I found in my grandfather's study yesterday evening." I pulled the portrait forward and held it in front of me.

Her eyes narrowed slightly, but her expression otherwise did not alter. "And so?" she said. "What does this have to do with me?"

"I'm not entirely sure," I answered. "My grandfather said that you sent the portrait to be reframed. Presumably you were the last to see the picture in its original condition. I was curious as to what had happened between then and now."

She shrugged and turned back to the mirror in front of her. "I've no idea. Why don't you ask the servants?"

"I shall," I said, my anger rising. "But I know of no reason why the servants would be concerned with it."

"And you do know of a reason that I should?" She leaned toward the mirror and ran a finger over a carefully arched eyebrow.

"You took it down. I must assume then that you also destroyed it."

She turned toward me, her eyebrows raised, her expression deadly. "Why on earth would I do such a thing?" she asked. "Why would I bother?"

I felt flustered at her icy calm and almost malicious indifference. I wasn't sure how to answer.

"I'm sure I don't know," I said. "I have no information whatsoever as to your motives. I am only concerned with the evidence as I see it and the possible consequences of your action."

"Evidence?" She gave me a smile that was almost frightening in its malevolence. "Are you some sort of lawyer now? And am I on trial? And what 'possible consequences' are we discussing?"

"I found this propped up in the study across from my grandfather's desk. You are surely aware that if he saw it, he would be furious. And you also know what might happen if he worked himself up in that way."

"If my husband chooses to indulge himself in childish temper tantrums, that is neither my responsibility nor my concern." She turned back to the dressing table and poked among the bottles, selecting one, putting it back, choosing another, a study in callousness.

"And for your information, my prim little busybody," she glanced at me sideways before turning back to the mirror, "I had nothing to do with the condition of the picture. It was in perfect shape when I took it into the study. I cannot speak for anything that happened after that."

She resumed the study of her face in the mirror, and I left the room, shutting the door hard, and standing in the corridor in a fury. I knew she was lying. I was as certain that she had destroyed the picture as I was that she was quite capable of destroying my grandfather through some calculating act of viciousness.

I started back toward my room, and then suddenly decided that having the portrait there was not a good idea. I turned toward the kitchen to locate Rosa. I would hide the picture in the cellars, I thought. My grandfather would never locate it, and meanwhile I had a plan to account for its absence.

241

I entered the kitchen and Rosa greeted me with a smile. Mrs. Malloy had her back to me, and I managed to hide the portrait from the view of anyone else for the moment.

"I need to go back to the cellars, Rosa," I told her, "I have something to put away down there."

She raised her eyebrows inquiringly, but she said, "Certainly. Come with me, señorita, and I'll let you into the pantry."

When we were out of sight of the others, I showed her the picture and told her briefly what had happened. She appeared shocked at first, and then angry.

"I would be willing to make a guess as to who did this, señorita," she said, her eyes blazing. "I know exactly who would be capable of such a thing."

"I have an idea, too, Rosa, but there is no point in making accusations. They would only be denied and meanwhile, I need to figure out a way to replace this. Don't mention it to anyone, will you?"

"Of course not, señorita." She opened the door and lit the lantern for me. "You can find a place to hide it among the old furniture. It will never be found."

I took the portrait into the cellar and went back into the rooms past the food storage area to the place where the old furniture was kept. Back against one wall was a very large old wardrobe, and I opened it and placed the frame with its tatters of canvas inside and closed the door. I felt that it was as secure a place as any, and it was unlikely that anyone would find it there.

At dinner that night, as if he had read my

thoughts, Grandfather brought up the subject of the portrait.

Sybil was having dinner in her room as she did frequently, and Lane was still in San Francisco, so the two of us were dining alone.

"Did you talk to Sybil about that portrait of your mother, Melinda?" he asked.

I was glad I had had time to prepare my story. "Yes, as a matter of fact I did, Grandfather," I said casually. "It had been returned from being framed, but whoever brought it out from San Francisco must have dropped it on the way. There was some damage done to the canvas."

"Damage, you say?" He frowned at me. "What sort of damage?"

"Nothing serious, as far as I know. A puncture to the canvas or some such thing."

"Careless rascals," he muttered. "They know I love that picture. Who did it, do you know?"

I shrugged. "I have no idea. Rosa said she'd ask, but chances are no one will own up to it; you know how it goes."

"Well, I'd better take a look at it and see what can be done about it."

"There's no need, Grandfather," I said, carefully cool in my desire not to arouse his suspicions. "I'm going to take it over to Evelyn Allen in the morning and see whether she can repair it. She's a talented artist. I'm sure she has had some experience in doing that sort of thing."

"Humph." He grunted, then nodded his assent. "You're probably right. Evelyn knows all about that painting stuff. If anybody can fix it, she's probably the

243

one. Be sure to let me know what she says."

Great, I thought to myself. Now I'll have to follow through on it. I had thought of asking Evelyn Allen to make a duplicate of the portrait so that I could put it in the frame and return it to the study and, I hoped, Grandfather would not be able to tell the difference. She had said she could copy the miniature I wore, and from the fragments of the portrait, I had been able to determine that the miniature was the same as the larger portrait.

I had hoped, though, to put off consulting with her for a while. I had no desire to face Jarrod Allen at this point. My suspicions were strong in my mind, and I wanted to search further, see what else I could find, see if I could get any information of a more conclusive nature before I had to face him again.

I lay in my bed that night and sorted through my thoughts for the thousandth time. What did I know about Jarrod Allen? Did I know for sure that he had been Antonia's husband? If only I had gone downstairs that night and had a glimpse of the man she was talking to, how different things might be right now!

But I had not. And so far, all I had was the diary, and the circumstantial evidence surrounding her death and the discovery of the body. And it pointed at Jarrod. Jarrod Allen, tall, bronzed, blue-eyed, the man whose mere presence set my pulse racing. The man who loved someone else. The man who may very well have murdered his wife. And I loved him.

You're a fool, Melinda Cole, I told myself again. It would indeed be much handier if I could simply turn my affections elsewhere. If I could be in love with Lane, how much happier for everyone concerned.

Of course, I knew my grandfather preferred Jarrod, but then my grandfather didn't know the truth about him. And never would, I decided. I suppose it was at that moment that I realized that I could never go to the sheriff with what I knew, even if I had any real evidence to incriminate him. I would never take it to use against him. The shock might be too much for my grandfather.

And one part of my mind said to me, cynically, are you sure it's because of your grandfather, Melinda? Are you very certain you aren't just protecting him because of the memory of that kiss and what it did to you?

I don't know, I answered myself. I just don't know. But I do know that I will protect my grandfather, whatever it involves. He lives in a house with a wife who hates him enough to attempt to trigger another heart attack, a cynical stepson, and a granddaughter who has very little capability for handling the dangers that surround him. Poor grandfather, I thought, I wonder if my presence here has caused some danger to him.

And with that thought, my mind took a new turn. Was it possible that he was actually in danger because of me? Was Sybil merely careless of him, or was she actively out to hurt him in such a way that he would not have a chance to make a new will?

I wished Mr. Matson would hurry and get here, I thought. I'd feel better if I could talk to him. Something strange was going on at the Mariposas, and my presence seemed to have triggered the process.

I finally fell asleep, my mind still turning over the

things I knew and those I suspected. There seemed to be something wrong, something missing, something I didn't know, and when I drifted off, my sleep was uneasy, and my dreams, confused.

Chapter Sixteen

I rose early the next day and left after breakfast to go to the Allen's ranch. I hoped to be able to get in to see Evelyn and avoid her son. I had not sorted out my feelings so that I could trust myself with Jarrod and I didn't know how to approach him.

I thought perhaps the most logical thing to do was to say nothing and simply pretend that everything was as it was before. After all, what choice did I have? I had no proof. I had only what made sense to me. But suspicion has a corrosive quality; I could feel it eating away inside me like acid.

It was difficult to face Mrs. Allen on the same basis as before, but after a few minutes of chatter, I managed to lose myself in my errand.

"I've come about the portrait," I said to her after we had talked for a bit. "I finally located it."

"Did you?" she said, smiling. "And what did you think of it?"

I hesitated for a moment. "There was nothing to think," I said finally. "The portrait had been destroyed when I found it."

"Destroyed!" Evelyn turned round eyes on me. "How? By whom? Why?"

"I only know the answer to one of those questions," I said. "I know that the canvas was slashed to ribbons—slashed beyond any question of repair. As to the person who did it, I have only guesses. And as to why, I don't even have that."

Her eyes narrowed as she looked at me. "I'd bet your so-called grandmother could clear up the mysteries for us in a matter of minutes."

"I don't know," I said, spreading my hands hopelessly. "I confronted her with it, even accused her of it, but she denied it. She is very cool, very controlled, you know. If she knows about it, she kept it to herself very well."

"Humph!" Evelyn snorted. "I don't doubt it. How did you happen to find it?"

I told her about finding it in my grandfather's study, set up so that he would see it, and about my suspicions that it had been set up to startle or anger him into another heart attack.

"How absolutely vile!" she said, almost shaking with anger. "That she would do such a thing— You know, there was talk that she killed her husband in San Francisco, and I never paid much attention to it, but I'm starting to think she did shove him down those stairs."

I shook my head. "I don't know, Evelyn. I don't know what to think. I'm starting to think you're right about that house, though. It does have secrets."

"I told you," she said. "Houses get to have personalities, just like people. That one is a bit sly. It looks like something it isn't. It has dark places."

"Well, be that as it may, I came to talk to you of something different." I reached for the chain around my neck and removed the miniature of my mother. "You have seen the portrait of my mother. It was like this, wasn't it?"

I handed her the miniature. She examined it and nodded. "Yes, this is the same picture."

"Could you copy this on a canvas the same size as the other portrait?"

She frowned and looked at the picture for a moment longer. "Yes, I think so. In fact, I'm sure I could. I had several opportunities to examine the original quite closely, and I think I could do a creditable job on it."

"I need it to be as close to the original as possible," I said. "You see, Grandfather asked about it the other night and I told him it had been damaged somewhat, and that I was bringing it to you to see whether you could repair it. I think any differences between the duplicate and the original could be explained by saying that those were the portions that were damaged. What do you think?"

"I think it might work." She looked at me for a moment, as if examining me. "I think you are also quite clever, young lady."

"Not so clever," I said. "If there hadn't been a competent artist within a close range, I'm afraid I wouldn't have been able to come up with any ideas at all."

"Nonetheless," she said, "I believe we can pull it off. And once we're finished with that, when can you begin sitting for me? You know I've wanted to do a portrait of you for some time now."

"I'm not sure," I answered. "Father Murphy has me involved in a project for him starting next week, and it may take up most of my time for a while."

"Oh?"

"He's starting a mission school, and I'm to teach in it."

"How marvelous, my dear. We've needed a school around here for some time now. Father Murphy has tried before to start one, but it does require a full-time teacher, and his duties kept interrupting. What does your grandfather think about it?"

"To be honest, I had forgotten to mention it to him. I've been so concerned about that picture that the school slipped my mind when I was with him."

"I hardly see that he could have any objections. Besides, you aren't the sort to sit about idle all day."

"No. I'm really used to having my time occupied."

"You're used to working, you mean." She gave me a stern look that was meant to mask a tone of concern. "You've had a difficult life, young lady. No point to lie about it, and you aren't one to complain, but you've not spent your days eating bonbons and crocheting antimacassars, either. Am I right?"

I looked at the carpet, then back at her. "It hasn't always been easy, but then it hasn't all been awful, either. And anyway, that's over now, isn't it?"

"I should hope so. Jim says he's sent for Steve Matson to change his will. You know what that means, don't you?"

"I think so. He has—indicated—that he would prefer to—make some changes."

"Don't be wishy-washy, Melinda. He's going to leave it all to you, and you know it. And you deserve it. It should be yours. But," she sighed, "there's many a slip between the cup and the lip, they say, and you know Sybil and Lane will do all they can to prevent it, don't you?"

"Well, I suppose they have reason to feel that it's unfair. I mean, after all, they've been there longer, and they have put some time and effort into the place, and—"

"Oh, poppycock, girl. Sometimes you're so busy trying to be fair that you simply won't call a spade a spade. Why do you think Sybil stuck that picture in your grandfather's study? If he dies before Steve Matson gets out here, they get it all, and you're out in the cold. It's as simple as that."

"Well, if that happens, then it happens, I suppose. I also suppose, that for that very reason I should be getting back to the ranch. I hate to leave Grandfather there alone with—well, without me for so very long."

"You were going to say 'with Sybil,' weren't you? Well, I think you're right to be concerned." She reached across and patted my hand. "Melinda, I hope Steve Matson gets there soon, because the ranch should be yours. It's yours by blood and by right. But if he doesn't, my dear, remember that you are always welcome here. You have a place to go if worse comes to worst. Do you understand?"

I nodded and squeezed her hand, close to tears. I truly believed that Evelyn Allen was my friend, and I had a hard time reconciling her to the position she seemed to occupy in Antonia's diary. Still, she might have a streak of snobbery I had never suspected. It was difficult to see it under the warm exterior she displayed to me, though.

I was convinced that no matter what my suspicions regarding her son, she was innocent of any knowledge of any wrongdoing.

I left the ranch and rode back along the road toward the Mariposas. I had hoped to escape without having to face Jarrod Allen, but it was not to be. I had not been gone from the ranch more than a few minutes when I heard the sound of hoofbeats behind me, and I turned to see a rider, whom I recognized as Jarrod, pursuing me at a gallop.

I stopped and waited, after checking the impulse to flee down the road. I couldn't outpace him, anyway, and it seemed silly to try. I'd just wait for him and try to behave as though everything was the same as it had been.

As he came close enough to me that I could see his face, I felt my heart turn over. Oh, please, I thought to myself, please don't be a murderer. Please be all I think you are. Marry Connie Robinson. Anything. Just don't be the one who killed Antonia.

He pulled up beside me and smiled at me the mocking smile I knew so well.

"You were running away without seeing me," he said. "Don't they teach better manners than that in Boston, Miss Cole?"

"Actually, they teach very good manners, Mr. Allen. Such as the one about not overstaying your welcome, and the other about hurrying home to check on your grandfather."

"As to the first, I'd say that was impossible. And as for the second, I'll ride with you and we'll both check."

It would have been difficult (and also untrue) to tell him I didn't want his company, so I turned back toward the ranch and he fell in beside me.

"Father Murphy says you're going to be teaching in the mission school. When do you start?"

"Next week, he says. I was just telling your mother about it. I think he's out gathering donations of money and supplies now."

"If we'd had teachers like you when I was in school," he said, glancing at me sideways, "I might have been more interested in attending."

"I doubt it," I said. "I'm a very stern teacher."

"Stern or not, you'd have been more fun to look at than Miss Hitchcock. She was my fourth-grade teacher. You've heard of a face that would stop a clock?"

I nodded.

"Well, hers would have melted the mainspring."

I laughed. "Actually, children think their teachers are so old anyway that they seldom think of how they look after the first few days. At least I always thought that was the case."

"Don't fool yourself," he said. "Most kids like pretty ones better."

"Maybe that explains why they loved my friend Mavis so much."

"Was she pretty?"

"Oh, yes. She had blonde curls and dimples and blue eyes. And she was dear. I miss her very much."

We carried on this light sort of conversation for a while, and I began to relax, surprising myself. Maybe Sybil isn't the only good actress around, I thought. Jarrod Allen could be remarkably

253

charming when he made the effort, and today he was making the supreme effort. Of course, I reminded myself, you are rather susceptible to his charms, aren't you, Melinda? I felt that he was being deliberately likeable today. Still, I was surprised when he stopped his horse in the shade of a huge oak tree that hung over our trail, and turned to me, looking at me intently.

"Melinda," he said, his blue eyes piercing mine, "there's something I need to say to you."

My heart began to beat so hard I thought it was going to crash through the walls of my chest. Was he going to tell me about Antonia? Was he going to explain to me what had happened?

"It's difficult for me to say this," he said. "I know that we've spent a lot of time—I mean, I don't know whether you still dislike me as much as you seemed to. I had hoped you would come to feel—" he seemed to be having a struggle with his words and I'm sure I was staring at him, as if in a trance. This couldn't be what it sounded as if he were trying to say.

"Damnit, Melinda," he said finally. "I'm trying to ask you to marry me. I'm not very good at this, but will you?"

I was stunned. "Marry you?" I asked stupidly.

"Yes," he said softly. "I'm asking you to marry me."

A feeling of utter frustration and confusion swept over me. How I would have loved to hear those words earlier, before the worm of suspicion had started eating at me! Now all I could think of were Lane's words, that Jarrod's proposal to me would be proof of his guilt, proof that what he wanted was Mariposas

254

and I was his means of acquiring it.

The pain was so great I wasn't certain I could bear it. I opened my mouth to speak and nothing came out. Finally, I managed to gasp, "I can't. I simply can't," and turned my horse and raced away from him.

He caught up with me quickly and grasped the reins and stopped my horse, turning it so that I faced him.

"Don't I even get to ask why?" he said, his face set, his eyes cold.

"I—I can't say why. I just can't, that's all." I felt helpless, and I wanted to get away more than anything. What could I tell him, that I couldn't marry him because I suspected him of murder? Impossible, I thought.

"Melinda Cole, *I am in love with you.*" He leaned across and grasped my wrist and his face was close to mine. "You are the one woman I want to marry, and I think I deserve some sort of an explanation besides just a flat 'no.' "

I could feel my eyes filling with tears, tears of pain and frustration and anger. "I simply don't have any other explanation," I said. "I just can't."

"Is there someone else?"

I shook my head and tried to free my wrist, but he held it tighter.

"You simply don't care for me, then, is that it?"

I shook my head again. "No," I said. "I mean yes. I mean, I don't know," I finished confusedly, avoiding his eyes.

Suddenly he released my wrist, and with the same arm swept me half out of my saddle into an embrace that crushed me to his body. His mouth, as it covered mine, was not tender—it was hard and seeking and demanding, and I felt my treacherous body respond with a fervor that left me shaken to the depths of my being.

As suddenly as he had embraced me, he released me, and set me back into my saddle, my body still shaking from the force of that kiss.

"You're a liar, Melinda Cole," he said, his voice harsh. "You love me as much as I love you, and I've just proved it."

"Yes!" I screamed at him, the tears streaming down my face now. "Yes! I love you." I grabbed the reins, sobbing as I tried to recover myself. "But I don't want to end my life like your first wife, that's why I won't marry you." In my pain I hardly knew what I was saying, but I knew I had been wrong when I saw the white line around his mouth.

"What 'first wife' are you referring to, Miss Cole?" he demanded icily.

I faced him, my chin up, the tears still streaming down my face, "Antonia Dominguez," I said, and his head snapped up. "You married her to get the Mariposas and killed her when she couldn't deliver it. I found her diary."

His face was as hard as I thought it must have looked to Antonia on the night she died. A muscle in his jaw clenched and unclenched and I suddenly thought how foolish I had been. If he killed her, what was to stop him from killing me to prevent my telling?

"You don't have to worry about me, though," I said, wiping my eyes with the back of my hand. "If I'd been planning to tell, I'd have done it before now. You're safe."

He stared at me a moment longer and then,

without a word, he spun his horse and raced off down the trail in a cloud of dust. I watched him ride out of sight, and then I leaned over the neck of my horse and sobbed for a long time.

During the next week, I threw myself into my work at the mission school. My students were as eager and excited as I was, and I knew we were going to enjoy each other. They welcomed the change in the routines of their days as much as I did, and it took my mind off Jarrod, at least in the daytime. At night, I couldn't avoid the thought of him, and the image of the contempt on his face when he had swung his horse around and left me on the trail returned to me in the darkness.

Lane had returned from San Francisco and appeared to have forgotten that I had refused his offer of marriage or that he had ever been upset by it.

He reported that Steve Matson had been ill, and this had accounted for his failure to come out to the ranch.

We resumed our daily rides, but we now scheduled them in the afternoon instead of the morning to accommodate my teaching duties. Grandfather thought the teaching was a fine idea; indeed, I sensed that he was rather proud of me.

"Give you something to do with yourself all day," he said. "My mother would have been proud to see it. She set a lot of store by book-learning."

Lane seemed to think the idea was a silly whim, but he appeared prepared to indulge me, if that was what I chose to do.

Father Murphy was delighted with the school. Enrollment was greater than he had anticipated, and support from the local residents was good. All in all, he was encouraged by our initial success.

I settled into the routine of my days at the school, and although things were going along quite smoothly on the surface, I couldn't shake a certain feeling of tension at the ranch. I didn't know what it was, but try as I would, I could not rid myself of the feeling that everything was, for the moment, in suspension. That the ranch, and its inhabitants, were waiting for something—and I was not sure what it was.

I came and went back and forth from the school, and each day I seemed to find some excuse for leaving the school later and later. Coming home to the ranch was no longer the pleasure that it had been for me. I found myself dragging myself away from the mission, slowly riding home, as if for some reason I didn't want to have to spend any more time there than I absolutely had to.

Twice in the next week I had the dream again, waking each time from its horror in shaking fear, and lighting the candle so that I wouldn't be alone in the dark. I didn't know what I was afraid of. I didn't know why that dream kept coming back to me. Each time I had the dream, more details were clarified, and each time now, my mother turned into Antonia, who laughed and laughed at me while I struggled to free myself from whatever was holding me back.

Each time I rose as early as I could and hurried from the house. Grandfather began to complain that I was not around to keep him company enough, and so for a day or two, I arranged to leave the school early so that I could come home and spend time with him.

Each day we expected to see Steve Matson, and each

day brought no sign of him. I had almost made up my mind to make the trip into San Francisco myself.

We moved through August with no word from him. Grandfather was getting restless and the tension in the house was becoming oppressive as the midafternoon heat. We were in the middle of a heat wave. There were no breezes from the ocean, and the cooling afternoon fog had ceased altogether. Each day was crystal clear and hot almost from when we arose in the morning to the time we went to bed at night. My students were restless and irritable. The mission was usually cool in the mornings; its thick walls provided excellent insulation against the heat. But in the afternoons, no relief was possible, even within the usually cool mission walls, and so I decided to keep the children for lessons only in the mornings, and I sent them home when the afternoon sun began to melt us.

One afternoon, I dismissed the class early and decided to ride home the long way around, along the beach first, and then through the redwood grove. I had never ridden through the entire length of the grove, and its cool dimness promised to provide some blessed relief from the oppressive heat.

I said goodbye to Father Murphy and headed down toward the ocean. As I reached the edge of the cliffs, I suddenly realized that there was a breeze ruffling my hair—the first I had felt from the sea in days—and it was very welcome.

Relief, I thought. The weather was beginning to cool down. The heat subsided, even as I rode, and I was grateful. I made the turn of the trail inland toward the grove, and slowed my horse to a walk as it came in sight.

Entering the grove felt much the same, I thought, as entering a cathedral. I dismounted and led my horse slowly down the path, gazing above me as I walked.

It was as cool and dim in the grove as I had remembered, and the gigantic trees towered above me. They were huge, with trunks that looked to be as thick as our small house in Boston. They seemed to reach into the air for a hundred feet before they began to branch out.

The floor of the grove was thickly padded with needles from the trees, and my horse's hooves were almost silent when we stepped off the trail. I could hear an occasional bird-call, but for the most part, the grove was silent.

A little sunlight filtered through here and there, and made patterns on the thick carpet of needles, but little of the light made its way through, and the grove was dim.

Looking about me, I could understand how an outlaw could hide in this place to rob a stagecoach, and then escape, slipping back among the great trees before he could be captured, out of sight in a moment, treading silently on this carpet-like forest floor.

The thought made me shudder and I quickly re-mounted my horse. I wasn't really frightened, I told myself. It's simply that there was no point in being foolish.

Suddenly the grove seemed to become dimmer yet, and I looked up, trying to see through the trees to determine if a cloud had covered the sun. I couldn't even see the sky. What I did see, though was mist—trails of fog creeping through the tops of the trees.

Idiot, Melinda, I said to myself. Of course there's fog. There would be now; the weather has changed. As soon as it began to get cooler, of course the fog would return.

I urged my horse into a trot, hoping to get through the grove and back onto the trail before the fog became so thick that I would have difficulty finding my way back to the ranch.

The fog was coming in rapidly, and filling the grove around me. I kept my horse moving as fast as I could for as long as I could see ahead of me for any distance, and then the fog swirled around me so thickly that I pulled him up quickly. I heard the echo of his hoofbeats sound in the forest.

I slowed to a walk, the mist swirling around me so that I was unable to see ahead of me for more than a few feet. I let the horse amble slowly through the trees. The mist parted, and I could see for a distance down the trail. I galloped for a way, and when the mist closed around me again, I pulled up, again listening to the echo of the hoofbeats die.

And then, slowly, an icy feeling moved along my spine as I strained my ears for those "echoes." It had taken a few moments for me to realize the truth. I had been too preoccupied with the immediate concern of finding my way out of the grove to recognize an obvious fact: there were no echoes in this fog-filled forest.

The sound here was muffled and flat. It didn't echo. I was hearing the hoofbeats of someone who was following me—following closely, at a distance close enough to hear me, and far enough away to remain unseen.

Panic overcame me and I urged my horse into a gallop. We plunged headlong down the trail, or down the direction I thought the trail took. The animal blundered into underbrush at the side of the path and almost sideswiped a tree before I regained my composure and realized that this course was likely to get me injured and left to the mercy of my faceless follower. I pulled him up and listened for the hoofbeats behind me, and heard them once more. I let the horse wander for a few moments while I looked over my shoulder and strained my eyes against the fog, trying to see who was there, and trying to decide what to do.

Then suddenly I decided on a course of action, and quickly dismounted and led my horse off the trail and into the underbrush. I moved as quietly as I could, leading him through the trees away from the trail.

I knew what a chance I was taking. If my pursuer discovered me, I was much more vulnerable off the trail than I would have been on it, where I could at least run for it. Furthermore, I was not at all sure that in this fog I could find my way back to the trail. That was less of a concern, though. The worst that could happen in that event would be that I would spend a miserable night wandering around in the forest. I had no idea what the worst that could happen would be if my unknown stalker caught up with me.

I tethered my horse to a bush and crept back in the direction of the trail. I knew that I was taking an even greater risk by doing this, but I hoped to get a glimpse of the person who was so carefully staying out of my sight.

The fog swirled about me as I made my way

toward the trail. I moved as slowly, carefully, and silently as I could. Within a few moments, I could see tracks at my feet and realized that I was back at the path. I backed off to the side and listened, but heard nothing. I peered into the fog in all directions, yet could see little in the dense fog.

Then suddenly I heard a horse snort, and it sounded so close I almost jumped out of my skin. I pressed my body against a tree and kept as still as I could, hardly breathing for fear any sound I made would carry.

The horse and rider moved slowly toward me through the mist. I could see the man's shape on his horse, but not his face. I waited, hoping they would move closer. When he stopped in the middle of the trail I strained to make out his features, keeping very still, knowing that if I moved he would be able to see the movement.

He turned his horse and moved down the trail. The mists closed about him and he was gone.

I let loose my breath in a sigh and slumped against the tree. My heart was beating hard and I put my hand on my chest as if to restrain it.

Who was he, I wondered, and what did he want? Was he really following me, or had my imagination run away with me again? No, I thought, not this time. There had been no doubt in my mind that he knew I was there, knew when I stopped and started again, and had come back to look for me when he thought he had lost me.

I found my way back to my horse and sat down beside him to wait for a few minutes more. I wanted to give him—whoever it was—time to believe I had raced on ahead of him out of his hearing. I didn't want to take a chance of meeting up with him farther on down the trail.

At length I mounted my horse, guided him back to the trail, and let him find his own way back through the fog. At length we left the forest and turned inland toward the ranch, and the fog began to clear. As it did, I pushed my horse to gallop at full speed, and I raced my sweating mount into the stableyard.

Chapter Seventeen

I must have betrayed my fright at my experience as I entered the house, because Lane, who was standing in the doorway to the sala, took one look at me and said, "Great Scot! what happened to you?"

I told him as briefly as I could what had happened and he frowned. "Are you certain that he was following you? He couldn't have been merely traveling in the same direction?"

I shook my head. "No. He was following me, I'm sure of it. He stopped each time I stopped. When I got off the trail, he came back to look for me. No," I sighed, dropping into a chair, "there isn't any doubt in my mind that I was being followed."

His eyes narrowed as he looked at me. He opened his mouth as if to say something, closed it, looked at me again, and finally said, "Does Jarrod Allen have any idea that you suspect him of murdering Antonia?"

I stared at him blankly. "Suspect him?" I murmured.

"Yes. You do suspect him, don't you? How could you help it with all you know about him?"

My mind darted from image to image as I tried to

take in what he was saying to me. "I'm afraid—" I began and stopped. "Yes," I said, a shudder in my voice. "Yes, he knows I suspect him," I said. "I lost my temper and I said—several things," I added lamely.

"It was not wise to let him know you suspect him," Lane scolded me, frowning. "No doubt it was he who was following you. You are probably in danger from him, especially if he thinks you have any evidence against him. Of course," he turned to the cabinet, poured me a glass of sherry and placed it in my shaking hand, "you really have no evidence that is not circumstantial. But he may not know that."

I sat like a statue, the glass clutched in my hand, my body suddenly as cold as if my veins were filled with ice water. "But I do," I whispered.

Lane wheeled on me. "You do?" he said, his eyes narrowing as he looked at me. "You have evidence?"

"Of a sort," I said, trying to remember exactly what I had said to Jarrod Allen. "I found Antonia's diary."

"Her diary?" he said, standing very still and staring at me. "She kept a diary?"

I nodded. "For several years, from before she was married. She never mentions her husband's name in it, but I told Jarrod I had it, and I didn't tell him that part."

"That was not wise of you, Melinda," he said, frowning over his sherry glass. "I can't imagine your being provoked enough to lose control that way. Why ever did you do it? What could he possibly have said to you to make you fly apart like that?''

I closed my eyes, and put my hand to my head. I didn't really want to think about this, and I certainly didn't want to talk to Lane about it. I shook my head. "What does it matter?" I asked, suddenly weary of the whole conversation. "I did it, that's all that matters. Obviously you think it was Jarrod who was following me.''

"Who else would it have been? I don't think you are taking this seriously enough.''

"Seriously enough! I've just been frightened out of my wits. That seems serious to me.''

"Nonetheless, I'm not sure you realize the danger you're in. Jarrod Allen killed a woman. He murdered her. Do you think he'd hesitate at killing you if you got in his way? After all, what would he have to lose?''

I realized then that I was shaking so hard I had to set the glass down to keep from spilling the sherry.

I rose quickly to prevent Lane from seeing how shaken I was, and said, "I think I'll go to my room. I'd like to lie down for a while before dinner.''

"Good idea," he said, lounging against the side of the fireplace. "Oh, by the way, did you know that Raul Marcos has been released by the sheriff?''

"He has? That's good news, anyway. Why did they let him go?''

"Insufficient evidence, the sheriff said. And as to its being good news, you may not think so if you have occasion to run into Raul. He swears that you are responsible for Antonia's death and he plans to make you pay, he said.''

I could feel the color leave my face. "He thinks I

killed Antonia?" I said incredulously. "How could he think that I—I scarcely knew the girl."

"Oh, he doesn't think you killed her. He just thinks your appearance here led to her death. He says that if it hadn't been for you, she'd never have been killed."

I was stunned. "But how can he think—I mean, I had nothing to do with Antonia. How can he possibly blame me for her death?"

Lane shrugged. "Who knows how his mind works? All I know is that there were those who heard him make the threat after he was released. He said you'd be sorry you ever came here, that if you'd stayed where you belonged, Antonia would still be alive."

I put a hand to my head which had suddenly begun to throb. "I find this whole thing so utterly absurd that it's almost incredible to me." I started from the room once more, then stopped as a thought occurred to me. I turned to Lane.

"When did they release him?" I asked.

"Yesterday afternoon. Why?"

"Then perhaps we're jumping to the wrong conclusion about the man who was following me. It may very well have been Raul Marcos."

He looked at me a long moment and then said, "Perhaps. At any rate, you should at least take seriously the danger you're in from either of them. Or both."

I nodded, then turned and left the room. I wanted to lie down somewhere for a while to gather my thoughts, to consider what was taking place.

I lay on my bed and thought over what I knew.

Someone had followed me through the forest. For what purpose, I was not sure, but it could not have been for any honorable reason; his movements were too stealthy. Raul Marcos had threatened me. Jarrod Allen had, perhaps, murdered his wife.

What was I doing here, I asked myself. How did I get myself into this? How could I get myself out? I seemed to feel the weight of events closing in on me, events over which I had no control, of which I was destined to be the victim through no fault of my own.

Suddenly I sat up on the bed, flooded with anger. "I've had enough of this," I said aloud, and I rose and went to my window. "I'm tired of being frightened by all the suspicion in this house."

I knew there was little I could do about Jarrod Allen, but there was something I could do about Raul Marcos. Threatening me behind my back, indeed. If he wanted to challenge me, he could do it out in the open. I would not allow myself to become the whimpering victim of subtle threats and innuendos.

I made up my mind to find Raul as soon as possible and face him with my knowledge about his threats. In fact, I reasoned to myself, it would make sense to do it in as public a way as possible. If it became public knowledge that he had made such statements, he might have to think twice before carrying out any injury to me, as he would be first on the list of suspects.

Having decided to handle Raul, I felt better as I went down to dinner. At least part of my problem did not appear to be beyond solution, and if I simply managed to avoid Jarrod Allen for a time—well, probably he would marry Constance Robinson and that would take care of that situation.

After a fashion, I said to myself, managing a wry smile at my inability to deal with the feelings I had for him. It will take care of at least part of your problem, Melinda, but only time will handle the other part.

At dinner that night, Grandfather asked about the portrait.

"Does Evelyn Allen say she can fix it?" he asked. "You never told me what she said."

At the other end of the table, Sybil was suddenly still, watching me with a curiously alert look on her face.

"Oh, yes," I said, elaborately casual. "She says there shouldn't be much of a problem. She's working on it now."

"What was the problem with it?" Lane asked. I looked across the table at him, but I was unable to read the expression on his face. Surely Sybil would have told him about the scene we had had.

"It was damaged in the trip from San Francisco. You remember. Sybil sent it in to have it reframed."

"Reframed." His face appeared utterly blank. "Yes, of course."

"At any rate, I took it to Evelyn Allen to see if she could repair it. She seems to feel that it will not be too difficult."

I glanced at Sybil, who wore the same blank expression as her son. If she longed to dispute my story about the "damage" to the painting, she obviously realized that she was in no position to do so.

Her eyes narrowed almost imperceptibly and she lowered her head to her plate.

"When does she think it will be finished?" Grandfather had not perceived anything odd about the exchange.

"I'm not certain, but I can ride out and check with her one day soon. She's had it quite a while now."

"I want her to do a picture of you, too. I'd like to have them both to hang in my study."

"She asked me to pose for her sometime. Maybe later when I'm not so busy with the school." Maybe later when Jarrod has married Constance Robinson and I feel safe to go there. "I think that having a portrait done would be—"

There was a strangled sort of sound from the end of the table and I turned to see Sybil shove her chair back, fling her napkin to the floor and stalk angrily from the room.

I turned to Grandfather, bewildered. The conversation had seemed to me to be innocuous enough. I wondered what had been said that had so angered her that she would behave in such an uncharacteristic fashion. It was not at all like the elegant Sybil to leave without even firing a parting shot.

My grandfather simply watched her leave the room, his mouth set in a grim line. Did I imagine that he seemed to have won a point in some sort of game I didn't understand?

I turned my gaze from him to Lane, who was regarding me with raised eyebrows and a sardonic smile.

"Merely one of our running battles in the continuing McCarthy-Harrington feud, Melinda," he said. "Nothing you should concern yourself about."

With that, he rose, excused himself, and followed his mother from the room.

I turned to my grandfather. "What was all that about?" I asked.

He looked at me as if he had momentarily forgotten my presence. "That? Oh, it was the talk of the portraits that brought that on, my dear. Nothing for you to worry about, though."

"That's twice in two minutes I've been told not to concern myself over something I don't understand in the first place. What, precisely, is it that I am not to be concerned about, Grandfather?"

He gave me a smile that was a trifle sly. "Well, as Lane says, it's merely one of our running battles."

"*What* is? Why won't you tell me what's going on?"

He looked at me for a long moment, then sighed, and rose from his chair. "Come into my study for a moment and I'll show you something."

I followed him into his study and sat down in a chair opposite him.

"You see the space on this wall where your mother's picture was hanging?" He indicated a place on the wall where the portrait had obviously been placed for some time. I nodded.

"Well, you see on the opposite wall where there's a space for another portrait."

I followed his gesture and saw that there was indeed a place where another picture appeared to have been hung at one time.

"Whose picture was there?" I asked.

"Susana's. My wife."

"The one that hangs in your room now?" I remembered having seen the picture when I was helping to care for him after his last attack.

He nodded. "When I decided to marry Sybil, I moved your grandmother's picture into my room to make a place for Sybil's portrait."

"Sybil's portrait?" I queried. "I've never seen it. Is it here?"

"Oh, yes. It's in Lane's room now. It is a beautiful picture. She had it done just after she was married to her first husband. It was supposed to hang in the ancestral home in England." He stopped and looked at me. "Of course, there wasn't any 'ancestral home.' You must have heard that story by now."

I said that I had.

"At any rate, when she moved in here, I had planned to hang that picture opposite your mother's. She didn't give me time to do that, though. First thing I knew, she had your mother's picture taken down and hers hung in its place."

He leaned back in his chair and looked at the ceiling for a moment. "That made me angry. I had your mother's put back and told her that she was to leave it alone, hers would hang opposite. She didn't want it that way. She didn't want to have to share the attention, so to speak.

"So, she took it down from that wall, and had it hung in the sala. I told her that if there were going to be any pictures hanging in the sala of this house, they would be pictures of the people who had a right to hang there, not pictures of some upstart. Well," he sighed. "I said a lot of things. Not all of them necessary, I suppose, but it's real hard to reason with Sybil when she gets her mind set on something. Sometimes she just has to be told how things are going to be."

He stared off into space for a moment. "Anyway, that's the first thing we had a run-in about, and things went downhill from there. She's pretty touchy on the subject of portraits. When I said I'd have yours in here, it really set her off."

"As you knew it would when you said it," I said.

He gave me a sheepish smile. "Well, I guess I did. Sometimes I can't resist poking a little fun at her, with those uppity airs of hers."

I shook my head at him. "Grandfather, I can't understand the two of you. Why can't you both just own up that you've made a mistake, and stop torturing each other like this? Why don't you just let her have her house in San Francisco and be done with her?"

His chin came up and he set his jaw in a way I recognized as symptomatic of his having made up his mind so nothing would change it.

"I wouldn't give her the satisfaction of beating me," he said fiercely. And then, in a softer tone, "Besides, Melinda, it isn't as simple as that. Life in the style she'd fancy in San Francisco comes dear, and as I told you earlier, our resources here are not exactly unlimited. It would require selling some of the land, or cutting the redwoods, or some other means of raising the money she'd need, and I can't see cutting into your inheritance like that." He frowned at me and said, "That reminds me. If it's

274

going to be your inheritance, I have to get Steve Matson out here. I can't imagine what's taking him so long."

"Nor can I," I replied. "But if we haven't heard anything from him by next week, I'm going to make the trip to San Francisco to see him myself. That would seem to be the only way to put your mind at ease about it."

He nodded assent and smiled at me. "You're a blessing to me, my dear. I wish we could have met each other sooner, but I'm glad to have you here for the time I can, at any rate."

The following day, after my pupils had left, I sought out Father Murphy to ask him for a favor.

He was alone in his study and he smiled at me and rose to greet me as I entered the room.

"Ah, Miss Cole," he said, extending his hand to me. "How are things going with the school?"

"Very well, Father, I believe. At least, attendance has been good, and the students seem to be learning and enjoying themselves."

"The parents appear to be delighted with your work. All of those who have talked to me seem to think you are a veritable treasure."

"I'm pleased that they think so, Father." I stopped, a bit unsure of how to approach my request.

"Actually," I began, looking across at him, "it isn't the school I wanted to talk to you about, Father. It's a problem that is a bit more—well, personal."

"Oh?" He frowned at me and indicated a chair

beside his desk. "What sort of problem, may I ask?"

I settled myself and groped for words to convey my concern and to ask for his help. "Father, did you know that Raul Marcos has been released from jail?"

His face brightened. "Oh, yes, we're all delighted. The sheriff finally decided he didn't have enough evidence to bring him to trial. Few of us ever believed in his guilt, anyway." He stopped and looked at me, his forehead creased in puzzlement. "But how does this concern you, Melinda? I was certain that you were not even acquainted with Raul."

"I am not, actually, Father. In fact, I've only seen him once—the night he and Antonia danced at my welcoming party. But you see, I've heard—" I stopped and looked at my hands. They were wringing themselves together in my lap, quite independently of any will on my part. I clasped them tight to still them and looked up at Father Murphy. "I have been told that Raul has made threats against me. He has said that he blames me for Antonia's death, that if I hadn't come here, she'd never have been killed, and I must be made to pay for that."

His eyes widened with shock. "But that makes no sense at all," he said, shaking his head. "What on earth have you to do with Antonia's death? Surely he made that statement without thinking. I can't imagine Raul saying anything so rash."

"Father, there is something that you don't know about Antonia's death, something Jarrod Allen kept secret when he found the body." I took a deep breath, clenching my hands even more tightly and looked at him directly.

"My butterfly—the Montoya butterfly—was found at the site of Antonia's death. It was lying near her body, and Jarrod Allen returned it to me without mentioning it to anyone."

"Your butterfly?" He looked at me, astonished. "It was found at Antonia's—"

"Beside her body. Jarrod Allen returned it to me. You see," I struggled to make him understand the circumstances. "I hid the butterfly in my room that night, and I forgot about it. Then when my grandfather had his attack, I didn't think to look for it for several days. It wasn't until just before Antonia's body was discovered that I found that it was missing. And of course, since I hadn't reported it stolen, well, you can see how it would look if it were known that it was found with her body."

His face was grave, and he nodded. "I can see that the implications would be very damaging for you," he said. "But Melinda, I must ask you this." He looked at me intently. "You did not have anything to do with her death, did you?"

I shook my head so hard my hair felt as if it would come loose. "Oh, no, Father. I did not. I swear to you that I didn't. Please believe me."

"Of course I believe you." He gave me a small, warm smile. "I was certain of it, but I must have it from your own lips, you know. However, this does raise some questions. Why did Jarrod not mention the butterfly? Raul was with him when the body was found. Does he know about it?"

"I had thought not until I heard about the threat.

If he does know, then that would explain why he is angry with me. But if he knows, why didn't he tell the sheriff?"

Father Murphy shrugged. "Who can say?" he said. "Perhaps he was afraid that if both you and Jarrod Allen denied having seen the butterfly, he would be more fully implicated. After all, if he had seen Antonia with it before she died, and if he did not know whether you had reported it stolen, that would place him at the scene, or close to it, at the time of her death. Knowledge of the butterfly could not have done him much good, either way."

"I suppose not," I said rather doubtfully. It didn't make much sense to me, but at that moment I was less concerned with Raul Marcos' motives than with the threats he had made.

"What I wanted to ask you, Father, was whether you would do me a favor. I thought that if I went to Raul and confronted him with what I had heard, in front of witnesses, that he might be afraid to carry out the threat. I mean, if doing so would make him a prime suspect in anything that happened to me—"

"Then he might be afraid to do anything. I think you're right, Melinda. But are you afraid that something is going to happen to you?"

I looked at him and opened my mouth to say no, and then closed it as the full realization came to me that I was indeed afraid something was going to happen to me. I had been afraid for a long time, and had consistently denied it to myself, but suddenly I was face to face with the knowledge of my own fear.

"I—I—I don't really know, Father. It just seems as if I've been frightened for a long time, and I don't know why, really."

"Is there anyone who might benefit from 'something happening' to you, Melinda?" He was looking at me carefully, and I couldn't bring myself to tell him what I knew about Jarrod Allen and Antonia, about why I thought Jarrod had returned the butterfly in order to keep me safe until he could propose, about all the things I believed and feared. He loved Jarrod Allen. He'd never believe anything bad about him, especially on as little proof as I had.

"Well, of course," I began lamely, "there's the ranch. I suppose if I died now, Grandfather would leave it to someone else, but surely no one would—" I couldn't bring myself to say the word "kill"— "harm me for that."

"One never knows. Has the will been made in your favor?"

"No, not yet, although I believe Grandfather intends to change it just as soon as he can get Mr. Matson, his attorney, out here to do it. He's made no secret of that, actually."

"Meanwhile, who are the heirs to the property?"

"Sybil and Lane, I believe. But surely, Father, you wouldn't suspect them of trying to—I mean, Lane is away from the ranch as much as he's there. And Sybil doesn't even like the place. Why would they care? Lane has a large trust waiting for him on his thirtieth birthday. I simply can't believe they'd be trying to frighten me."

He sighed and was silent a moment, as if thinking. Then he looked at me as if he'd made a decision about something.

"Melinda, I have no knowledge that leads me to

believe that you are in imminent danger, and yet I believe that you must have some reason for feeling as you do. Perhaps you know something you are not admitting to yourself, or that you are not telling me. I've no way of knowing. I do know this, though. Things may not always be what they appear." He looked at me for a moment, his face grim.

"My feeling is that it would be wise for you to be very careful for the next few days or so, at least until you've had a chance to see Mr. Matson. If I were you, I'd discuss my plans with no one. I'd be careful about what I said to whom, and I'd stay out of places which could prove to be dangerous. Do you understand me?"

I said yes, but I wasn't certain that I did.

"Has anything specific happened to cause you concern recently?"

I recounted for him the incident in the redwood grove and he nodded, but said nothing.

"Who is it that you are warning me against, Father? Do you think that someone really means me harm?"

"I'm not certain, although what you have said to me would certainly indicate it. I will go to Raul myself and warn him away. Certainly he has no desire to return to jail at this moment, so that should be easy enough to handle. Is there some place you can go for a few days without causing alarm at the ranch?"

"I really don't think so, Father. I hate to leave Grandfather alone. There have been things that have—happened that I'd prefer not to recur. I'd like to be there with him."

"I see." He looked past me and then down at his hands. "Well, my dear," he said, "do be cautious. Perhaps when Mr. Matson has been to see your grandfather, the problem will lessen somewhat."

"I hope so," I told him. I certainly hoped so. In spite of his warnings, I left feeling somewhat better. At least, I thought, I wouldn't have to worry about Raul, whatever else I had to be concerned about. I could not know that I had not yet begun to learn the meaning of the word fear.

Chapter Eighteen

My conversation with Father Murphy had left me with mixed feelings. It seemed to me that he suspected that I was in danger from Sybil and Lane, but then I had deliberately withheld from him any information about or accusations of Jarrod Allen. With no more proof than I had, I couldn't bring myself to tell him what I suspected. If only I had some real proof, I thought. If I could only find, say, the marriage license or something valid. If I could prove that Jarrod had been Antonia's husband, I would be able to go to Father Murphy with some sort of evidence.

As it was, I had nothing, or at least nothing that was of any real value.

When I returned to the ranch, I was given a note from Evelyn Allen saying that she had almost completed the so-called repairs, and that I should bring the frame for the picture as soon as I could.

I went into the kitchen and found Rosa to ask her to let me into the cellars.

She smiled when she saw me. "Ah, señorita, I have missed you. Since you have been the schoolteacher, I don't get to talk to you any more."

"I know, Rosa. I've been very busy. But I've missed you, too. Why don't you come up to my room tonight? We can have some of your special hot chocolate and talk after dinner."

"I'd like that, señorita," she said.

"Now I want you to let me into the cellars again. I have to get something I put down there."

"Of course, señorita. Come with me."

She let me into the pantry, lighted the lantern for me, and opened the door above the stairway. I took the lantern and went down the stairs, holding my skirts so that I wouldn't trip.

I went directly to the old wardrobe where I had hidden the shredded picture, and reached inside to pull it out.

The frame was rather heavy—it was an ornate, elaborately carved frame—but when I pulled it from the wardrobe, it seemed heavier than I remembered. As I dragged it into the light, I saw why. I had apparently set the frame on an old garment of some sort, and as I pulled it out, the cloth had caught on the frame and was being dragged along with it.

I reached for the ragged material to toss it back into the corner of the wardrobe, when something about the color of it caught my eye. I set the frame down and shook out the pale, lavender-pink fabric.

It was my dress, the dress I'd had made in San Francisco. It had been ripped to pieces, and tossed into the wardrobe to be hidden from sight.

It had not been lost through a mistake of the dressmaker. Someone had torn it to shreds and hidden it. I was never to have seen it, but I had found it.

I felt so sickened by the discovery that I felt my knees give way and I sat down on the floor, the torn folds of the dress in my lap. The fright I had thought I was putting behind me rushed over me in an icy wave, and I realized that I was shaking, my body almost convulsed by tremors.

Did they truly hate me so much? And was it "they"? Or was it "she"? In the ferocity that had destroyed my dress and my mother's picture, I could see only one hand—that of Sybil Harrington.

I sat on the floor a moment longer and then I stood up and picked up the lantern. I returned to the bottom of the stairway and called for Rosa. When she came, I asked her to join me at the foot of the stairs, and I held out the dress before me.

"Rosa," I said, looking at her intently, "do you know anything about this?"

Her eyes widened with shock, and she looked at the dress, then at me, then back at the dress. Finally she said, "What is this, señorita? I do not understand."

"This is the dress I was to have worn to the Allens' party," I said, folding the shreds into a tight ball. "Someone has done what you see and has hidden it in the old wardrobe." I paused for a moment. She didn't look at me. "You said no one except me had been down here. That wasn't quite true, was it?"

She was twisting her hands against her skirt, and she did not meet my eyes. "I—I'm not sure, señorita. Perhaps someone came when I was not here. I am not always here, you know."

I could feel my anger mounting. "Nonsense,

284

Rosa. You know everyone who goes into these cellars. It was Sybil Harrington, wasn't it? She tore the dress and she put it down in the old wardrobe. Am I correct?"

Her face was frightened and miserable. "Please, señorita, if she thinks I told you, she said I would have to leave. Please. I have been at the Mariposas all of my life. I don't want to have to leave."

"Rosa, you know my grandfather would never allow you to be fired. Was it Sybil?"

She nodded hesitantly. "She brought it down here the day it was delivered. She said she'd see whether your grandfather could do anything about that. She said he'd made her take you to get it, but you'd never wear it, she'd see to that, and if I told you, she'd see that I was sent away. I am very sorry, señorita."

I sighed. "Rosa, if it hadn't been for you, I wouldn't have had that lovely lace dress to wear to the party. You didn't do this, you know. And you know very well your job is safe. My grandfather—"

"But your grandfather is old, señorita, and not well. After he is gone—" She shrugged and spread her hands in a gesture of futility.

"After he is gone, I will inherit the ranch, and you will have a place here as long as I have anything to say about it."

"But as it is now, señorita, you will not inherit unless the will is changed. The señora and her son will have the ranch."

"I know, but as soon as Mr. Matson gets here, Grandfather has said he will change the will."

She shook her head from side to side slowly, and

raised worried eyes to mine. "If he gets here in time, señorita. She has vowed to me that you will never inherit the ranch. She said she will see to it."

Again I felt the curious chill creep over my body, but I said nothing. I turned from her, picked up the frame and carried it up the stairs and out to my room. I was shocked to realize that even Rosa was in the power of my grandfather's wife. Fear for her job, for the loss of her place, had made her vulnerable.

I had to face the fact that the time had come to go to San Francisco myself and see why Stephen Matson had not responded to our messages. I was beginning to fear that I already knew why he had not, but I refused to give way to speculation for the moment.

I was beginning to feel the weight of a suffocating burden of fear. All around me people seemed to be changing. Nothing was as I believed it to be. It was as if the outlines of familiar objects were blurring and changing into other things. What had seemed to me to be a haven when I had first come, was suddenly a place where I was not safe at all, where I myself was seen as a threat, and where my life might very well be in danger.

And yet, I found it difficult to believe, in spite of all I knew, that Sybil could be guilty of more than a bad temper and a wicked disposition. Granted, she was mean, but I did not believe her capable of murder.

Still the fact remained, that someone around here *was* quite capable of murder, had committed it, and might be willing to commit it again if the circumstances led them to it. And from my point of view, I stood a very good chance of becoming the victim if I didn't do something to alter the situation in which I found myself.

I put the frame in the wardrobe in my room and told myself that I would take it over to Evelyn Allen in a couple of days. Meanwhile, I had to get to San Francisco as soon as I could. I decided to leave early the following morning and see if I couldn't get Stephen Matson to the ranch the following day. If I were in any danger, so was my grandfather, and any delay at this point was to be avoided.

I left my room and went down to the stables to arrange for a buggy to take me to the city the following morning.

As I entered the stable, the man named Lou who had taken my message to Stephen Matson before was just leaving.

"Oh, Lou," I said, as he smiled and lifted his hat. "I'm glad I ran into you. I wanted to arrange for a driver for tomorrow."

"Sure thing, Miss Melinda. Where were you figuring on going?"

"San Francisco. I need to make a trip into the city for a few things." I tried to make my errand sound as casual as possible. "I'd like to have someone drive me, if possible."

"I'm pretty sure that's possible, ma'am. In fact, I can probably do it myself if you would like."

"That would be fine with me," I said. "I'd like to leave early."

"No problem, ma'am. By the way, did you get things straightened out about the message to Mr. Matson?"

I frowned. "Straightened out? I'm not sure I understand. Did you have some trouble delivering it?"

"Well, no, ma'am, no trouble, exactly. I never delivered it, was all. I thought you knew about that."

"You never delivered it?" I made what I'm afraid was a futile effort to keep from sounding shocked.

Lou's weathered face was puckered into a puzzled frown. "Well, no, Miss Melinda. I was sure she told you. She said she was going to."

"Who?"

"Why, Miss Sybil. Miz McCarthy, that is." He tilted his head to one side as if trying to comprehend my confusion. "You know, when I left you, I was gonna go see your grandfather and make sure it was all right for me to be gone a day to San Francisco. But I never did get to see him, I ran to Miss Sybil—Miz McCarthy—in the house and when I told her what you said, she said it wasn't important, that I didn't need to go. She took that message you gave me and said she'd tell you to send it with the supply wagon next week. Didn't she do that, ma'am? Shore hope I didn't do the wrong thing."

I struggled with a variety of emotions and thoughts. I didn't want Lou to know what Sybil had done—no point in involving the hired help in the family squabbles—but I suppose I had already made it plain that I had not known about the message not going to Steve Matson. I attempted to put the best face on the situation that I could.

"I'm sure you didn't do anything wrong, Lou. I suppose Sybil just forgot to mention it to me, that's why I was surprised. I can't see that it makes much difference." I forced myself to maintain a calm appearance in front of him.

"At any rate," I continued, "I'll be in town tomorrow and that should be sufficient. Can you arrange for a rig and driver for me?"

"Oh, yes, ma'am, I'll do that." He gave what I thought was a relieved smile. "Don't you worry about it. I'll take care of it."

I turned and left, my mind in a turmoil. I felt the walls of fear closing in on me for the second time that day. Sybil had shredded the picture. Sybil had destroyed my dress. Sybil had intercepted the message to Steve Matson. Sybil seemed to be waiting like a giant spider to catch me in her web.

I found myself gasping for air, as though I had been running hard, and I realized how effectively she was controlling me. I felt as if I were battering myself against her web, a silly butterfly caught in her clutches, and all she had to do was sit on the edges of the web and wait, because sooner or later I'd entangle myself so that I was trapped, or batter myself to bits trying to oppose her.

How stupidly you're behaving, Melinda, I said. After all, she's a woman, not a black widow. And you're a human being with a mind of your own, not a helpless butterfly. So far, she's done very little, actually, but she's winning this war of nerves, isn't she? She has you scared silly.

I refused to be intimidated any longer, I told myself. Tomorrow I would go to San Francisco and explain the situation to Mr. Matson myself. I would see that he came out as soon as possible and after that everything would be all right.

Somehow I didn't see past that point. Somehow, I thought, Mr. Matson would make everything smooth again, and would solve the problems. Things would be well, I didn't know quite how I expected him to accomplish that minor miracle, but I felt that if the will were changed, somehow my position in the family would be, too.

I went to bed early, expecting to have difficulty falling asleep, but surprisingly, I dropped off quickly. I must have slept soundly for several hours, but I awakened sometime in the early morning hours and sat up with a sudden start.

Sybil Harrington was standing beside my bed, a candlestick clutched in her hand.

The light from the candle cast a ghastly glow over her face and over the objects in the room. Her eyes were shadowed and her face looked like a death's head in the feeble light. I drew the covers around me and in a voice I hoped did not sound as frightened as I felt, rasped, "What do you want?"

She smiled, her features oddly contorted in the strange light. "I? What should I want, my dear Melinda?" Her voice was soft, almost crooning. "I think the question is what *you* want, is it not?"

"I don't know what you mean," I said, trying to gather my wits. I have always been slow waking up, slow to get my mind together, and I felt my sluggish brain struggle to cope with this situation.

"Of course you do, my dear." That awful voice! "What you want is very simple. Everything. That's all you want. Of course, I can sympathize with that." She smiled again, that smile that the light so distorted into a hideous grin. "That's precisely what I want, too. But it must be obvious, even to a simpleton like you, that we can't both have it, am I right?"

I didn't answer. I just stared at her.

She moved closer to the bed and continued in the same soft, soothing voice. "And that's why you must not be allowed to go to San Francisco to bring the lawyer out here. If you do, your grandfather will change the will and leave everything to you." Her voice grew harsher. "As you very well know, my greedy little orphan. And you will not have it. I need this ranch and the money it will bring. My son needs it. And I've worked for it."

She was breathing heavily now, and she leaned over the bed so that I could see that her face was contorted with anger, her teeth clenched, her knuckles white as she grasped the candlestick.

I felt like screaming but it was as if my throat were paralyzed. I felt mesmerized by her mad, burning eyes.

"I've put up with that crude old man for five years now, and every cent he has, I've earned." My gentle, gruff old grandfather!" "He can't possibly last much longer. And indeed, he wouldn't have lasted this long but for you, you interfering little watchdog." She leaned back from the bed, her breath harsh in her anger.

"And so you see, my dear Melinda," she smiled again, that vicious smile, "no trips to San Francisco for you. Another week should do the trick and then you may go anywhere you like. Indeed," she paused and gave me a significant look, "after that you will

291

have to go somewhere. You certainly won't be allowed to stay on *my* ranch." She turned and started from the room and I finally found my voice.

"How did you know—that I was going to San Francisco, I mean? I only told Lou."

She turned and the smile she affected now was total contempt. "Not everyone on this ranch thinks you're so wonderful, *granddaughter*. Some of the people here are mine. Lou happens to be one." So, I thought, that explains the "Miss Sybil." I should have been more alert. Only her old employees would have called her that.

She turned and swept from the room, her white robe flowing about her. I heard a key turn in the lock as she left.

I sprang out of my bed and turned the handle and pulled, but it was indeed locked. I had been locked into my room. I panicked for a moment and pounded on the door with my fists and screamed—until it came to me that no one could possibly hear me at this time of night, and certainly not in such a remote corner of the huge house. I ran to my window and threw open the curtains, only to be confronted with the ornate grillwork. So lovely, I had thought, and now so confining.

I put my hands to my face and gave way to a moment of despair, but only a moment. In a few minutes, the part of my mind that always stood a bit apart and watched me do foolish things asserted itself and said to me, Straighten up, Melinda. How silly of you to be standing here crying! How long do you think it can be before someone comes?

I straightened up, ashamed of myself. Of course

someone would be here in the morning. Rosa would miss me, and so would Grandfather. Someone would come and check. Sybil must be quite mad to think that locking me in my room would accomplish anything lasting. Except—what did she have planned for Grandfather?

A week, she had said. A week should take care of it. What did she have in mind?

I returned to my bed and lay down. I could feel my heart pounding as I lay there, and I stared up at the canopy for a long time, but eventually I dropped off into a light sleep.

I awoke when the dawn was just breaking, and I rose and washed and dressed. I paced my room and looked out the window and waited for someone to arrive. The house was strangely silent. I looked out the window onto the landscape below me. It was empty of anyone I could call, but then it usually was. Seldom did anyone come to this corner of the house. The stables and corrals were all on the opposite side and the courtyard was to the front. This was the most remote section of the house.

I'll bet, I thought, that this was Sybil's idea, too.

When I felt that someone must surely be up and around, I went to the door and pounded on it and screamed and called. Then I waited. There was no answering sound. I pounded and called again, but the heavy oak door seemed to absorb the sounds of the blows, and my voice, behind the thick adobe walls, went no further than the threshold.

I went to the window, opened it, and called. No answer. I listened for a few moments and heard nothing. The house was silent.

I felt strangely as if the house was conspiring against me, as if it held me prisoner of its own volition. I seemed to feel it closing in upon me, as if I were in a cocoon which would open in time, but not until it chose.

My, aren't we imaginative, Melinda, a part of my mind said to me. A cocoon, indeed. There is nothing mysterious going on in this house except what has been arranged by a greedy and half-crazy woman.

By noon I was tired from trying to make noise and attract attention. I left the window open and tied a white scarf to the grill, hoping that someone might see it and come to check and see why it was there. I left it open in case someone came around to this side of the house; I should be able to hear them with the window open.

I lay down on my bed and dozed for a while. In the dream that came as I lay there, I again saw my mother's face. It was frantic, and she reached out for me, trying futilely to reach me as she receded from my desperate grasp. I struggled through the water that soaked my skirts and pulled me down, to try to get to her, but she faded even as I reached for her, and I failed once more in my attempt to get to her.

I thrashed about suddenly and woke myself. I was covered with perspiration and even with the windows open, the room was stifling. I rose and washed my face and hands again. I looked out the window. The shadows were lengthening, and the afternoon was growing late. Why had no one come to look for me? Surely by now I would have been missed—by Father Murphy at the school, Rosa,

Grandfather—surely someone would have thought to look for me.

Suddenly it occurred to me that I had set up my absence myself so neatly that there was no need for Sybil to do anything other than let my plans be known. I had said I was going to San Francisco. Lou would verify that I had gone, and no one would question my absence. I had even mentioned to Grandfather that if we'd heard nothing by this week, I would be going. They must believe I had gone.

But Sybil knew that I had not. Did she intend to simply leave me here? What was going on in her twisted mind? The San Francisco trip could not last more than three days as an excuse. But perhaps that was sufficient for her plans. Perhaps in three days—I turned my mind from that thought. I couldn't stay here three days. I'd think of something.

The sunset faded and the sky began to darken. I was quite hungry, although I had water, thank goodness. I paced the floor for a while, thinking that if I had not been released by the time it grew dark, chances were not good that I would get out that day. I'd probably spend another night there at least, because no one would be here after dark.

When I could see the stars outside my window, I lay down on my bed and fell into a restless sleep.

I was awakened by the sound of a key in the lock. I sat up in bed quickly and reached for the vase on my bedside table. She would not get away so easily this time.

I slipped out of bed and walked to the door as

quietly as I could. As the door opened a crack, I raised the vase, ready to hurl it at my jailer and dash from the room.

The door opened slowly, and I tensed myself to fling the vase, but the shadow that loomed in the doorway was too large to be Sybil.

"Melinda?" It was Lane's voice. I lowered the vase with a sigh of relief.

"Lane! Thank goodness you're here! I thought it was your mother again. How did you know I was here?"

"She told me what she'd done this evening. Everyone believes you're in San Francisco."

"I guessed that after no one came all day. Thank heaven you came. I'm half starved and I've only been here one day."

"I can imagine. Listen to me. We're going to have to get you out of here. I think my mother's a little crazy." His voice was tense, and I couldn't see his face.

"A little! I've almost decided she's quite mad. What on earth could she have been thinking of, locking me up in this room?"

"Who knows? Mother gets these strange ideas. But we have to get you out of here in any event. I'll take you to Father Murphy until we can find another place for you to stay."

"But why should I have to leave?" I was angry at the thought of sneaking away in the night because some crazy woman had taken a notion to get rid of me. "I'd rather just go to her and tell her I won't have any more treatment like that, and I'm going to

San Francisco tonight."

"Melinda, you can't." Lane's voice was tight, and he seemed unusually tense. "She has Lou looking out for you in case you managed to get loose. You'd never make it to San Francisco."

The meaning of his words stunned me. "You mean she would have me—"

"That she would have you killed. Yes. I mean that. I told you she's a little crazy. She wants this ranch, and she's become obsessed with the idea of it. The only way you can stop her is to get out now and leave for San Francisco as soon as you can. But not tonight."

"I see," I said, fear replacing my resolve again. "Where's Lou now?"

"He's out in the courtyard. We can't go out that way."

"Then how?" The courtyard was the only entrance to the house. I didn't see how we could get out past her guard.

"There's another way." There was an odd note in his voice and I turned to him quickly. I could not make out the expression on his face.

"How?"

"I'll show you. First come down to the kitchen with me, and we'll get you something to eat. Then I'll take you to the mission and you can leave from there when it gets light."

I followed him to the kitchen and lit a candle so that I could look through the cupboards for something to eat.

I rummaged around and found some bread and

meat for a sandwich. I was ravenous. I found a pitcher of milk and poured myself a glass. Lane paced back and forth as I ate, glancing occasionally at the door and stopping to peer out the windows.

I ate rapidly in response to his apparent haste, and stood up, brushing the crumbs from my skirt. He was standing by the counter, drumming his fingers on the top of it impatiently.

"Now," I said, turning to face him. "I feel up to making the trip. Which way do we go?"

He looked at me for a long moment, his face expressionless. "Through the cellars," he said.

"Through the cellars?" I think my face must have been as blank as his own. "But there's no way. Didn't you tell me they were blocked off? An earthquake, you said?"

"It was an earthquake that blocked the tunnel and probably a tremor that unblocked the tunnel. I discovered some time back that the passage was tight, but not impassable. One can get through."

"But how did you happen to find it?" I asked, puzzled. "Why were you in the cellars in the—"

I stopped. His expression was now very strange. He was standing close to me now, and he appeared to be waiting for something, waiting as the knowledge of what he was telling me sank into my mind, waiting for me to realize what he had just told me.

It took a few seconds for the implication of what he had said to become clear to me, but as it did, I felt my eyes grow wide with understanding and fear. He had been in the cellars, and not through the kitchen entry. He had gone into the cellars through the ocean entry. And the only reason he would have had for going into the cellars was to meet—Antonia! He had been meeting her in the cellars. He had been her husband. And he had killed her.

As if he could read my thoughts, he smiled suddenly, a mean, twisted smile and I felt myself shrink from him as he stepped closer to me.

"I see that you understand the situation, Melinda. You know how it is that I know those cellars, don't you? My *wife*—" how contemptuously he spat the word!— "and I used to meet there. It was through her that I discovered the passageway to the sea, the open tunnelway. She knew about it. Not much of a bridal chamber, down there, but—" He shrugged, and anger swept over me. Anger for poor Antonia, so callously used, and so carelessly discarded.

"But then you weren't much of a bridegroom, were you?" I said venomously. "Poor Antonia."

He looked at me, hatred in his eyes. "Poor Antonia, indeed. Antonia and her 'proof' of her birth. 'Proof' of her right to inherit. Stupid little fool. If she hadn't held out for marriage, she'd be alive right now. It wouldn't have been necessary to—get rid of her."

"You did kill her, didn't you? Did you leave the butterfly there to make it look as if I had done it?"

"It seemed a good enough idea at the time. She steals the butterfly, you run after her, she stumbles off the cliff trying to escape. Even the fact of your accusation might have been enough to push the old man over the edge. But then, I hadn't reckoned on

299

Allen finding the body. Or on his being in love with you."

My heart sank at the thought of Jarrod Allen and the wrong I had done him, but I hadn't time to dwell on that thought at the moment.

I was concerned with keeping Lane talking until I could come up with some plan for escaping him or of rousing the rest of the household.

"And what of Antonia's so-called proof? Did she actually have proof that her father was Don Diego's son? Or was she lying about it?"

"Oh, she had proof of that, all right. She had a letter Don Diego had written, acknowledging that he was the boy's father."

"And wasn't that good enough for you?"

"No. Not good enough for two very good reasons."

"My existence, you mean."

"That's one of the very good reasons. Of what purpose is an illegitimate line, when the legitimate one exists? But there was more to it than that."

"Oh?" I was half listening to what he was saying. My mind was working furiously, trying to devise a means to get past him to the door.

"Antonia wouldn't have stood to inherit this ranch at any rate. She wasn't even an illegitimate descendant of Don Diego."

"Not even—are you saying that—"

"Antonia wasn't the daughter of Antonio Dominguez. She was the daughter of Paul Durango."

"Paul Durango! and Rosa!" I couldn't conceal

my astonishment. No wonder Rosa had been so anxious to have her daughter forget about the ranch. Poor Antonia. If she'd known the truth, she'd be alive today. Poor Rosa. What a load of guilt she must be carrying.

"Paul Durango was something of a rake, I gather. Your mother was well out of any marriage to him. He managed to seduce Rosa not long after your mother eloped, but unfortunately, she had Antonio Dominguez standing by, more than happy to marry her. He never knew Antonia wasn't his, so he convinced her of her right to this place. Rosa knew, of course, but what could she do about it? She could hardly own up to the truth. Although it would have been better all around if she had, I suppose."

"How do you know all this?"

He leaned against the doorframe and looked down at me. "Rosa told me. After I saw the letter, I was going to take it to your grandfather and use that and the fact of our marriage to try to get him to make over the will in our favor. I knew he was planning to change it. After the fight he'd had with my mother that started over the portraits, I knew he'd never leave it the way it was." So that was her mistake, I thought. The fight over the portraits. It wasn't Evelyn Allen that Antonia had meant, at all.

"It was only a matter of time," he continued. "But if Antonia were a true Montoya—At any rate, I went to Rosa to ask her to help us convince him, but I got no further than the letter when she broke down and told me the story."

He snorted. "Idiot. If she'd kept her mouth shut,

it would have worked anyway. No one else would have known. But she has a misplaced loyalty to the Montoyas, and she wouldn't go along with it. So I never told her we were married. I just made up my mind to get even with her in the process."

The last words were so vicious that I shuddered, chilled by the cruelty in his voice.

He took out a watch and glanced at it, and then smiled his twisted smile. He came toward me, around the table. "It's time to go, Melinda," he said softly.

I uttered a strangled croak and dashed around the table past him toward the door. He reached for me quickly, and grabbed my hair, pulling it savagely and yanking me almost off my feet. Then he struck a blow to the side of my head and everything went black.

When I came to, I was in a narrow passageway that led steeply downward. I was being half-carried, half-dragged along the damp corridor, and the smell of the sea pervaded the air.

As I realized where I was, I began to struggle, but my hands had been tied and I was held fast in Lane's grip.

He jerked me to my feet and shoved me ahead of him down the corridor.

"You can walk now," he snarled, "but don't try to run. You'd never make it."

I said nothing. I stumbled along in front of him, feeling my way through the shadows thrown by the lantern he carried high over his head. The walls of the tunnel were damp and the floors were covered with green slime that went an inch or two up the walls, also. The slick stuff made walking difficult, and with my hands bound I had trouble staying on my feet.

Once I stumbled over a rock in the darkness, and he jerked me to my feet and pushed me forward again.

"You could have avoided this, you know, Melinda. I did ask you to marry me."

"Considering the fate of your other bride, that was hardly a generous offer, now, was it?"

I couldn't see his face, but his voice was icy. "She got just what she deserved, that greedy little— It would have been different with us."

"Would it? You were only interested in me for the ranch. You would probably have come around to this sooner or later, anyway." I had nothing to lose, I thought. I could afford to be reckless. I twisted my hands in the ropes, trying to free myself.

"Probably not. You'd have been amenable after a while."

I wondered briefly what he meant, but I didn't want to consider it at length.

"What will you do with me now? Shove me off a cliff like Antonia?"

"Not quite. You'll see in a few minutes. If the carriage in San Francisco had been more effective, it would have been quicker, but this is more certain."

"The carriage—you mean it wasn't an accident? You had—"

"I had actually very little to do with it. I merely paid some small boys to toss firecrackers under the

303

horse's feet when I signaled. It was rather crude, but would have been effective had it worked. It didn't, so we've come to this. A bit harder on you, I'm afraid, but rather more sure."

"Your concern for my well-being is very touching, but it comes a bit late."

"No need to be sarcastic, my dear. I am concerned for your well-being. I'm simply more concerned for my own. And since you were unwilling and unable to help me achieve my ends in one way, you shall do it in another. Now," he stepped in front of me and raised the lantern. "Follow me through here carefully."

"Carefully? Are you afraid I'll get hurt?" Something about that struck me as so funny that I knew I must be close to hysterics. Lane looked at me blankly. He saw nothing incongruous in keeping from harm a woman he was about to murder.

We had reached the place where the walls and part of the roof had collapsed, but Lane led me around one end of the mass of dirt and rock that was piled to the ceiling of the tunnel. Along the end of the mass was a niche in the pile and by climbing up and bending almost double, we could go over the obstruction and down the other side.

Lane led the way, holding the torch so that I could see to follow. It occurred to me to simply sit down and refuse to move, but I knew he would not hesitate to drag my inert body across those rocks, and I liked the thought of that even less than I liked having to climb up. So I followed, balancing myself as well as I could with my hands tied.

As I climbed, I made myself go as slowly as possible, trying to find a way out of the situation. I thought that if I could knock the lantern out of his hands, I might have a chance in the darkness to escape, but I wasn't sure that I could outrun him, bound as I was, even with the advantage of darkness.

We came down the other side, and I could see past him a large door, sealing off the tunnel. It was obviously quite old; the bottom of it seemed to be rotting, and the hinges and fittings rusted. Lane reached for the handle and pulled it toward him.

"This was my biggest obstacle in getting through this tunnel," he said. "The hinges were quite rusted. The lock is useless, but it has a bar on the inside that holds it quite well."

I could see, high on the walls, marks that indicated the water level, and it was obvious that the sea came all the way up, over this door. And then I looked past the door to the far end of the tunnel where light was beginning to show, and I could see the faint outlines of the metal grating my grandfather had placed over the entry to the tunnel. We had reached the sea. We were in the smugglers' cave.

Much worse, we were in the middle of my nightmare tunnel. I turned to Lane, suddenly immobilized with fright. This was the dream. He was going to leave me in here, and let the tide come in. I would be drowned.

I screamed, overcome by hysteria, and thrashed out at him, striking him a blow with my bound hands. He staggered and almost dropped the torch, but recovered and dealt me a blow to the head that sent me reeling across the tunnel. I slumped down against the wall.

He hung the lantern on a bracket on the wall that had once held torches, and came to where I was lying.

"There's no point in fighting it, Melinda. The tide will be in soon, and when it has gone out, I'll come back and pull your body outside the grate so that it will appear that you drowned by accident."

"I don't think anyone will believe that," I said, my voice filled with all the disdain I could manage between sobs. "Why on earth would I be down here? It simply makes no sense."

"Oh, it'll make perfectly good sense when you're discovered down the road where it goes near the cliffs. You should never have tried to ride horseback all the way to San Francisco. It's well known that you are not an experienced horsewoman. Your horse threw you over the edge of the cliff. Then he came home without you. Very simple. Unfortunate, but those things happen."

"And Grandfather will have no choice but to leave the ranch to you. Is that your plan?"

"The ranch has already been left to us in the will. All we have to do is see that it isn't changed."

"He may change it anyway, just to keep it from you."

"He's not likely to have the chance. Your death should just about finish him off." He had knelt beside me and was unfastening the ropes on my wrists. "I have to take these off. It wouldn't do for you to be found wearing them, you know."

As I watched him loosen the ropes, a thought occurred to me and I asked, "What about your trust? Do you need all of this? Why do you have to have the ranch, too?"

He smiled at me. "The trust is, shall we say, less than adequate to keep me in the style I prefer. Besides, most of it will go to cover certain—ah, debts of honor I have incurred over the past few years."

"Debts of—do you mean gambling debts? You have gambled away your trust?"

"Let's just say I have certain claims against it when I come into it. Substantial claims. And now, Melinda," he said, looking at his watch again, and tucking the rope in his pocket, "I think it is time for me to leave."

I could not believe what was happening to me. This couldn't be happening, not now, not to me. I held my hands to my mouth, tightly clenched. I looked around me at the walls of the high-arched tunnels, chiseled from the rock more than a century before. The dreamlike feeling was so strong that I half-expected to awaken any moment.

Lane stood and glanced down at me, then turned to look at the grating. It was becoming light outside the tunnel now, and I could see the ocean some way past the barrier at the end of the tunnel. He turned back to me and said, "I *do* regret having to do this, Melinda. However, you did have your chance. This shouldn't take long. The tide should have turned already, and it's very high this time of year. It doesn't ordinarily fill the cave to the top of the door, but it will today. You must have seen the dampness where the water comes in around the cracks in the doorway.''

I turned my gaze from the ocean to his face, and the seriousness of what he intended finally dawned upon me. "Lane, I simply can't believe you would do this. A fight with Antonia is one thing, call it a fit of passion, whatever. But this is coldblooded murder. You can't be doing this, Lane, you can't do this!" My voice had risen almost to a scream, and I stood up, reaching for his arm.

He stepped back from me toward the steps that led up to the door "I am sorry, Melinda. I would prefer another way, but I'm afraid that you have left me almost no alternative.''

He stepped toward the door, the lantern in his hand. "No!" I screamed. I leapt for him, but he was too quick. He shoved me back against the wall and opened the door and slammed it in one swift motion, and I heard the bar fall into place on the other side.

Panic overcame me, and I beat on the door and screamed until my fists were bleeding and my voice was almost gone. Then I turned and ran to the grating at the end of the tunnel and shook it and yelled as loud as I could. But my screams didn't carry over the sounds of the surf, and I collapsed in a heap on the stone floor of the tunnel and sobbed into my hands.

I was brought to my senses by the water that began lapping around me as I sat there crying. I looked out and saw the tide was coming in rapidly;

already waves were racing across what had been a wide strip of sand between me and the water, and entering the mouth of the cave.

I gathered the remnants of my courage and began to look at my situation as calmly as I was able. I went back to the door and turned my attentions to it. It was old and the salt water and time had done much damage to it. It appeared to be rotting at the bottom and that fact offered me some hope. I pulled at some of the loose splinters to see whether they would come loose, and a few of them did.

That the door should have survived all these years at all was amazing to me, and I thought in passing that it must have been made of some extremely durable and water-resistant wood to have withstood the conditions in the cave. I looked around for something to aid me in my attempt to batter the lower section of the door. I thought it might be possible to make a hole large enough to crawl through before the tide reached this level.

I found a rock with a sharp corner and began to bash at the section of the door that seemed the weakest. I hammered and scraped as hard as I could for what seemed to be a long time, and was beginning to make a small opening in the decaying wood on the bottom of the door, when I turned to glance at the tide.

My heart fell when I saw it, and I felt the panic rise in me again. The water was lapping at the bottom step.

I suppressed the urge to scream, and renewed my efforts to hammer a hole I could squeeze through.

By the time the water had reached the step where I

was kneeling, I knew with a sickening feeling that my efforts were in vain. I had an opening I could barely get my hand through and the water would cover it before I could enlarge it to any greater size.

I threw the rock into the water, and stepped down into the tunnel again. I thought now that my only chance was to try to scream loudly enough that someone on the road above the cave might hear me.

I waded through the water to the grating and tried to rattle it, and screamed as loudly as I could, but it seemed to me that I could barely hear myself over the sound of the waves crashing against the rocks and spreading into the cave. My skirts were soaked to my waist now, and I had more than ever a sense of living my own nightmare. I felt hysteria rising within me, and I held onto my reason with as tight a grip as I could manage.

Suddenly a huge wave swept into the cave, and almost washed me off my feet. I turned and retreated to the steps at the door where I could climb out of the water and postpone what now seemed to me to be inevitable.

The water rose inexorably. I crouched against the door at first, but as the waves splashed higher, I had to stand. I pounded on the door as I stood there, knowing well that I was beyond the hearing of anyone in the house, but refusing to give up as long as I was able to make some noise.

When the water reached my waist, I began to press my mouth to the crack of the door and scream as loudly as I could. I alternated pounding and screaming until the water reached my armpits. Foam and bits of seaweed floated just beneath my face. I was having difficulty staying on my feet. As the water swirled around me, it tugged at my wet skirts and pulled me off balance.

I grabbed the torch bracket beside the door to keep my balance, and as the water rose, I could feel my feet swept from under me. I closed my eyes and forced myself to think about drowning. I had read that it was a painless way to die, and I forced myself to concentrate on facing it without fear.

After all, if my father could face his death, I could face mine. But I had regrets. I would never be able to tell Jarrod how sorry I was. I could never be with my grandfather again. I thought of my mother, and wondered why I had had the dream about her and this place.

Why had she come? What had it meant? How could my mind have pictured a place I had never seen? I hadn't recognized it when I saw it from the outside, because I was seeing it backwards, but from this direction, every detail was the same. How could I have dreamed about it? I was never to know.

The water had reached my chin, and I was floating, holding on to the bracket, and almost reaching the top of the door. My head was nearly bumping the ceiling. I heard the sound of the surf and a scraping of some sort. I had hoped for so long to hear the sound of the bar on the other side of the door being lifted, that in my state of near-delirium, I could almost convince myself that I heard it.

Then suddenly, I knew that I *had* heard it, and at the moment I knew it was true, the door was flung open, and I was swept by a wall of water into the arms of Jarrod Allen.

Chapter Nineteen

In later years, Jarrod would tell our children that I swept him off his feet, and I would always protest that I had a bit of help from the Pacific Ocean. The water threw the door back so violently that it was ripped from its ancient hinges, and the two of us were flung to the foot of the incline, where Father Murphy was stretching out his hand to help us up.

I don't remember much after that, except that Jarrod covered my face with kisses, rushed me to Rosa's competent care, and instructed her that I was to be put to bed and not disturbed. Rosa saw me to my room, and when I was safely in bed, went back to the kitchen to make a cup of her special chocolate for me. I thought that I wouldn't be able to sleep because of the excitement, but I was out before she returned.

When I awoke, the sun was close to setting, and the light was growing dim. I looked across the room to where Evelyn Allen was rocking placidly and knitting. She heard me stir, and glanced up and smiled at me.

"Well, hello!" she said, putting the knitting aside

and coming over to sit next to me on the bed. "How are you feeling now, my dear?"

"Fine," I answered. "Perfect. I feel as if I've been asleep for a year." I sat up in bed, a hundred questions running through my mind. "Evelyn, what happened? How did Jarrod find me? And for that matter, why would he even bother to look? I was so beastly to him. Where's Lane? And Sybil? And—"

"Now, now, my dear," she patted my hand and smiled at me. "Not so fast. You've had quite a shock, you know, and besides, Jarrod is waiting downstairs to see you. I have orders to fetch him the minute you wake up. He can answer all your questions."

"Jarrod—" Almost involuntarily my hands flew to my hair, which hung lank and matted around my shoulders. "I can't let him see me looking like this."

Evelyn's eyebrows went up in amusement. "Of course not. Some things are important. But I can tell you quite frankly that he wouldn't care if you looked like the Loch Ness monster, he's that much in love with you."

I turned my back as I got out of bed to cover my pleasure and confusion. "You must think me an absolute idiot, Evelyn. I thought he was in love with Constance Robinson."

"Not her, thank goodness," she said vehemently. "Constance Robinson and all her 'socially prominent' friends back East? I should hope not. Of course," she added, a note of mischief in her voice, "he did hope you'd be a bit jealous of her. But there's never been anyone for him but you since the first time he laid eyes on you. *He* may not tell you that, but I will."

I smiled at her, my eyes brimming with tears, and then turned to my dressing-table. When I had made myself as presentable as I could, Evelyn left to find Jarrod after making me get back in bed and lie down.

He must have been waiting at the foot of the steps, because they were back in what seemed to be only a moment.

He crossed the room in two swift strides, sat beside me on the bed, and took both my hands in his.

He gazed into my eyes for a moment, and then he asked, "Are you all right?"

"I'm fine," I answered, "thanks to you. But how did you know where I was?"

"Lane told us."

"Lane? But why would he—how did you convince him—"

"I didn't. The sheriff did. But I'd better start from the beginning, if this is going to make any sense. When you accused me of marrying and murdering Antonia, it simply didn't make any sense to me. I had hardly known the girl, but I knew that you must have some reason to think as you did, and the only way to convince you of my innocence was to find her real husband."

"Which was Lane."

"He was. But you see, they weren't married in this county, or there would have been a record of it. I took a chance that they were married in San

Francisco. If it had been somewhere else, there would have been a problem, but fortunately, I was right. The records were there.''

''You went to San Francisco to look up the record?''

''And to talk to Steve Matson. He needed to get down here, and fast. Turns out he'd never received a message of any kind.''

''I had guessed that.''

''I also learned that Lane is up to his ears in gambling debts. He had borrowed against his trust, but he now owes more than the trust will produce. His only hope was to get some money out of this ranch. At any rate, when I learned that, I knew you'd be in danger, so I got back here as fast as I could.'' His face was grim. ''I'd never have forgiven myself if I'd been too late.''

''It would have been my own fault,'' I said softly. ''If I'd trusted you, if I'd gone to you in the first place—''

He touched my cheek with one fingertip. ''How could you have known? With what Lane was telling you? Well, it doesn't matter now. I went to the sheriff as soon as I got back, and we stopped and got Father Murphy. It seems Father Murphy had already been in to see him with his own suspicions after the incident in the forest—''

''That was Lane, I suppose?''

He nodded. ''With the information I had, it didn't take long for him to see what was going on. He's the one who got Lane to tell us where you were.''

"How did he manage that?"

"He told him he'd go to jail anyway since we knew about Antonia, but that if he'd tell us where you were, that would be all he would be charged with. Sheriff said Lane could probably get off with a jail sentence for Antonia's death—crime of passion and all that—but if you died, he would hang."

I closed my eyes and shuddered at the realization of my narrow escape. "Thank goodness he did," I said. "Did Lane write that letter to the sheriff about Raul?"

"Right. He wanted to throw suspicion elsewhere, and at the moment, Raul looked like a handy scapegoat. Until he thought of me," he added.

"What about Lou? He was supposed to be guarding the place to keep me here."

"Gone. We'll never see him again, I'd wager."

"And Sybil?"

Jarrod glanced at Evelyn and she frowned. "I don't think—" he began, but Evelyn said. "You might as well tell her now. She's not the sort to get hysterical, Jarrod."

He turned back to me and his face was somber. "She killed herself after Lane was arrested."

"Killed herself?" I felt the blood drain from my face.

"She knew she was implicated, if not in Antonia's death, then in the plot on your life. Lane told us about her locking you away in here. She couldn't face the scandal, I suppose. Before the sheriff took Lane away, he placed her under a sort of house arrest, pending an investigation. She went to her room and took some kind of a sleeping concoction she had. They found her when the sheriff came back to talk to her."

"How awful!"

"It is," he said, reaching up to tuck a strand of my hair into place, "but somehow I can't work up a great deal of sympathy for Sybil Harrington after what she tried to do to the woman I plan to marry."

"You'd still marry me," I whispered, "after all the awful things I said to you?"

"He'd best," Evelyn interrupted acidly, "if he doesn't, he'll have to find a new place to live, for I won't let him back in the house."

"You see, Melinda," Jarrod gave me a tender smile, "you have to marry me. You can't leave me homeless."

"Of course not," I said, my face serious. "I couldn't have that on my conscience. I suppose there's nothing else to do, then." And then another thought crossed my mind, and I sat up in bed. "My grandfather! How is he? How has he taken all this? Is he all right?"

"As a matter of fact," Evelyn said, "we sent for the doctor to come up before we broke the news to him, but he seems to have taken it very well. We didn't tell him about your scare, though. We thought that might be too much. We told him you had suffered such a shock at Lane's arrest that you'd been put in bed. That satisfied him. Men always expect women to go to pieces at times like this."

I smiled at her. That story would explain any pallor I might show.

"Do you think he's well enough to handle some good news for a change?" Jarrod asked. He stood up, but he held onto my hand.

"I think it would probably be better medicine for him than anything the doctor has," she said, heading for the door. "And I think you'd better speak to Father Murphy about performing the ceremony as soon as possible." She gave us a look of mock severity. "For one thing, if you wait very long, Jarrod Allen, you'll be in danger of damaging this child's reputation."

I giggled, and she gave me a sudden wicked grin. "And for another, you've promised me I'll be a grandmother before another year's gone by."

And she was.

TEMPESTUOUS, PASSIONATE
HISTORICAL ROMANCES!